DISCLOSE

JOELLE CHARBONNEAU

HARPERTEEN
An Imprint of HarperCollinsPublishers

ISBN 978-0-06-280365-8

Typography by Jenna Stempel-Lobell
20 21 22 23 24 PC/LSCH 10 9 8 7 6 5 4 3 2 1

First Edition

For Nellie Bly, who defied rules and faced danger in order to report the truth.

And for all journalism students. Your passion for following the facts where they lead will change the world.

DISCLOSE

ONE

Some old poem claims that patience is a virtue. I know because Dewey has quoted it to me at least three times a day for the last week and a half. Each day means another without people knowing the truth. Worse, another day of not finding those who were taken—if they can still be found. Another day of planning and of realizing that despite the risks those I care about are willing to take, we still might never succeed.

How am I supposed to be patient?

"One thing at a time," Dewey has stated so many times that I want to scream. "Patience is necessary if we want success," he said when he handed me my new government-issued ID under a new name. "Patience and careful planning," he advised when I cut and dyed my hair to change the way I looked.

Perhaps. But it isn't comfortable. It doesn't matter that I am busy training and meeting secretly with my best friend, Rose. She and her mother have agreed to take some of the biggest risks of all. We have a plan now that I hope will put people on the path to finally seeing and accepting the truth. Those meetings are why I filled out an application for Mrs. Webster's company—one that she will make sure is accepted. They're why I sat for a phone interview for a job she and Rose coached me through. All of it is necessary if we have any chance for success, but it all means I am sitting in a house that isn't mine, reading the history of those who tried and failed in decades past to bring truth to those who weren't interested in believing it, and remembering things that I wish I could forget as I count the days until finally I can try again.

Now it is nearly here, and I'm not sure I am ready for the things we will do and the choices we have agreed must be made.

Golden sunlight warms the bright azure sky as I walk down the sleek concrete sidewalk. I scan every face while attempting to appear as if I belong among the dozens of people commuting to work. After all, I'm one of them, walking to my new "job." I roll out my aching shoulder muscles, shift the turquoise bag on my shoulder, and wince at the way the matching boots Rose gave me pinch my toes.

"Suck it up," she told me after the package with the clothes she and her mother sent arrived at my door. I tried on the footwear while she waited for the verdict on the phone. "If you're going to work at *Gloss* you have to look like you belong there."

Apparently, fitting in at Mrs. Webster's fashion e-zine meant wearing skintight black clothing, a lot of eye makeup, and super-uncomfortable high-heeled footwear. "What happens if the Marshals come and I have to run?" It was not just possible, but probable considering what I have done and what we are about to do.

"The Marshals are looking for Merriel Beckley. That's who you used to be. Your government identification and the *Gloss* records show you are Merriam Adams," Rose assured me. "As long as you act as different as you look, no one will question a thing."

I used to struggle with the correct meaning of the word "irony." Now that my eyes have been opened—now that there is zero chance of my ever returning to my high school, of resuming a normal life, of being asked to define irony again—it does not escape me that it is deeply ironic that the very thing I am fighting against—people's willingness to accept whatever the government says as the truth—is the very reason I am able to walk down the street in plain sight.

Rose is right, I tell myself. Because words like "verify" were removed from our language, people simply believe what they are told. No one will question that I am who my new identification claims me to be. Two months ago, I would never have thought to question it myself.

Merriam Adams. I repeat the name in my head like a mantra, hoping that doing so will help me remember that's who I am supposed to be now. "Merriam" for the book that contained the meaning of the words that changed my entire life and brought me to this point. "Adams" for a woman I read about recently. She created ammunition for soldiers who had almost no supplies left to fight.

I stop at the light at the corner of the street and shift my weight. A brown-suited gentleman with a bushy salt-and-pepper mustache smiles at me. My shoulder muscles tense. I glance down at his footwear. Just plain brown loafers. Not the military-style running boots that would have signaled for me to flee.

I let out the breath I was holding and attempt to shake off the anxiety-tying knot in my chest. If I can't handle this walk, how am I going to deal with what I will eventually have to do? Atlas insists it won't be necessary, but . . .

Someone bumps me. Another snaps something impatient and I look up to see the light has changed.

One step at a time, I remind myself as I make my way across the busy intersection. The glass and steel of the Chicago skyline glisten against the background of blue. Cheerful flowers of white and yellow bloom in large urns stationed along the sidewalk. Impatient car horns blare nearby, drowning out the public screens reporting news about a car that drove off Lake Shore Drive and had to be pulled out of the water. I spot the entrance of my destination in the distance, glance around for signs of anyone who might be watching me, then hitch my bag firmly onto my shoulder and approach the off-white stone and rose-gold building.

The word "*Gloss*" shines in gold letters above the door, but it is the small, colorful image painted on the glass of the entrance that causes me to hold my breath. For a heartbeat, the city around me drops away, and the anxiety gnawing at my stomach disappears. All I can see is the design in front of me. Black curved lines fan outward from a center point—creating the image of partially opened pages of a book or magazine. Coming from the center of the pages are licks of brilliant yellow, fluorescent pink, electric blue, and bright orange.

I trace the painted lines of the wide V created by the open book with trembling fingers. Just weeks ago, this image lived only on my tablet—created from the desperate desire to keep fighting when everyone said it was time to retreat. I only had a hint of what that fight would look like then. Only a glimpse of what I, or others, might have to do.

The inspiration behind the design was the tattoo worn by the Stewards. They were the ones who taught me the word "verify" and the truth behind what that word revealed.

I'd drawn thousands of images over the years—honed my skill in the hope that one day I could follow in my mother's artistic footsteps. In all those years, nothing I had created was as personal as this image. Nothing had mattered as much as the moment when I sent it to Rose and waited for her to show it to her mother, hoping she would agree it was right for *Gloss.*

That was weeks ago, and now here it was—paint swirled onto the glass—the new logo for the top fashion and entertainment e-zine.

And a target Mrs. Webster has knowingly placed on her back.

"The Marshals will recognize the inspiration for the logo," Atlas warned on the day I explained my new plan to Rose and her mother. It took some doing to safely meet face-to-face. The Marshals' search for me included watching Rose and her mother. If it weren't for the network of buildings with alternate exits that Dewey and Atlas had unearthed from their work with the Stewards, we would never have managed it.

I paced the length of the room, unable to sit in the worn, mismatched orange and red armchairs the Stewards had placed in the room—as I waited for them to arrive. I worried the Marshals would stop them from coming. I was terrified to meet with Mrs. Webster after my part in her son's disappearance. If I hadn't stolen Isaac's identification to verify the information I'd been given by the Stewards, Isaac would have never been taken by the Marshals. He would be safe instead of imprisoned—or worse. City officials had told Rose and Mrs. Webster that he was still alive—kidnapped by a fictitious criminal gang. It was a lie. And despite all of that, I needed to ask not just for forgiveness but also for their help.

Mrs. Webster should have screamed or slapped me. I wouldn't

have blamed her. The angry click of her needle-thin, gold-and-black-swirled heels as she crossed the gray tile floor toward me made me brace for both. Instead, she pulled me against her in a fierce hug and when she finally let go and removed her gold-framed sunglasses there were tears glistening in her deep brown, perfectly made-up eyes.

As Rose stepped next to her mother's side, I hurried to say, "I'm sorry."

Mrs. Webster held up her hand. "Stop right there. Rose and I have talked. I know the truth about what happened to my son."

Not the story the police and the mayor gave her about Isaac being kidnapped by a dangerous gang actively working to undermine the city's security and disrupt everyone's lives, but the real truth, where Isaac was taken by the Marshals because the security card he was given for his summer job was used to enter a room that held government secrets. The security card I "borrowed" without Isaac's knowledge.

"Isaac's gone because of me." I force myself to look into her eyes.

"You didn't take my son. You didn't lie to me about why he is gone," she snapped.

"My father did that." Rose stepped beside her mother. "My lying-for-the-government-means-more-to-me-than-my-children father."

"And now—" Mrs. Webster straightened her shoulders. "I'm going to do whatever I have to in order to get my son back."

Which is why we have a real plan—a plan that if everything goes right has a real chance of working—and why my design is now on the *Gloss* door.

"It looks amazing, right?"

I jump at the voice behind me and turn to see Rose standing on the sidewalk, her thick, dark hair framing a face that, despite the stress and lack of sleep, is still beautiful. She smiles from mere feet away—where she is not supposed to be—and I stand still as a stone trying to decide how to remind her that Merriam Adams and Rose Webster aren't supposed to know each other.

"As of this past Monday that's the new logo for *Gloss*. We're refreshing our whole image," Rose says to fill the silence between us, then holds out her hand. "Sorry, I'm Rose Webster. I'm a summer intern. I was told another intern was starting today. That's you, right?" When I still say nothing her smile falters. "Or did I just make a total idiot of myself?"

"No. You surprised me." I smile now that I finally understand what Rose is doing. "I'm Merriam—new design intern."

Rose grins. "I think we are going to be great friends, Merriam. To prove it, I'm going to show you around. Ready to take the fashion world by storm?" she asks, her eyes serious as she opens the door to the *Gloss* offices.

Am I ready?

Two weeks ago, I refused to leave the city. I was determined to stay and continue the mission my mother started before the government had her killed. I wanted to help restore censored words to the country—to find Rose's brother, Isaac, and all the others the government had caused to disappear. And this was a key piece of the puzzle—using *Gloss* to bring truth to a country that thinks it already knows what the truth is.

It is the first step. One I've been impatient to take, and yet, I hesitate as I look at the open door.

The last time I helped create a plan, it failed.

I failed.

For months, I dreamed of my mother's death. Her wrapped in her red coat standing on the beige-gray concrete sidewalk. The bright gold headlights of the car shining against the dark of the night. The scream that must have cut through the unseasonable cold. In the last week, new faces have joined that dream. Several members of the Stewards appear in my restless moments of sleep. I see Flap's pink hair framing a lifeless face as she is dragged along the stone-paved concourse of Navy Pier. I can almost feel each bullet strike Stack's chest before she falls to the ground—her eyes turning blank and cold. The other four are less clear. I have been told their names, but I can't pick out their faces. It all happened in the hours before we set off for the mission I convinced everyone would spark a revolution. And so, their memories haunt mine.

I was told the time wasn't right, yet. By those who were older than me, who had known the truth about what the government had done. They said we should wait.

Perhaps they were right. Perhaps I should have gone with my father, who was secreted out of town by the Stewards to I'm not sure where with nothing from our old lives to bring with him. Our house was packed into a moving van. My school and dad's work were told that he took a new job in Washington state. From what I can tell, not one person doubted the information they received.

My father was offered a tablet to bring with him. It was loaded with a picture of my mother and me. It could be used to send messages the government wouldn't track. He left it behind. Unlike Rose's mother, Dad blamed me for ruining his life. Rose told me it was just the alcohol talking. I couldn't find the words to tell her it was his way of choosing the alcohol instead of me.

I adjust the backpack that holds the tablet Dad refused. Rose's dark brown wide-set eyes are filled with a determination that matches mine. Rose and her mother are willing to risk everything to get Isaac back. I have to do the same.

"I'm as ready as I'm ever going to be."

"Good, because with the new campaign there's a lot of work to do," Rose says as she escorts me through the doors toward a mosaic-tiled counter comprised of various shades of pink, cream, and blue glass. The name *Gloss* is written in gold and silver in the center of the turquoise wall behind it. The other reception walls are filled with cleverly positioned screens displaying past *Gloss* covers. Silver chairs are clustered in the corner of the perfectly polished white floor. A runner of the exact blue as the walls is unfurled in front of the counter—like a small patch of water in the middle of an otherwise frozen pond.

Anna, the receptionist, turns toward us. Her eyes narrow behind her purple rhinestone-encrusted glasses. The last time she saw me was several months ago. My hair was long and dishwater blond then. Nothing like the short red-and-white-streaked style Rose created for me. Still, I hold my breath as I hand over identification with my new name and picture so I can be signed in.

After studying me for several long seconds, she says, "You're early, but someone should be in the design department if you want to go back now."

When I assure her that I do, she adds, "Your eyeliner is wonderful. Blue is definitely your color."

She issues me a temporary pass, tells me to come back after lunch to exchange it for a permanent one, and loses interest in us as the phone behind the counter begins to ring.

Once we pass through the door that leads into the main section of offices, Rose quietly says, "I understand that I'm not supposed to know you, but Mom needs the new images you worked on last night. She's shuffled some of our advertising space around and instead of tomorrow, she is going to launch the new campaign this afternoon."

"But that wasn't the plan." My stomach lurches. "Atlas hasn't returned, yet. We don't know what he's learned or whether he's convinced anyone else to help."

If we have any hope for success, we will need more Stewards willing to take a risk.

Rose frowns. "I thought you said he'd be back yesterday."

The worry I've been trying to hold at bay storms through me.

"He just . . . got delayed," I say, hoping that it's the truth.

Atlas broke the rules to invite me into the Stewards. He introduced me to "verify," and the other words the government removed from the electronic versions of our books. Words no one remembered. Words that made it easy for everyone to forget.

Atlas knew my mother. He hoped that I might know something that could help him find his father, and the other people who were suddenly killed or disappeared because they understood what those missing words meant for our country. He gave me paper books to read. He helped me question everything I had been told, including what the police said about my mother's death.

He was there for me as I came to terms with her murder. It wasn't pretty, but he supported me. And in doing so, he claimed a piece of my heart.

For the last week, while I've been working to get ready for today, Atlas has been zigzagging around the city trying to uncover Unity Centers where the government holds those that disappeared. He's also been looking for Stewards who stayed aboveground and might be interested in continuing to fight for the truth. His success is important, but so is his return.

"Have you heard from him at all?"

I shake my head. He was supposed to leave a coded message if he needed more time so we wouldn't worry that he had been captured by the Marshals.

"He'll be fine," I say, irrationally hoping that saying the words aloud will make them true.

"He'll be more than fine when he sees the logo appear on public screens," Rose insists.

"I hope so," I say, but what I really mean is that I hope Rose and her mother will be fine. Even if I wanted to put a stop to our plan, now that everyone inside *Gloss* has seen the logo, Rose and her mother are in danger. Eventually the Marshals will hear about the design that has too many similarities to the Stewards' tattoo to be ignored. The only way *Gloss* will be allowed to continue—the only way Rose and her mother will be safe from disappearing like Isaac—is for us to follow the plan and display the logo in full sight of the general public as soon as possible. Once everyone has seen it, it will be harder for the government to shut *Gloss* down over it. Not without lots of unwanted questions. About why the symbol is so terrible. About what the symbol means.

Questions the government will not want to answer.

"Is everything else ready?" I ask.

Rose nods. "Everyone involved in the rollout has been told our former designer Chris Tapper created the logo and Mom has the paper trail to prove it. We've got this."

With Rose's help, Mrs. Webster spent the past weeks creating a false electronic trail that would lead anyone questioning the origins of the logo to Chris Tapper, a real *Gloss* designer who abruptly resigned via email a few weeks ago. According to his res-ignation message, he was moving across the country to take a job at a friend's company, but not one person has been able to reach him since that day.

Our guess is that the designer had been made to disappear by the Marshals. If we're right, the government won't be surprised when they discover he is credited with the new logo design. If he, like Isaac, is in their custody, we are counting on the Marshals not believing his denials. If not—it's all so much easier.

Mrs. Webster and Rose are counting on me to continue the fight. I hate that for their sake I am hoping Chris Tapper is dead.

Loud conversation causes us both to glance down the hall as a few *Gloss* staff members head to their work spaces. Soon the entire floor will be buzzing with people. Before I lose the chance, I ask, "Did you see your father last night? Did he say anything new about Isaac?"

Her eyes harden. "Nothing new. According to him, the mayor is negotiating Isaac's return from the *gang*. It doesn't look like he's get-ting much sleep. I'd feel sorry for him—if I didn't know he's lying. If he just told us the truth and was willing to help us . . ."

"The only thing that matters right now is that Isaac's still alive," I say. Part of me wonders if I believe that. The other part is certain Mr. Webster wouldn't be losing sleep, worrying, or spending so much time perpetuating the lie if he knew Isaac were dead.

"I keep telling myself that whatever else my father has done, he loves Isaac—so he's not going to let anything happen to him. Right?"

"Right," I agree, because I tell myself that, too.

Rose takes a deep breath and nods as two more employees come down the hall. "Let's get you settled and working. Things are quiet now, but they are going to be busy around here today. A new intern will want to be a part of it all."

I hand Rose the *Gloss* design tablet Mrs. Webster gave me to work on the logo. She leads me through the blue-gray cubicles and glassed-in offices used for tech support, sales, and customer service until we finally step into a large space filled with drafting tables, silver and blue stools, and dozens of wall screens displaying e-zine pages. Standing at one of the drafting tables is a woman with lots of dark brown hair piled on her head. She is wrapped in an oversize off-white man's dress shirt, baggy denim pants, and beat-up blue sneakers that look seriously comfortable—nothing like the fashions advertised in *Gloss*. The woman stabs at the screen several times and appears ready to jab the design tool at Rose when my friend says, "Mrs. Meacham, this is the new design intern. I was told to bring her to you."

"Well, she's here. I'm sure you have something else you can do now."

Rose gives me an encouraging smile and then bolts, leaving me alone with my boss. Mrs. Meacham moves around the design table and crosses the room with long, comfortable strides that make me yearn for my normal sneakers.

"What's your name again?" she asks.

"Merriam Adams."

She gives me a tense smile. "Nice name. Don't expect me to remember it. Mine's Nicolle, but I probably won't answer to it and if I'm working to meet a deadline I won't answer no matter what you call me."

I blink as the telltale sounds of people arriving for work float into the space.

Nicolle shakes her head at my silence and heads back to her worktable. "So what's your story? Can you actually draw or are you hoping to become a model and took an intern position in my department as a way of getting discovered?"

"I can draw," I say.

She glances down at my uncomfortable shoes as two twenty-something women in bright button-down tops, jeans, and heels come into the space. They are followed by a slightly older guy holding an almost impossibly large, steaming orange mug.

"For both of our sakes, I seriously hope so. We're doing a public rollout of the new logo today. If you can make yourself useful, good for you. If not—pick a table in the corner, stay out of our way, and keep your mouth shut. Everyone!" she shouts as several more designers come through the door. "Let's get to work."

Every time I had visited *Gloss* in the past, there had been an upbeat energy and a low hum of conversation as people calmly went about their business. Today, it was as if everyone had plugged their fingers into a light socket.

The designers shout at others across the room, drink cup after cup of coffee, and pace while they wait for word to come from Mrs. Webster and her team about the rollout of the new *Gloss* logo and design. More than anything, I want to do what they're doing— debating accent colors and shadows and shifting lines so that the viewer's eye will be drawn to exactly the right place. Instead, I fetch coffee, crawl under tables when a stylus goes missing, and watch as the sharp angles and sweeping curves that for the last several weeks I've changed and changed and changed again fill the wall screens.

Tweaks for my design are debated. Adjusted. Lines shifted slightly to the left or right. Thickened. Sent back upstairs for everyone to wait again. Until finally, Nicolle claps her hands to get everyone's attention and announces, "We're locked!"

The design team stops working and exchanges smiles and high fives. A guy with spiky blond hair wearing a bright green shirt slaps his hand on one of the tables and says, "I knew we nailed it."

I smile even as I clench my hands under the design table. When everyone quiets, Nicolle continues, "The ads are being uploaded to the public screens. They will go live in two hours. Mrs. Webster has asked that we all meet her outside to watch when that happens. I'm giving you ten minutes to celebrate and refuel. Then I expect you back at your stations working on the layouts for next week's issue."

Designers grumble, but I get the feeling it is exactly what the team expected to hear. A few of them wander off to grab a snack or coffee. Nicolle heads to a meeting and the rest settle back in to work. No one seems to remember that I exist. I glance at the clock—one hour and fifty-two minutes until the *Gloss* ads with the new logo go live across the country. I'm glad Nicolle didn't let any of us go to lunch or I'd be throwing up.

I shift in my seat and doodle on the screen in front of me as the minutes tick by in the ever-thickening air. I've been anticipating and dreading this moment with equal weight. We have all agreed it is the best way forward—but . . .

"Well look at that."

I crack my knee against the table as I jerk around to see Nicolle looming. Her pale, hazel eyes narrow as they shift to my screen. Streaks of electric blue, pink, and yellow wind over a backdrop of silver. In the center of the image is a large handbag, like the ones pictured on dozens of advertisements on the electronic pages of *Gloss*. The black lines are woven to give the bag texture. Sharp, hard gold colors the geometric fastenings lending them weight. But it is the handles of the bag that I spent the most time on. Each line created to lend depth to the braids. But if anyone looked closely in the shadows and empty spaces, they'd find fanned out V's like the ones in the new *Gloss* logo. V's that formed the open pages of a book. V's for "verify."

I hold my breath as Nicolle studies my work. Takes in the details. The flaws—because there are dozens of them. So many places to refine and rework and reimagine. If I had several more hours, it would be better. I could . . .

"Huh," Nicolle says, shifting her intense gaze from the tablet to me. "You *can* draw. Maybe by the time the summer is over, I might actually try to remember your name."

Before I can react, she turns her back on me.

The crawling minutes speed up as the end of the day approaches. I drop my stylus several times and can barely draw a straight line by the time Nicolle announces, "Okay, everyone. It's time!"

My stomach flips. I shut down my screen, retrieve my phone out of my bag, and hold it tight to my chest, then hurry after everyone as they stream into the hallway. We join the rest of the *Gloss* staff as they make their way out of the office.

The sidewalk is jammed. I shove through clusters of *Gloss* workers and look for Rose. I spot her hurrying across the street to the other side, where her mother stands at the edge of the sidewalk surrounded by several fashionably attired individuals I assume are top *Gloss* executives. Sunlight gleams off Mrs. Webster's jewelry as she stares at the enormous public screen far above the *Gloss* entrance. A blond man in a ruby-red shirt moves to the side as Rose walks beside her mother. Without looking at her daughter, Charity Webster reaches out and clasps Rose's hand tight in hers. They know the risks they are taking even if the others chattering excitedly around us don't.

"Any minute!" someone shouts from nearby.

I shove my way through the crowded sidewalk and step between two cars parked at the curb just as the chirpy brunette on the screen ends her broadcast. She tells everyone to stay tuned for the five o'clock news that will start after the commercial break.

The credits roll. I clutch my phone tight. Everyone around me holds their breath. Then a rainbow of brilliant color explodes onto the screen. Music blares. Lights pulse as if dozens of photographers are taking the images that follow one after another. Shots of the American Dream pop band, women walking down Michigan Avenue in high fashion as if they are on a catwalk, the president of the United States and her husband waving from the balcony of the White House—the American flag fluttering behind them. The images pass too fast for me to catch them all. Smiling families. Tourist attractions. Sports. Models in stunning dresses walking on a creamy-white beach with a compelling female voice narrating over the kinetic images and music and the excited shouts of the staff around me about how *Gloss* is always where you want to be.

I stumble and have to catch my footing, but I look up in time to see the flashes of colors—pink and blue, orange and yellow. They alternate faster and faster as the music grows louder until there is a cymbal crash and the new logo for *Gloss* appears.

It isn't exactly the same image that I drew. It's better. The designers worked their magic so the colors almost leap off the screen, which will hopefully make it impossible to ignore.

Down the street, in the distance, other public screens are filled with the same image as the narrator's voice says: "A new *Gloss*—so you can be a brand-new you."

The *Gloss* staff cheers and exchanges congratulations as the next commercial, one praising the stepped-up recycling program, plays followed by a Pepsi ad.

Employees on the sidewalk start to stream back into *Gloss*. Several cars honk their horns. I step back onto the sidewalk and spot Rose and her mother waiting at the crosswalk for the light to change.

My new phone vibrates. With an unsteady hand, I punch up the text message.

THEY'VE AGREED TO MEET. SEE YOU TONIGHT—STEF

Satisfaction flares. Step one is done. Now we have to move on to step two and hope that nothing goes wrong.

I start to text Rose, when I notice the shoes of the woman strolling past me on the sidewalk. They are the same as the man in the gray suit that appears on the sidewalk across the street—and the woman who comes to stand beside the bus stop only a few feet away from me.

Black running boots with metal straps.

The Marshals—the people responsible for taking Isaac, and killing my mother. The people who have been searching the city for me—are here.

TWO

A female Marshal dressed in gray slacks, a crisp white dress shirt, and carrying a large brown handbag stops in front of *Gloss*'s front door.

I hold my breath and prepare to run.

The last time I faced the Marshals I survived, but Spine and so many other Stewards did not. When the Marshal's eyes sweep my way and she doesn't immediately show any sign of seeing the real me under the makeup and fashion-forward hair, I stay put and attempt to take normal breaths.

We knew the logo would gain unwanted attention. We knew there was no avoiding Marshals asking questions when they saw the ad. But we never dreamed so many would arrive just moments after it played for the first time.

The female Marshal steps around a twentysomething couple who are hurrying down the sun-streaked sidewalk. Then she turns in my direction.

Don't stare, I tell myself. *Pretend not to notice the male Marshal in the suit who is currently crossing the street to this side—right behind Rose who has no idea he is there.*

The bus stop Marshal moves in my direction. Her leather bag brushes my side as she walks by. There is something hard inside that bag. I'm pretty sure I can guess what it is.

"Watch it!" I snap, stepping away from the woman, trying to get some distance between us, and hoping she only hears the annoyance I am trying to convey and not the fear pounding in my heart.

"Sorry," the woman murmurs. She doesn't bother to look at me. Instead, her eyes stay focused on Rose and Mrs. Webster who are stepping up on the sidewalk on this side of the street.

Fingers shaking, I type the message THEY'RE HERE on my phone, but stop myself from sending it because the Marshal behind her has moved. Now he can see over her shoulder. They move toward the entrance to join the rest of the *Gloss* employees heading back to work. I can only watch helplessly as that Marshal and another who appears beside him follow Rose and her mother into the building. The Marshals are not in the reception area when I finally make it through the door. And I don't see them in the hallway as I head back to work or in any of the nearby cubicles. Mrs. Webster's office is on the second floor. Maybe—

"You—intern!"

I turn and see my new boss, Nicolle, standing in the aisle between a bunch of cubicles. She points behind her and sighs. "Design room is this way."

"Right." I turn my back on the stairs and follow Nicolle into the design room. The screens are now filled with images of page design options for the next *Gloss* issue. Once again, I am told to sit in the corner while the others work on making the interior page design reflect the new logo and color scheme.

After about ten minutes, Nicolle declares everyone useless. She tells the team to go celebrate the launch of the campaign and to expect to work late every day until the new issue is put to bed. No one reminds Nicolle that it is already past time to leave as they gather their things. While they head out, I look around the work-room for an excuse to stay.

"I can take the coffee mugs back to the break room." I jump up and start gathering the mismatched ceramic mugs that haphazardly decorate the tables in the room.

Nicolle places her hands on her hips. "Do you think cleaning coffee mugs is going to impress anyone?"

"Not if they like drinking coffee out of dirty cups."

She stares at me, her eyes hard and narrow behind the large frames. I stand perfectly still hoping she cannot see how desperate I am to stay. Mrs. Webster said she could deal with the Marshals, but if she and Rose are in trouble, I have to try to help them.

Finally, Nicolle nods. Her lips twitch. "You have a point. Clean up. Don't touch anything you shouldn't or I'll know. Be here early tomorrow. It's going to be a long day." With that she heads back into her adjoining office and shuts the door.

Juggling six mugs, I hurry to the break room. Some people are cleaning up their desks or calling for friends to meet them for drinks. Others are hunched over computer screens or tablets—clearly plan-ning to work into the evening hours.

I wash and put away the mugs in record time and go back into the hall. No Nicolle. My heart hammers as I head up the steps and

I hold my breath as I slowly open the door and step onto the second floor of the *Gloss* offices.

The offices and cubes are bigger on this level. I can see the outlines of people moving around behind opaque glass and hear the low murmur of voices as I take slow steps down the royal-blue carpeted aisle. Mrs. Webster's office takes up the back corner of the floor. I am almost to the door when someone touches my arm.

I jump, and swallow down my yelp as I face the woman whose large brown leather bag bumped me out on the sidewalk. Standing beside her is a tall, lanky man in a blue button-down dress shirt. I don't have to look to know what shoes he is wearing.

"I didn't mean to startle you," the Marshal offers with a quick smile. "We got turned around. We're looking for Chris Tapper's office. Can you direct us?"

"Chris Tapper?" I repeat the familiar name and look down the hall toward Mrs. Webster's office.

"You seem kind of jumpy," the man says. My heart goes still under the man's piercing gaze. "Is there a reason you're nervous?"

Only dozens of them.

"Today is my first day working at *Gloss*," I say, hoping they won't question that truth. "I'm an intern."

The two exchange a look as Rose steps out of an office and into view far down the hall behind them.

"I'm sorry we startled you," the female Marshal says with a toothy smile. "I hope you enjoy working here."

Rose takes a step toward us and begins to gesture—clearly wanting to know if I need help—as the Marshals begin to turn.

"He's not here!"

The Marshals' heads swivel in my direction before they can see

Rose and make the connection between the two of us.

"Excuse me?" the woman asks.

"You said you were looking for Chris Tapper," I say. "He doesn't work here."

"You started today and you know everyone in the building?" the male Marshal asks, taking a terrifying step closer.

"I wish." I force a laugh that sounds stupid even to me as Rose ducks back into the doorway she came out of. "Everyone was talking about him because he came up with the new logo that debuted today—just before he moved."

"Did anyone say where he went to?" the woman asks.

I shake my head. "I don't think so. Just that he got a new job." Hopefully, my story will help confirm the cover Mrs. Webster created.

The two exchange another look before the man says, "Well, that's too bad. We really wanted to talk to him. We appreciate your help."

This time when they turn away, I don't stop them. I don't move. Not when they step into the stairwell and the door closes behind them. It isn't until an older woman I recognize as one of the *Gloss* editors emerges from her office and smiles as she passes that I finally head down the hallway to the door Rose disappeared behind.

"Holy crap," Rose says when I close the door behind me. "Mom is meeting with two Marshals and some guy from the City Pride Department right now in her office. I didn't realize there were others walking around."

"Do you know what they're saying to your mom? Are they going to make her change the logo back?"

"Not unless they want people to ask why the government

insisted the design be changed," Rose says with a smile. "Dozens of people have called Mom to compliment the new logo since the meeting started. Mom's secretary has been interrupting with an update on the number of congratulatory messages every few minutes. Some of the messages Mom arranged in advance so she could demonstrate that the design has already made an impression. The rest are unsolicited. Most from high-profile people in the industry."

As long as they believe the documentation Mrs. Webster has about the designer and that she has no knowledge of the Stewards, it will be impossible for the government to justify asking her to change the logo back without drawing even more attention to the design—and the change.

"I'm going to meet Dad tonight and drop how strange it was for government people to meet with Mom after the reveal."

Rose and her mother were certain Mr. Webster would use his influence to get the Marshals to back off—if only because family scrutiny would continue to make him look bad after Isaac being taken. If Mrs. Webster's correct, those things combined should keep her and Rose and the rest of the *Gloss* staff safe—but for how long, it's impossible to say.

I tell her about my meeting for tonight. She assures me again that her mother has everything under control and that I shouldn't worry. But I can't help it when I spot another Marshal watching *Gloss's* front door from a café table across the street as I walk away.

My phone chimes. I stop midway up a sidewalk flanked by a line of blue and white flowers. The burgundy brick three-story house it leads to is now my home. Rose's message is short: Goons gone. Mom's good. Going to meet Dad.

I grab the railing and climb the steps up to the porch. A group of baseball fans walk by in their blue-and-white-striped jerseys. I mutter, "Go Cubs." The excited group gives me a thumbs-up, as I pull out my house key and let myself inside.

The house I lived in with my parents wasn't large, but it was filled with cheerful colors—each selected when I was little by my mother and me. Sunny yellows edged in white, brilliant blues, and dusty pinks. The fabrics were worn from use. The floors a bit scarred. I didn't realize how much I loved that house until it was gone. This place couldn't be more different.

The sand-colored tiles where I gratefully shed my shoes are cold despite the warmth of the sunlight streaming through the glass window above the door. The foyer walls are stark white. So are the ones in the adjoining living room with its impersonal brown leather chairs, steel and glass tables, and wrought-iron lamps. It may as well be the lobby of a midrange hotel. The pictures that fill the screens on the living room walls provide the only personality in the room.

There is a shot of the baseball field from just blocks away. An image of a man wearing a dented gray hat that is only slightly different from the one that I've actually seen him sporting playing a guitar in a pop band—as if he would ever do anything that fun. There is also a picture featuring me with my short red-and-white-streaked hair and heavily made-up eyes standing at the edge of Lake Michigan. The sky is impossibly blue. The water shimmers in the background and I am flanked by two smiling people that I have never met. But if asked I am to say those people are my parents and that the man in the hat rocking out on guitar is my uncle.

A fake photo history for "Uncle" Dewey and I that took almost no time to create.

Quickly, I walk by the pictures, through the dining room, which is furnished with an unused long black table and six high-backed black leather chairs.

Faint strains of classical music and the rich scent of coffee greets me as I step into the stainless steel and gray-ceramic-tiled kitchen. A mostly empty pot sits on the warmer. The bowl of sugar and a spoon rest on the linoleum counter. The coffee calls to me, but it'll have to wait since I'm running late and there are things I have to do before tonight's meeting.

The flowing orchestral music grows louder as I head up the stairs to the bedroom I've been using. The plush carpet is not quite dark enough to be called beige. The bed has a high oak headboard. The only real color in the room is the ruby-red comforter I found buried in the closet and the electronic map of the city displayed on the wall screen.

I shed my work clothes, and making sure I check for any tags I might have missed, change into workout gear and slip into my not-quite-broken-in pair of running shoes. Then, shoving my phone in my back pocket, I head for the bedroom door, open it, and yelp.

"When Lord Byron spoke of children that only scream in a quiet voice, he was not speaking of you." Dewey shifts the battered brown hat on his head and sighs. Unlike mine, Dewey's clothes aren't new. His brown pants are faded and the plaid green-and-yellow button-down shirt is worn at the elbows. As a Steward, Dewey rarely left the underground Lyceum and its hundreds of thousands of books. But according to Dewey, just because he spent thirty years of his life underground didn't mean he believed he would always be safe there. Which is why he bought this place years ago and had Atlas's father maintain it.

It has been weeks since I returned to the building the Stewards used as an exit station—a location we could use as a safe house that would also covertly allow us to reach our underground headquarters—the Lyceum. I will never forget how my father reacted when I came through the entrance after making the decision to continue to fight for the truth. His hands were shaking, but his eyes were mostly clear when he gave me an ultimatum: "If you make the choice to stay, you're on your own."

I still can't decide what hurt worse—those words or watching him walk out the door the next morning knowing that the dad I'd counted on most of my life had left long before that moment. My mother's death and the drinking that he used to cope had changed him. Still, realizing he didn't love me enough to stop drinking—or to stay and help me when I needed him the most—made me feel as if I were being pulled underwater.

The whispered click the door made as it shut behind my father on that day almost sent me to my knees. Then Dewey said, "It goes on."

His matter-of-fact tone cut through the emptiness and had me turning to look at him. He was holding his hat in his hands, giving me an unshadowed view of the greenish-yellow outline of a fading bruise on his cheek. The last signs of the injuries he had received at the hands of the Marshals because of the plan I insisted would work.

"What goes on?" I asked him—wishing my father would come back through the door and say he made a mistake.

"Life," he said simply. "No matter how dark the moment or deep the pain, life continues. The bravest are those who are willing to face the new day uncertain of what will come with the dawn."

"Who said that?"

He placed his hat on his head and adjusted it before saying, "I did. And while you face the uncertain dawn, you will stay with me."

"Where?" I asked, looking around the now-abandoned Steward exit station we had been using. "We didn't go along with the lockdown. Do you think we should still stay here?" The exit station had been a refuge, but after everything that happened it no longer felt safe.

"I don't think making camp in a Steward station is a good idea." Dewey shook his head. "I doubt Scarlet would react well if she found us here."

I doubted the current head of the Stewards would be happy to run into us anywhere. Not after we convinced dozens of her members to defy the lockdown she'd ordered. It was her anger with us that revealed how she betrayed Atlas's father to the Marshals simply because they disagreed on the future of the Stewards. Scarlet was willing to sacrifice anyone—even friends who trusted her—when she believed she was right. Since I was most definitely not her friend, I could only imagine what she would do if we ever met again.

"Not to fret. I took the advice of Miguel de Cervantes to heart." Dewey smiled at me. "'Forewarned, forearmed; to be prepared is half the victory.' Which is why I arranged to have a station of my own."

I shake off the memory and frown at Dewey, who now is standing in my bedroom doorway waiting for me to recover from my surprise. "Mrs. Webster decided to launch the new *Gloss* campaign today."

"I know," he says, pulling a piece of paper out of his pocket. "Between the two news channels and a variety of websites, I've seen the *Gloss* advertisement over a dozen times. Mrs. Webster already contacted me through my alternate email. Our cover is holding."

"A Marshal was watching the building when I left."

"There is no turning back for Mrs. Webster or her company now."

Which means there is no turning back for me. "Stef contacted me just after the new ad launched," I say, thinking of the girl Atlas and I helped save from the Marshals weeks ago.

"And?"

"And Stef's friends have finally agreed to meet—tonight at eight."

I wait for Dewey to smile or nod or say something positive about finally getting Stef and her friends to consider helping us. Instead he glances at his watch, then holds out the paper in his hand and says, "You don't have much time."

I grab the paper, unfold it, and study a map of a small section of the city, the route I should take and the stops I need to make along the way.

"Our package will be ready when you arrive at the first stop," Dewey says. "Don't forget . . ."

"I know where to go and what to say," I snap, even though I am grateful for the carefully drawn directions.

Dewey merely lifts an eyebrow and calmly says, "I will have food waiting for when you return." For some reason, that only stokes my annoyance.

Grabbing my backpack, I brush past Dewey and head downstairs and out the door. On the porch, I double-check to make sure I have the money and ID cards, then swing the bag onto my shoulders and start running.

A bunch of girls I went to school with used to gush about their love of running. How each day they did it made them love it even more. I don't know who they were trying to impress or if they were just insane, but after running every day for several weeks I can honestly say I despise it more now than ever. When my dad left the city, I ran hoping I could out-distance the crushing ache. After ten minutes, each breath of air was like shards of glass scratching at my throat. But I refused to stop. I knew I would need to be faster and stronger now that everything had been taken.

My family.

My home.

Even my name.

I won't let them take anything else.

Rubber slaps against sidewalk. My breaths come high and fast. After three blocks my calves ache. Not stretching before starting out was a mistake. Just one more thing to add fuel to the frustration churning inside me.

The memory of the Marshals appearing outside *Gloss*—the looming threat of what they could do to Mrs. Webster and Rose— makes me run faster. Past the corner market. The hair salon. A gelato place with a sculpture of David eating ice cream standing proudly next to the front door. Not a scrap of gum on the walkway or a scratch on any of the signs that I pass. Everything looks perfect. Everyone I pass doesn't understand the price being paid for the illusion.

Finally, I reach a narrow doorway. A bright blue sign with white scripted lettering reads Screen It. A bell jingles when I push the door open. I step into the air-conditioned space filled with screens of every shape and size—from small handhelds to one that takes up most of the store's back wall.

"Can I help you?" the tan, dark-haired man behind the counter asks.

I glance around the store. There is a customer absorbed in the task of selecting a cable. Other than him, the place is empty.

Keeping my voice low, I ask, "Can you verify if you have an item on hold for a friend of mine?"

The man behind the counter sits up straight. "I'm always glad to verify information." He reaches under the counter and comes up with a white plastic case. "Everything is in here. Tell our friend I had to make it a bit bigger than what he asked for, but it was necessary to handle both functions." He drops the case in the palm of my hand and says, "Tell him I can guarantee at least a hundred hours of battery life. It should go a little longer than that, but—" The man sighs. "Just make sure he doesn't try to push it much further."

A hundred hours. Just over four days.

I shove the case in my backpack and ask, "May I use the bathroom?" as the customer approaches the counter.

The man behind the counter smiles. "In the back to the *right*."

I nod and leave him to deal with the guy and his cables, head to the back hallway, and instead of going through the left door marked Restroom, I follow the clerk's directions, which are a match for Dewey's, and open the Employees Only door on the right.

Despite the Stewards going into lockdown, underground in the Lyceum, this switching station is still open for business. This clerk was willing to help with our package and is allowing me to use the back exit in defiance of Scarlet setting the rails to red. Unlike a lot of Stewards Dewey has reached out to, this one is still committed to the cause. With any luck, Atlas will return with news that he has found more. Their help, combined with the reach of *Gloss* and the device I carry with me, will finally allow us to uncover what happens to the people the government has disappeared. We're going to learn what we don't know and share that information in a way that will make everyone in this country see facts they won't be able to deny.

I jog down the alley. When I reach the end, I turn south past a line of brown and white brick apartments and red-and-white-checkered sidewalk tables filled with people. The tangy scent of oregano and garlic wafts from their plates. Mitch Michaels, a movie-star-handsome news anchor I've grown up watching, smiles from the public screen halfway down the block. He's replaced by a commercial for TRAVEL USA and its upbeat, sea-to-shining-sea celebratory music. I tune out the sales pitch of majestic images of the Grand Canyon, Mount Rushmore, and the Mississippi River and keep running. It's only when I reach the next block and the screen changes to the bright colors of the new *Gloss* logo that I come to a stop. I take the moment to watch it without the threat of the Marshals or the chatter of everyone from *Gloss*.

Thrill and anxiety bubble inside like one of Mr. Reid's chemistry class experiments. No matter how carefully I measured the light blue crystals or the sugar-like white powder or the acrid-smelling clear liquid, the combination was never quite right. Everyone else's experiments turned pale pink or opaque. My vials gurgled and overflowed onto the blue-orange Bunsen burner flames.

The new *Gloss* logo flashes once again on the screen and then changes to sports news.

If this experiment goes wrong, more than a few chemicals will be spilled. I—

Something shuffles on the sidewalk behind me. I wait for the sound of footsteps to tell me the person has moved on. Someone shouts in the distance. Cars whoosh along the street. And whoever is behind me is still there—waiting.

I ease one strap of the backpack off my shoulder.

"You don't want to do that."

My heart leaps at the familiar voice even as I get a tight grip on my bag. "That's what you think." With that I pivot, swinging the bag as hard as I can at Atlas's face.

Atlas lunges to the side and has the nerve to grin when the bag barely glances off his shoulder. Before I can recover my balance, he grabs the free strap and pulls. I pitch forward. The bag hits the ground, but Atlas's arm wraps around my waist before I can land next to it.

"Your weight wasn't balanced over the balls of your feet," he says into my ear. My back is pressed against him. His arm still holding me tight. "A Marshal wouldn't have stopped your fall."

"A Marshal wouldn't have expected me to swing my bag. You taught me that trick." I lean my head back against Atlas's warm chest. The arm around me relaxes and I smile. "You also taught me this." I stomp down on Atlas's foot, then jam my elbow into his stomach. He lets out a satisfying yelp with the first and a grunt with the second.

"Good to know you haven't forgotten while I've been gone." Atlas rubs at his side, then grins. The sharp lines of his features soften. The contours of his deep brown face catch the light differently, creating something too compelling to be called something as ordinary as handsome.

He's here. Safe.

I take a step toward him.

"Are you going to hit me again?"

Before he finishes his question, I lock my arms around his neck and pull his head down to meet mine. His lips are warm and strong.

He pulls me closer and I lose myself in the liquid heat spiraling through me, thankful for this moment filled with excitement, sparks of color and light, and the tugging need for what could come next.

Atlas gasps with pain and the moment shatters into a thousand tiny shards of reality. Atlas rubs his arm where the Marshals shot him weeks ago.

I'll never forget that moment. The bullet piercing him. Atlas launching himself into Lake Michigan to convince the Marshalls he was dead.

Somehow he had the strength to swim through the bone-chilling water and get back to the Stewards' meeting point. He was lucky—the bullet passed clean through the arm. But that doesn't mean it wasn't a close call—and a sign of what could come for any of us.

"Did you reinjure it?" I ask.

Atlas shakes his head. "I had a close call yesterday and strained a muscle. No big deal."

"What kind of close call?" For the first time, I notice the purple shadow of a bruise on Atlas's jaw.

"The Marshals found one of the old Stewards' stations. There were two Stewards who didn't make it to the Lyceum in time for the lockdown hiding there. I could only get one of them away from the Marshals. The other . . :" A haunting emptiness fills Atlas's eyes. "I was going to follow them to wherever they took her, but she used the deadman's switch before they could put her in the car."

The ever-present worry that his father might have taken that same life-ending step shines in Atlas's eyes.

"We'll find your father and Isaac," I say, picking up my fallen bag and checking to make sure the plastic case inside escaped damage.

"Is that the tracker we—"

"Yeah." I let out a relieved sigh and tuck it back into the bag. "Dewey is going to run some tests and make sure it's ready to go."

"I thought I found the Unity Center. That's why I was out of touch longer than planned," Atlas explains. "Only it was a dead end. The City Pride Department started renovations on the site two months ago. The guy at the hot dog stand across the street said the building had been empty for a few months before construction began."

Which meant that the Marshals' holding facility had been closed and the City Pride Department had begun erasing any sign of their work long before Atlas's father went missing.

I used to dream about working for the City Pride Department— just like my mother. City Pride dedicates government resources to making every part of a city beautiful, nationwide. It originated from a pilot program in Chicago based on the theory that an attractive place to live would create a sense of pride for residents in the community, and a desire to keep the neighborhood both attractive and safe. Everyone cheered when crime plummeted in the Chicago neighborhoods where the program had been implemented. Streets that had been neglected for years were brought to life by government artists and designers. Suddenly the area that had once been considered the most dangerous in the country was an example of how to make a city both beautiful and safe.

For years, I envied my mother for the positive impact her art had on the world. I was thrilled when she encouraged my own artistic inclinations and couldn't understand why she suddenly told me I should shift my future dreams to something less demanding. I thought she felt I wasn't good enough. Now I know it was because she had found out the truth.

It wasn't that I wasn't good enough. Still, after everything I know, I have to consciously remind myself of that fact.

"How about the Stewards you visited?" I ask.

"I found nine." Atlas stops walking. "None of them are willing to work with us. At least not yet."

My heart sinks. "None of them?"

"They still believe in the cause, but . . . they heard about what happened. On the pier. They don't want to put themselves in that kind of danger until they know for certain we can make a difference."

My fault. I pushed them to move forward. I convinced them that sharing the truth would change everything. I was wrong. If I were them, I wouldn't want to work with me, either.

"How did you find me?" I ask as we walk to the end of the block.

"Dewey." Atlas gives me a ghost of a smile. "He gave me the training route you were taking. He'd have something to say about you stopping to admire your work."

"Dewey has something to say about everything."

"He also said Stef and her friends made contact."

"I'm meeting with them after I drop off Dewey's package and change clothes," I say.

"Well, then we'd better get moving." Atlas drops my hand. He smiles, but there is frustration and worry behind his eyes as he says, "I bet you're still not fast enough to beat me back to Dewey's place."

Hitching my bag onto my shoulder, I let the conversation about the future fade and do the only thing I can do—I take Atlas up on his bet and run.

THREE

Atlas wins, but only by a half block.

I'm getting stronger, I think as I tug on a forest-green T-shirt and a pair of jeans.

Atlas holds out a beat-up blue baseball cap as I come down the stairs. "Ready?" he asks.

I take the hat, run my thumb over the edge of the repair I recently did on the lining, and nod.

Dewey steps out of the shadows of the living room with several CTA cards. I place my "Merriam" card on the small entryway table so I don't mistakenly use it, and take the ones offered by Dewey.

"Change the cards you use with every stop and—"

"Don't do anything stupid," I finish the thought, knowing that if I do anything stupid, it will be Mrs. Webster and Rose who pay for my mistake.

"Good advice, but not what I was going to say." Dewey puts his hand on my shoulder and looks into my eyes. "Before you so rudely interrupted me, I was going to remind you of James Thomson's words. 'More firm and sure the hand of courage strikes, when it obeys the watchful eye of caution.' Do you understand what I'm telling you?"

I want to say yes, but if I do I am pretty certain Dewey will call my bluff. "Not even a little bit," I admit.

Dewey smirks. "Rest assured we will discuss that deficiency." He shifts his hat lower on his forehead and turns to Atlas. "I shouldn't have to tell you to be careful, but as Meri has demonstrated, just because I understand something doesn't mean someone else will." With that he disappears up the stairs.

"I'll meet you on the corner by Wrigley Field," Atlas says. When I nod, he goes to the back door to avoid notice by anyone who might be on the street. I tuck my hair under the battered baseball cap, shove Dewey's new CTA cards into my pocket, and step onto the front porch.

The last vestiges of sunlight have faded into the horizon, leaving behind a chill that whispers over the night air. I walk quickly down the quiet street and turn onto the next perfectly maintained, tree-lined block, moving from the quiet neighborhood into the one bustling with pedestrians and cars and eventually vendors selling royal blue, red, and white T-shirts and hats. Organ music and cheers drift on the breeze as Wrigley Field rises in the distance.

The crowd inside the stadium is roaring when I reach the corner closest to the historic lipstick-red with white lettering sign that my father made Mom and me pose beneath years ago. My father used to have the picture displayed on a screen that sat at the edge of his office desk. When he looked up from his work, he could see the green steel stadium and its memorable sign in the background with Mom and me grinning like idiots. Someone must have removed the screen with that photo from his office. Who knows what happened to it.

Since Atlas isn't here yet, I stare up at the sign and wonder—is Dad watching the game right now from wherever the Stewards took him to hide? If so, is he thinking of mom and me and our picture? Or has he turned his back on that memory the way he walked away from me?

"You okay?" Atlas appears at my side and I shake off the cobweb of emotions.

"I'm fine," I say, even though I'm not sure I am. I never heard Atlas approach. Never saw him coming. If he had been a Marshal . . . "We should get moving."

Atlas doesn't ask the questions I can see in his eyes, which is good because I'm not sure I have answers. It's easier for us to focus on making our way to the L. We'll get off at the next stop, and take the bus three more stops away—using a different CTA card at every one so anyone looking at transit card travel patterns can't trace us back to Dewey's safe house.

Finally, we climb off the final bus and hurry down the quiet block toward the destination I was given. We pass a small coffeehouse whose windows glow with an inviting warmth. I spot a man in jeans, a white button-down shirt, and a brown dress coat standing next to a silver-and-ruby-red bench at the end of the block.

Atlas takes my hand and gives a deliberate nod.

Marshal.

I can't make out the man's shoes from here, but I don't doubt Atlas's instinct. Hand in hand, we cross to the other side of the street. Then we walk at an agonizingly slow pace along the sidewalk that hums with life while the last gasps of dim sunlight give way to the midnight blue of night. When we reach the next block, Atlas looks up at the public screen that is playing a popular game show. In it, contestants have to perform impossible and often embarrassing or disgusting stunts in front of their former significant others in order to win cash and possibly a second chance at love. Almost everyone I know watches or has applied to be on the show.

I used to think people who applied were crazy, since I never found anything remotely interesting about a guy smearing himself in honey and standing in the center of a bunch of beehives to prove his ex should give him a second chance. After living with Dewey, I know this kind of show is on-air for a reason. "Bread and circuses" is what Dewey called it—giving a sense of security through everyday essentials like food and at the same time providing outrageous entertainment to distract the mind.

I guess if people are busy passionately debating whether Jane should have taken back the guy smeared with honey, or if she was a witch for sending him away, they won't think too hard about the world around them. They're too distracted to question. A kind of conditioning for the masses.

The studio audience's bubbly laughter grates on my nerves even as its mesmerizing effect on those watching on the public screens gives us an opportunity to make sure we haven't captured unwanted interest.

I chance a glance back toward the coffee shop. The Marshal scans the area, then spots a woman in high heels and a tight black dress. He smiles when she waves. The two kiss while we pretend to watch the woman on the screen dissolve into tears after watching her ex get stung by a dozen bees. Once the Marshal and his date head off into the night we continue down the block.

I check the time when we arrive on the street of our meeting place; the storefront with a bright sunflower on the sign is near the end of the block. The store has already closed for the night.

Just weeks ago, Atlas directed us to take refuge inside this shop. We were being chased by the Marshals for saving the very girl I'm meeting tonight—a girl the government was trying to make disappear.

The off-white glow of the streetlamps and the illumination from the still-open restaurants cause the shadows to retreat from the sidewalk. No other Marshals are in sight, but just because we don't see them doesn't mean they, or others, aren't nearby—watching. We won't be able to hang here for very long without drawing attention.

"Do you see her?" Atlas asks.

I shake my head and walk up to the bright blue-and-yellow painted doorway, which currently stands empty. The other businesses housed in the same building are also closed.

"Maybe she got cold feet?" Atlas frowns. "There are a lot more Marshals on the streets since we last saw her. That might be giving her and her friends second thoughts."

My stomach ties into a knot even as I insist, "She said she would be here."

"I also said you were supposed to come alone."

Atlas and I spin toward the clipped words. A tall, lanky figure with a black baseball hat pulled low over her forehead appears. She yanks off the cap and shakes out the long dark hair I recall from our brief but terrifying first meeting.

Then she turns toward Atlas. "You weren't invited to this party."

"I invited him," I say. "He's the reason you're standing here now instead of in the hands of the Marshals."

"That's not exactly the way I remember it." Stef shrugs. "And I'm not objecting to his presence. I'm just surprised that he's here at all." She looks back at Atlas. "Rumor has it the Stewards have gone into hiding. We haven't seen any signs of your friends since all those books and papers were handed out. And you're right." She gives Atlas a wide, slightly gap-toothed smile. "My friends are having second thoughts. You being late won't help convince them otherwise."

"There was a Marshal . . ."

"Save it for the others." Stef checks her watch and says, "Let's go."

Stef disappears around the building and Atlas and I have to hurry to keep up as we go down the alley we all traveled once before, across the street, through the park, and finally into a residential block. Stef keeps the pace brisk as we pass tall two- and three-story brick houses all guarded by perfectly pruned bushes of evergreens, which alternate in height. Stef frowns at her watch again.

"What's the big deal?" I ask. "We were only a few minutes late." Nine, to be exact.

Stef glances at me, but doesn't slow. "For some of the people you're meeting, a few minutes means the difference between being part of the action, or taken out of commission for a week or more. Seeing the symbol on the screens today convinced them you were serious. They're willing to listen, but if we're not there soon, they won't stick around and wait."

We move on to the next block filled with bungalows that are painted in shades of yellows and blues that glow in the moonlight.

"If time's a factor, why tell us to come here? Why not give us the real location of the meeting?"

Stef smirks. "Like you and your friend here would tell me the exact location of wherever the Stewards hang out? This way." She trots down the sidewalk of a two-story white house trimmed with yellow and blue—windows completely darkened—and heads to the gate that leads to the backyard. She glances back at the street, pauses for several heartbeats, then says, "I swore they could trust you. Don't make me a liar."

She grabs hold of the fence, places her foot in one of the chain-link sections, and climbs. Atlas grins as Stef awkwardly swings her leg over the top and eases herself to the other side. I return his smile. We both take several steps back. He nods and I race toward the fence first, judging the distance and the height the way he instructed. When I am about two feet from the barrier, I inhale and leap up and catch the top of the fence with my hands and stick one foot in the links over halfway up. Without pausing so I don't kill my momentum, I use my foot and arms to push myself up and over the fence. I land with an *oof* on the other side.

I have to take two steps forward to regain my balance. Within seconds, Atlas sticks his own landing.

Stef gives us a long look. If she's impressed, she doesn't show it. Instead, she turns and walks along a stone path through a garden of flowers toward the back door of the house. She raps three times. There is a scuffling noise followed by two knocks. Stef knocks one more time and the door swings open. She jerks her head and we follow her inside a narrow laundry room with a door to our left that empties into a dimly lit kitchen. Another well-lit entryway with a set of stairs leads downward.

A stocky young man is there—maybe Atlas's age or a year older—with a sharp chin, deep brown skin, and narrow glasses. He crosses his arms over his chest and blocks the steps. "You didn't say there would be two."

"I didn't say there wouldn't be," Stef says sharply. "Are the others still here?"

"Most of them," the guy says, not moving from the doorway. A line of diamond studs in his right ear twinkle as they catch the light. "Jake and Chris left. Joy and her cousin are going to have to head out in a few minutes. It was hard for any of them to get away tonight. A lot aren't sure the risk was worth it." The guy shifts his attention to me. "Stef says you saved her from the Marshals. They must have been punier than the ones I've seen."

Atlas stiffens. I smile. The words aren't the same as those spoken by Dewey on our first meeting, but their purpose is similar. "Are you trying to insult me?" I ask sweetly.

The guy's dark eyes narrow behind his metal frames. "I am if it's working." He steps out of the way and performs an arm flourish toward the steps.

"You're going to have to work a whole lot harder," I say as Stef walks past him and down the stairs. "I'm pretty sure I've been insulted by the best."

He gives me a slightly crooked smile. "I'm Ari. You'd better get down there or you'll lose your audience to curfew."

I glance at my watch. We still have several hours before the mandatory overnight road curfew, which makes me think some of our audience must have come from a distance if they are worried about making it home.

The government claimed the curfew—which prohibited driving between the hours of midnight and five—was put into place because so many crimes were committed during that time of the night. Once crime was no longer an issue, the curfew remained to allow the City Pride Department to make road repairs without threat of creating traffic jams.

Before learning the word "verify," I believed the curfew contributed to the safety and prosperity of the city. Now . . . I'm not sure what I believe. Maybe once it was about safety. Now, I suspect the rule provides cover for the moving of people and things under the radar.

Atlas's father? Rose's brother? They might already be miles away. We won't be able to find either of them unless others around the country understand what is happening—what has been taken—without them even being aware.

Which is why I'm here.

I head down the brightly lit, unfinished, and slightly unevenly spaced steps. Voices float up from below as Atlas's footsteps sound behind me. My nerves stretch taut.

I know Stef wants to fight back. It's the reason she thinks less of the Stewards—because they have always operated on the fringes—storing and protecting the truth instead of exposing it. She had heard rumors of the Stewards, but her group wasn't interested in waiting in the shadows. They wanted to create change no matter the cost. That's why Stef was shocked when she saw the symbol of the Stewards tattooed on Atlas's arm. We had prevented Marshals from taking her off the streets and almost were killed in the process. It was the first time anyone had heard of a Steward risking anything to come to the aid of someone who wasn't one of their own.

I follow the stairs as they turn into the basement doorway and take the final scarred wooden step onto the concrete floor of a large unfinished basement filled with faces that are all turned toward me. The reason Ari mentioned the curfew hits me square in the chest.

"You can't be serious," Atlas says from directly behind me.

I can't help thinking the same thing because several of the people crammed into the underground space are younger than I am. They aren't worrying about the *driving* curfew. Their curfews are imposed by parents.

Stef's friends, the ones I have been counting on to help fight the government—are children.

FOUR

At least a dozen twelve-year-old kids are sprawled on black-and-white zigzagged rugs or seated on sunken blue and brown couches. There are some my age standing along the gray, pocked concrete walls. Here and there are a few that appear to be older, like Stef. But not many.

"These two helped me escape from the Marshals," Stef says, draping her arm around a girl with a cascade of long, dark braids. In her oversize orange-and-white football jersey she looks maybe as old as thirteen. "They're Stewards."

A low murmur of disapproval colors the tense room. A pair of twins with slightly angular hazel eyes and mops of curly red-brown hair sit cross-legged to my left. They might be as old as fourteen, and they glare with open hostility. One of them says, "Is that supposed to make us trust them?"

"Only if you're foolish," I shoot back, taking a step away from the stairs. Atlas moves to stand at my side. "I doubt you could know what you know and still be sitting here if that was the case."

The twin boys roll their eyes, but the girl standing at Stef's side grins. Considering some of the dumb things Rose and I did a few years ago, I'm not sure that's a positive sign. But I'll take what I can get.

"Stef says you fought the Marshals for her." A scrawny boy with a bruise blooming sickly yellow near his left ear pushes away from the wall. He crosses his arms in front of his puffed-out chest. "She said you know how to beat them, but how do we know you didn't just get lucky?"

"Really?" We don't have time for this, but it's clear by the way the others are nodding that they think we do.

By Stewards standards, I'm not all that skilled, but I've learned enough in the last few weeks that I am certain I can put on a decent demonstration. "Fine. If you back up, Atlas and I can spar for you," I say, pulling off my hat.

"I don't want you to fight him." The kid smiles. "I want to see you fight her." He points to a woman in her early twenties standing in the back of the room. She is solidly built and only an inch or two over my height, but holds herself as if she is at least a foot taller. Her brown-and-blond-streaked hair is pulled into a high ponytail. Long gold hoops dangle at her ears. Anger gleams bright in her eyes.

"We're not here to fight," Atlas says.

"Because Stewards don't fight," Hooped-Earring Girl snaps, weaving around the couches until she comes to stand in front of me. Now that she is up close and personal, I'm certain she could kick my ass, and her predatory smile says she knows it, too. "Stewards hide."

Atlas shifts, but I shake my head. "I've got to do this," I whisper. Atlas is bigger. Stronger. The one they expect to fight.

48

For a heartbeat of a moment, I'm transported deep in the Lyceum standing in front of Spine. She mopped the floor with me, and didn't give me warning before doing it. With her in my mind, I jab at Hoop Girl's face. Everyone gasps. As I'd hoped, instinct causes her to jerk back. Her balance shifts just enough that when I hook my leg around hers and pull, I send her to the ground in a less-than-graceful heap.

"She took down Joy!" rings above the other shouts of outrage, excitement, or both.

The girl's name is *Joy?* The girl scrambling to her feet doesn't look all that joyful to me. In fact, she looks seriously pissed. She faces me again, then snarls and curls her hands into fists.

Atlas and Dewey have drilled me on a lot of fighting techniques. The first is never be where your attacker thinks you'll be. Which is why when Joy puts all her weight behind her punch, I dart out of the way. She yelps and sails through the empty space I vacated, then crashes into the wall next to the stairs. If Joy were a Marshal, I'd use the opportunity to do the smart thing and run. But there's no running now. Instead, I shift my weight to the balls of my feet while Joy grunts, shoves away from the wall, and comes at me again.

I dive to the side, but not before Joy's attack glances off my ear. Head ringing, I dive to the cold, hard concrete floor.

"Enough!" Stef calls. "This isn't playtime."

There are snickers. A few mentions of Joy being in trouble before a pair of scuffed running shoes come into view, followed by Atlas's hand. I take it, let him haul me to my feet. Joy has retreated to the far side of the basement, alone. Face flushed, she stands with her arms crossed over her chest, watching me with narrowed eyes.

"This is a waste of time," Atlas says into my ear. "Come on." He takes my hand and turns toward the stairs.

"Where are you going?" the girl with the long braids demands. One by one the others in the room fall silent. "Stef said you wanted our help."

Atlas grabs the stair rail. "We made a mistake."

"Why?" the girl yells. "Because Joy doesn't like you?"

"Joy doesn't worry me," Atlas says.

"Then why are you leaving?"

Atlas runs a hand over his short-cropped hair and turns. "How old are you?"

She lifts her chin. "Fifteen."

"And you?" He looks down at a wisp of a girl with almost colorless hair and skin that I am certain would turn an angry crimson if she ever spent more than a few minutes in direct sunlight.

"Thirteen."

He shakes his head and looks at me. "That's why we're leaving."

"We're not good enough for the Stewards?" one of the twins asks.

"They think we're too young," the other sneers.

"No," Atlas shoots back, then sighs. "Look, it's just . . . your age means we can't in good conscience ask for your help. It's too dangerous."

"And what we've been doing is safe?" the girl with the braids snaps. "Tell that to my uncle. Or to Ari's cousin. Or Stef's boyfriend."

When I blink my surprise the girl looks over at Stef and asks, "Do the Stewards even *know* what we've been doing? Do they even care?"

Stef waits as bands of silence stretch tighter with each passing second.

Finally, I break the silence. "I don't think most of the Stewards do know who you are or what you have been doing. Do you?" I look to Atlas.

Ari turns to Stef. "You said they knew about our hacking into government systems and the code we've been working on to keep them from locating people who are discussing the truth online. You said they had a plan that could help stop the government from taking our friends and family."

"We do have a plan," I say. "And we are going to stop them."

"Merriam." Atlas places a hand on my arm. "This isn't what we expected."

"No, it isn't," I admit. "But I wasn't what you thought I would be, either."

I turn back to look at the faces scattered throughout the room as something clicks into place.

Yes, a bunch of them are younger than me. Yes, I hate the idea that what I'm asking will put them directly in harm's way. But I was being watched by the Marshals before I saw the faded ink of the word "verify" on the Stewards' rain-soaked page. I was already in harm's way long before Atlas decided to give me the "train ticket" and take me to the Lyceum. I just didn't know it. My mother never told me the truth. No doubt she believed she was protecting me, but I never had the chance to learn what she knew. Because it was too late. She died. Murdered by the government I was taught to put my faith in.

Being unaware of the truth didn't mean I was unaffected by the consequences of the lies that surrounded me. It simply kept me from making my own decisions about how I wanted to deal with it.

"I didn't know about the missing words—the parts of history

they took away—until a few days before I saw the Marshals go after Stef. Atlas taught me the meaning of the word 'verify' and introduced me to the Stewards. If you asked most of them, I doubt any would say I belonged with them. They thought I was like you." I turn toward Atlas. "The Stewards believed I was too young, too."

He steps to the floor beside me. "Meri. You can't be okay with putting these kids in danger."

"I'm not," I snap. Whispers echo through the basement. "I had the same reaction you did when I came down those stairs. But they'll be in danger whether they help us or not. So, if they want to fight with us to change the world for the better, who are we to tell them no?"

Atlas looks from me to the faces scattered throughout the basement. His eyes shine dark and hot. Desperate for an answer of glistening white. One that absolves him. But the truth is never that clean. As far as I can tell it's always made of shades of gray.

"The Stewards weren't wrong to want to keep me safe," I say quietly. "They were just mistaken to think I was ever safe in the first place. Or that they had the right to choose whether I should have the chance to fight for my future."

I keep my eyes on Atlas as he struggles with what he was taught to believe by the Stewards—by his father and grandfather—and the plan we have embarked upon.

Mrs. Webster and Rose won't be able to hold off the Marshals forever. They have sacrificed everything to give us this chance. We can't squander it.

Atlas's hand tightens on mine. A weight I barely recognized on my heart lifts. This is a decision I do not make alone. We are in this together.

"Merriam is right," Atlas says. His sigh tells me everything I need to know about how much he hates that phrase. "The government changed all our futures when they took away the pieces of our history they found inconvenient. They stole our choices. I would never try to do the same thing to you. You have a choice."

The others in the room exchange looks. A few of the younger boys leaning against the wall roll their eyes. I smile, remembering that I wasn't exactly impressed by Atlas when we first met, either.

"Can we get on with it?" A tanned boy in ripped jeans and a Voices of Freedom tour shirt shatters the moment from his place on the floor. "If I'm not home in twenty minutes, my ass is going to get grounded."

"I guess your parents know that's the only part that needs to be grounded since it's where your brain is located," a blond girl about my age giggles.

He crosses his arms defiantly over his chest. "You only wish you had my skills."

"Enough!" Stef calls and the room goes silent. "Shep has a point." She looks at the smug boy in the ripped jeans. "Although not about your skills. If you had been more careful, Shep, Merriam and Atlas wouldn't have had to rescue me from the Marshals in the first place, and they wouldn't be here now."

"But we are here," I say. "And we're going to uncover and expose the truth about what happened to the people the Marshals have taken away."

"We know what happened to them." Ari pushes away from the wall. "They're dead."

"No," I say as Atlas stiffens beside me. "At least, not all of them." Aware time is slipping away, I quickly run down how I broke into the City Pride Department archives and the Unity Center plans I discovered there.

"We were right! We knew they had to be using paper!" the blond girl from before exclaims. "That's why we haven't been able to find anything useful when we wormed our way through a crack in their firewalls."

"Being right also means we're screwed." A guy with buzzed hair and two gold hoop earrings shoves himself out of the sunken, faded blue couch. "We can't hack information if it's not sitting on servers waiting to be hacked. And everything about the truth we've put online gets taken down by their software in minutes."

The room explodes with frustration and angry words.

"Even if you had found information to share and managed to put it online long enough for people to read it, it wouldn't have changed anything!" I shout.

"How the hell would you know?" the guy shoots back.

"Because we tried." I swallow my own anger at the loss and my naiveté. "We put information right into people's hands that explained everything to them, and most of them refused to see it. The news told them it was all a Hollywood stunt so that's what they believed. I thought if we gave people access to the truth they would embrace it. I was wrong."

People died because I was wrong.

"So, we're screwed," the guy in the back reiterates. "We can't get the information we need, and even if we did no one would believe it is real."

"Not if the source of the information makes them uncomfortable," I say.

"The truth *is* uncomfortable."

"You're right," I agree. "Which is why we have to present it in a way they seek out and automatically trust. We're going to use *Gloss* and we started today."

"We recognized the Steward symbol in the logo," Stef says,

stepping forward. "The Marshals will, too. They'll shut it down."

"We have that covered," Atlas says with more confidence than I feel.

"So what? You created a logo for a magazine that is all about fashion. Congratulations." Joy scoffs. "You'll now have the ability to change the world one smokey eye at a time."

"*Gloss* is popular," I say, deliberately not looking at Joy. I will not take the bait and get into an argument with her and waste what little time we have left. "People pay attention to things that are popular and no one wants to feel like they're missing out—especially when it's the thing everyone is talking about. We're going to get people talking about *Gloss* so that even people who don't read it feel as if they have to pay attention. We're going to make it so talked about that the government can't risk shutting it down without drawing notice. Then we're going to start including some of the government-erased words inside the pages."

"And the software programs the government has designed will find the content in their scans and shut the whole thing down," Ari says with a sigh. "Bubble busted."

"Their software scans articles." I smile. "Not artwork." Mrs. Webster had me add a word into one of the ads two weeks ago as a test to see if the programs would flag the magazine's image files. No alarms. No Marshals. And a softening of the ground under the readers for the information that, if we do this right, will change everything.

The two who were fighting about hacking exchange a look.

Stef glances down at them. "Are they right?"

"Maybe," the blond girl says. "The software might be able to recognize block letters, but stylized ones would be hard, if not impossible, for it to detect when the magazine is scanned, especially if it's uploaded at the same time as the rest of the content. The most aggressive programs are reserved for external additions to known sites and web searches."

Something I know all too well from my online search of the word "verify." Had my query not come back with error messages and alarms, I might have simply recycled the "ticket" the Steward gave me and never thought about it again.

"So putting stylized words in artwork could actually work," Ari confirms.

The blond girl and the boy in ripped jeans nod.

"Eventually, someone in the government will notice," Stef says. "And *Gloss*'s popularity will only stop them from shutting it down for so long."

"We know. *Gloss* will publish the truth long before that happens," I say. "But we have to move fast. The quicker we get everyone paying attention to *Gloss*, the better chance we have of getting out the facts we need them to hear. In a way they can accept hearing it."

I will uncover more of those facts once the next phase of the plan is in motion.

"*Gloss* is the e-zine they trust—that everyone they know loves. When we give them the truth, they'll pay attention."

"But none of that will work if we don't draw new attention and readers to *Gloss*," Atlas adds. "That's where we need your help."

Stef looks around the room, then says, "Most of our team has to leave, but I want them to hear one answer for themselves before Ari, Joy, and I make any decisions about partnering with you. The Stewards have been rumored to have been working in secret for dozens of years—while many other people, including those who we have known and loved—have been captured and killed for trying to make people relearn how to question what our government is doing. In all that time no one from the Stewards has made an attempt to be a part of that effort. You've given us a lot to think about today, but the Stewards have never aided us. So why should we put ourselves on the line to help with your plan now?"

A hundred responses leap to my lips, but I turn to Atlas and wait for him to answer. His grandfather was one of the first in the city to see the implications of the government's push to remove words from public use, then textbooks, and finally all sources of printed words. He and his friends went against the popular recycling push and not only collected and preserved books, they created the Lyceum under the city to house them until the time came when people were ready to embrace those books and the truth inside them again.

"My father dedicated his life to the Stewards in order to gather and protect the truth. He carefully recruited others to that mission, hoping that eventually the right moment would come where everyone could be told about the lies the government has told." Atlas's eyes narrowed. "The Stewards were hunted. My father was taken. I don't know if he is dead or alive, but if he were here I think he'd give you the same answer. Why should you put yourself on the line to help us? Because the truth has to win. It's why we'll still do what we believe is necessary no matter what you say."

"But you'd have a better chance with us. Right?" Shep quips.

The others around the room nod.

"Time's up!" Ari shouts. The youngest in the room complain, but they immediately get to their feet and start for the stairs.

"Wait," I insist.

"We heard you out," Stef says. "We'll talk it over and let you know our answer."

"When?"

"When we're ready," Joy offers with a smug smile.

I walk to Joy and look her square in the eyes. "Some Stewards believed their way was the right way and were willing to destroy anyone who expressed different ideas. This is your chance to prove you're better than them." I unzip the bag on my shoulder and upend the spray-paint canisters of neon pink, yellow, orange, and white on the ground. "Or maybe," I add, turning toward the stairs, "you'll prove you're more like them than you want to think."

FIVE

Atlas says nothing as we walk back to Dewey's street. I can tell by the set of his jaw that he has already written Stef and Joy and the others off—like the Stewards who have refused to help. Are they simply afraid? Or are they like Scarlett—who cared more about being right than about the freedoms we have lost?

I have no illusions. I know our plan isn't perfect. Getting people to read *Gloss* in even greater numbers is a good start. And while I told the truth about hiding the words in the *Gloss* images, what I didn't say is those words were only a last resort. The dozens of designs on my tablet will only be used if the third step in the plan doesn't go the way we hope. And only if Mrs. Webster can continue to keep *Gloss* open through her cunning and connections.

I see only one Marshal sitting at a café down the street from *Gloss* when I report to work the next morning, but there is no time to worry about him as everyone dives into work getting the new issue up and running. It isn't until late in the afternoon that Rose finds me in the bathroom to let me know the mayor called her mom personally this morning to congratulate the magazine on the new look and to make sure she wasn't inconvenienced by the surprise Media Quality spot check from the night before.

"My father must have talked the mayor into getting involved," Rose whispered while we ran the water in the bathroom sink. "Mom told me to tell you that we're fine and will be ready when you are."

Will I be ready? I wonder hours later, long after Mrs. Meacham finally releases the team with the warning we will be working late again tomorrow. But while everyone else is probably long asleep, I stare at the city in the shadow of a large pedestal. Atop the concrete block is a stunning Native American warrior rider seated on an intricately detailed steel horse.

The driving curfew makes the night seem impossibly quiet. I shift the bag I carry on my shoulder. The clink of the paint cans rings loud in the silence.

Golden lights gleam from the windows across the skyline, brightening the shadows of the silver and black steel buildings that carve out a distinctive silhouette against the black night sky. The well-tended, well-spaced trees sway in the gentle breeze that carries with it the scent of the lake and whatever flowers the City Pride Department planted in the dozens of rounded-edge square stone planters in the paved plaza.

On a sunny, warm day, this area would be filled with tourists and Chicagoans alike. Currently, there are a few strolling along the sidewalks of Michigan Avenue. Not far from me, a lone couple is sitting on one of the benches, wrapped around each other in a way that makes it clear they have no interest in anyone around them. Across a twisting road from me, a lone runner pounds the pavement near my warrior's twin statue. When I turn toward the lake, I spot three people on bicycles, taking advantage of riding in the moonlit, temperate late-night air. If I didn't know the truth about "verify" and the Marshals and the missing people who dared to look too closely or question too much, I would feel completely safe here in the heart of the city.

But I do know. I know as I study the streets and the trees that lead to the lake, then the buildings to the west that stretch into the embrace of the velvet sky.

The city is beautiful. It's the place my mom dedicated her life to making attractive and welcoming. Painting over whatever the government was doing. Kidnapping and oppression and death. Anger fills me as I look up at the warrior with his bow pulled back, ready to strike.

The Native Americans fought in the war that created this country. They helped fight for freedom, and while I only know a tiny fraction of the history removed from our modern textbooks, I know that the government betrayed them. They didn't give up their land willingly as I was taught. They refused to conform to what was convenient for the government and were slaughtered. Their land was stolen. Their freedoms. Perhaps it shouldn't be a surprise that even Dewey's textbooks only dedicate a few paragraphs to their story.

"History is written by the victors," Dewey said when I noticed the lack of words used for such horror. "And people are happy to let them. No one wants to consider whether their happy lives came at a terrible cost."

Maybe he's right. Despite everything I know, I still find myself wanting to believe in the things I've been proud of all my life. That scares me more than anything. And it's why I can't let them win.

Squaring my shoulders, I turn and start toward Michigan Avenue. Gusts of wind accompany my footsteps as I cross the normally bustling street. I briskly walk along the wide expanse of currently empty road, first under the covered walkway of an old stone building, then on the open sidewalk—away from the lake and into the city.

I flinch at every sound as I travel the handful of blocks to my destination. Each shift of a shadow has me looking for signs of the Marshals or the Chicago Police. Atlas wanted to be here with me tonight to guard my back—to act as my eyes when I am too busy to see. But there is no reason for both of us to be at risk until it is absolutely necessary. And if I am honest, this walk—one that will strike at the heart of everything the city stands for, and that my mother dedicated her life to—is something I need to do alone.

Finally, my destination comes into breathtaking view. In the distance, high arching iron and tinted glass windows are filled with a beautiful blue-green light. The same vibrantly colored light shines atop a roof elaborately decorated with aluminum sculptures of owls and intricate metal foliage that my mother first pointed out to me when I was barely old enough to walk. Next to the darkened buildings around it, my target shines like a beacon.

High-pitched laughter from somewhere nearby makes me jump. I pull my cap low on my forehead, cross the street, and walk the streetlamp-lit sidewalk that runs parallel to the building. The hum of an engine catches my attention and grows louder with every step I take. I glance over my shoulder as a street sweeper rambles through the intersection, then disappears. When I reach the end of the block, I duck around the corner of the beautifully lit building and scan the area.

No one's in sight.

Carefully, I unzip my bag, remove one of the cans of paint Dewey purchased, and shake it. The clicks and clatters hammer in my ears. My breath comes fast and sharp. My heart pounds as I wait for someone to appear—to understand what I am about to do.

Once the can is ready, I go still.

No one comes running to see what caused those sounds. No one is close enough to see or stop me.

I run my free hand along the rough, reddish-brown stone and stow the cap of the spray-paint can in my bag. Then I step back, take a deep breath, and try to forget everything I was conditioned to believe about the purpose of the City Pride Department. Even still, regret grows deep in my chest. Which is stupid. This is my plan. There is no reason to feel bad about marring the government's veneer of perfection. The fact that I do, despite everything I know, chases away any lingering doubts about what must be done.

The paint can is cold in my hand. Fixing the image of the logo in my mind, I clutch the hard metal, raise the canister, and press the nozzle.

Vibrant pink hisses a terrible and triumphant song as it streaks through the air onto the section of wall in front of me. Color seeps into the stone in an imperfect curved line, which irritates me because there is no fixing it and even if I could, there isn't time. So, I step slightly to the side and start spraying again.

Squiggles of pink.

Fast yellow swirls.

Shots of orange that are supposed to resemble licks of flames.

Then I reach for the black to create a quick outline to make the other colors pop.

The majority of art is created on screens. It was the medium my mother taught me to draw on. It was the one I watched my mother's hands work with every day as she created magic with colors and shapes. Yet, despite her skill with modern design tools, my mother's first love was applying paint to canvas. I remember the way she held the brush—as if it were an extension of her hand—much like the way I feel about my stylus. When I was little, I sat on the stool in her studio and watched her work for hours, saying nothing as she danced with color on the canvas, creating meaningful beauty where there was once only a sea of shapeless white.

My father never approved. He felt painting on canvas was not much better than using paper. A waste of resources. Selfish. Perhaps that's why I didn't try harder when my mother let me take the brush and spread the color on the small square of stretched fabric. Or maybe it was because no matter how hard I tried, the colors smeared and created images that were nothing like the ones I had designed in my mind.

"Painting requires more care than the drawing you do every day. And it should," my mother said when I grew frustrated and threw down my paint, sending spatters of crimson across the yellow of my shirt. "Mistakes on the screen can be removed with just a stroke of a stylus or a push of a button. What you do with a brush and canvas—it's harder to make disappear."

I wish I remembered exactly what I said in response, but I don't. Instead, I remember her picking up her own brush and walking to the painting that had become an unpleasant mess of muddy browns and iron-gray streaks despite my desperate attempts to create the beach scene my imagination had conjured.

"Painting can be frustrating, but to me it is wondrous. I feel as if I didn't just create the work, but instead I'm a part of it. That who I am comes alive in the texture of the work."

I didn't understand. Not then. Not years later when she gave voice to that same thought. How anything could be more real than seeing a design come to life onscreen where the color choices are infinite and precise, and mistakes could be removed with no more effort than the blink of an eye? It didn't make sense to me. Until now.

For the first time, I think I feel what my mother experienced when she painted the canvases that led me to the La Salle Street Bridge—to Atlas and the Stewards—to this moment here at the back of a structure that once housed thousands upon thousands of paper books.

My heart beats fast. My hands work faster, slashing color in long and short bursts of air. Drips of paint bleed downward from the design where my hand lingered too long. The drips are mistakes. Flaws that everyone will see. I don't care. Maybe it isn't perfect, but neither am I. And this painting, as destructive as it might be perceived, is part of me. Maybe that is why the color on these stones means more to me than anything else I have ever created.

I spray for the last time, shove the can back into my bag, and step back to look at what I have done. Artwork where it didn't belong. An image that wasn't carefully discussed and reworked and approved by the government.

"Hey!" someone shouts somewhere in the distance, and I don't wait around to see if he's yelling at me. I run.

My feet pound the pavement as I zigzag through the city blocks until finally, I slow, walking to where I have stashed the maroon-and-black bicycle I found sitting on the porch this morning. Neither Dewey nor Atlas claim responsibility for the gift, but I'm grateful. I pull it out of the rack, throw my leg over the bar, and pause to listen for sounds of sirens or approaching cars. In the distance, there is the faint beeping of a truck backing up followed by the *rat-a-tat-tat* of a jackhammer. Comforted by the normal sounds of roadwork, I put my foot on the pedal and ride north through the city to the second of the three locations whereI plan to make my mark tonight.

My legs are tired and my skin damp with perspiration by the time I ride down the block to Dewey's house—the other logos painted without any sign of the Marshals. Tomorrow, I'm sure I'll be happy about it. Tonight, I'm too tired to be anything but relieved. The porch light glows—welcoming me back—as I wearily carry the bike up the steps and lean it against the house. The door isn't locked. I open it slowly and find Dewey sitting beside an illuminated brass lamp in an otherwise darkened living room. He is fingering the battered gray fedora, which rests in his lap.

"I didn't think you'd wait up."

Dewey studies me as I step into the room. "I had company until an hour ago. Atlas was quite insistent on being here to make sure you returned safely, but all his pacing was making it hard for me to read, so I kicked him out. Whoever said we need more togetherness really missed the mark." He shrugs. "I messaged him when you came up the porch steps in case he was still inclined to worry."

"I told Atlas to wait at his house." Although I can't help wishing he was here instead of staying at the house his father inherited from Atlas's grandfather.

"You had to know he wouldn't listen," Dewey says quietly. "He didn't understand why you didn't want him with you tonight."

"He said he did." I drop my backpack onto the other armchair and notice specks of pink, orange, and black paint dotting my fingers. If the Marshals had caught me, my hands would have given my guilt away.

66

"He lied. People dedicated to the truth still do that, you know. It's not the only thing he's lying about." Dewey pushes to his feet. "I tried to explain to him using small words so he could understand how difficult tonight was for you."

"I practiced a bit with the paint cans before I left. I was able to work fast when I was out in the open."

"That's not what I am referencing." He looks down at his hat. "Your mother would be proud of what you did tonight, Meri. And of what you are going to do next."

My throat grows thick and dry.

"Atlas grew up believing everything about our government was wrong. You were raised to think the world was exactly right. It is not surprising that actively putting a mark on the thing you were taught to honor and respect would trouble you."

I shrug as if it couldn't matter, but Dewey isn't done. "Perhaps it will help for you to remember that something must break before it can be rebuilt. Change isn't easy. It's not supposed to be, if it truly means something. And sometimes the breaks make things more beautiful. Did you cover Kintsugi in your art class?"

I blink. "No. What's that?"

"It's the Japanese art of repairing broken pottery. When fixing something, most people try to do it in a way that hides the fact that it was ever broken. They think the break means the piece is flawed." Dewey smiles. "But with Kintsugi, artists don't attempt to camouflage the damage. They highlight the location of the repair with powdered gold or silver in celebration of the piece's unique history. By doing so they transform it into something even more special and give it second life."

If our efforts work, I plan on looking up Kintsugi pottery.

"So," Dewey says. "Your outing was successful?"

I nod.

"Tomorrow's . . ." He glances at the clock; it's post-midnight, and corrects himself. "Tonight's adventure will be easier for your heart if not your body. The Marshals will no doubt be made aware of the situation. By this weekend they will be on high alert."

"Which is what we are counting on."

"When your friend Stef and the others meet you on the La Salle Street Bridge, the Marshals will be scouring the city in greater numbers than they were tonight. Odds are some will be swept up by those Marshals."

Spine's lifeless face flashes in my mind.

"Atlas doesn't think they'll agree to help," I say, picking at a dot of paint on the back of my hand.

"He doesn't want them to help. There's a difference."

"I don't understand."

His eyes meet mine. "I think you do. After all, if it is just the three of us painting the logo, it will take more time for *Gloss*'s popularity to grow. That would alter the timeline and buy him a few extra days to find information that will make it unnecessary for you to take the next step."

I shake my head. "We don't have a few extra days. His father and Isaac might not have much time left." *If they aren't already dead.* "Atlas knows we have to do this now or we could lose this chance for good."

"Just as he knows Stef and the others will join because they are young—like you."

"Which means what?"

"People your age lead with their hearts instead of listening to what's in their heads—although I suppose you don't have all that

68

much in your head anyway, comparatively speaking." He glances down at the hands I have fisted at my sides. "Taking risks is hard for those worried about losing what they already have. It's the reason Scarlett and many of the other Stewards spoke of change even as they resisted it. It's that same fear that drove your father to leave you even when in his heart he knew he should stay."

The unexpected mention of my father jabs past my defenses. Tears burn hot in my eyes and I'm too tired to push them away.

If he notices the emotional blood he's drawn, Dewey's detached expression and bland tone don't show it. "I suppose that is my long way of saying I have no doubt Stef and the others will join us because the future means more to them than their past. They will come for the same reason that you will make the choice Atlas wishes you didn't have to make."

His words hang in the air and his eyes lock with mine. Understanding and fear swirl behind his eyes. Then he shrugs and whatever I saw is gone when Dewey says, "That is a conversation for another night, seeing as how I have wasted much of this one."

I shove aside my own fear that I have been pretending for days hasn't been growing and say, "I hope you're right, Dewey. About the others joining."

"You should have realized by now that I am more often right than not." Before I can come up with a biting response, he places his hat on his head and starts toward the stairs. "You'll find rubbing alcohol and nail polish remover in the bathroom upstairs. They should help you remove all evidence of tonight's adventures. Tomorrow, I will buy gloves."

"Dewey," I say. Slowly, he turns and I scramble to try to come up with the right words for what I want to say. Only, I can't seem to find them, so all I can offer is, "Thanks—you know." I shrug and jam my hands into my pockets. "For waiting up."

With his face covered in shadows, it is impossible to tell what Dewey is thinking in the silence. Finally, he clears his throat and sharply says, "It's not like I did anything out of the ordinary. It was just as easy to read in the living room as it would have been up in the library. Make sure you turn off the lights."

It isn't until he disappears up the stairs and I am reaching for the light switch that I realize Dewey wasn't carrying a book. He had lied about why he was downstairs and I blink back tears.

I couldn't remember the last time anyone cared enough to wait up for me.

SIX

I am barely awake as I work on the assignment Nicolle gave me, to familiarize myself with competitors' page designs, when I hear one of the designers working behind me say, "You have to see this! City Pride was just arriving to scrub it off the walls, so Mica took a picture to prove it was there."

The excitement level spikes in the room as the designers all make a beeline for the picture. By the end of the day it's clear everyone in the building has seen the photos of the spray-painted logos. Most are upset that public buildings were defaced, but there are several who are more disappointed to learn the images were removed before they would get to see them in person.

Their disappointment is short-lived.

By Friday, all anyone can talk about are the mystery paintings throughout the city that Atlas, Dewey, and I have lost sleep creating. *Gloss* employees have started to get up early to hit the streets looking for where the logo turns up next. They will all be gone by the time I grab my next spray can, but hopefully that will change if Stef and her friends make the choice to show up tonight. The cover story of the logo's creation and Mrs. Webster's insistence that the spray painting was the work of overzealous fans has held—for now. Dewey and Atlas had created a few dummy online accounts to back up Mrs. Webster's claim, though two sets of Marshals have returned to question Mrs. Webster and various members of the marketing team about the painted images.

"They wanted to know if we arranged for someone to do the paintings as part of our marketing campaign," one indignant woman huffed to several colleagues, who were huddled over a community box of doughnuts. None of them noticed the snaillike pace of my coffee pouring as they reacted to the news.

"That's crazy!"

"But cool."

"Cool?"

"That we have passionate fans—hell yes. Have you seen the things people are posting online?"

"It's against the law. It's wrong."

"So what? You want to go back to the old logo, so whoever is doing this will stop?"

"That will just encourage them to do it even more. That's what the ones who questioned me said."

But that isn't what's going to happen, I think as I take the coffee back to my team's design room. Not if I can help it.

Weeks ago, Dewey quoted someone named Ovid who said that water could burrow a hole into rock if given enough time—or something to that effect. I think of that quote now standing next to the rust-red steel girders above the dark, flowing Chicago River. I have already watched two navy-and-powder-blue-uniformed police offi-cers and an alert, athletically compact dark-haired woman in the Marshals' distinctive footwear stroll by. Tonight wouldn't be as easy. And it would get harder and more dangerous from here, but the only way to drill a hole through to the other side of the rock was to keep the water steadily dripping.

I spot Stef, dressed in dark skin-tight pants, a black long-sleeved shirt, matching baseball cap, and dark sunglasses, standing at the northern end of the bridge.

Relief swirls with dread.

She came. Dewey was right. A fact that I am sure he will remind me of.

Stef nods, then steps around several other pedestrians and strides toward me. In her wake are the curly-haired twins in match-ing denim shorts and gray T-shirts. Beside them, the girl with the long braids, who's dressed in baggy blue jeans and a tight white T-shirt.

I asked for four people. Part of me thought the older ones would come. I guess I should have known better.

"I wasn't sure you would be here," I call as they approach.

"The future matters more than the past," Stef says, stopping in front of me. The others take up positions just behind her. "You should know that Joy still doesn't like you. She's planning to kick your ass once this is over."

"I hope she'll have the chance to try." I toss her a backpack filled with spray-paint cans. "I guess we'd better get to work."

I keep my voice down as I quickly sketch out their part. Each person will visit two or more public locations with the supplies we provide. Between the traffic and the laughter and conversation and wind, no one can hear us speak, but I still take care to avoid certain words. "More and more people are coming out at night, so working fast is important."

Stef nods. "We get it."

"We even practiced with the cans you left behind to make sure we can do it quick," the girl with the braids adds.

"We did," Stef confirms. "And we have a few ideas for next time. If you're willing to let us make some suggestions."

"Any and all ideas are welcome. It's going to take a lot of effort to get people ready for what we have to tell them," I admit.

"We aren't afraid of doing the work." Braid girl lifts her chin.

"Good," I say. "Then you're with me tonight." Quickly I explain that Atlas and Dewey are working on the south side of the city. Their efforts should pull the Marshals to that area, leaving us free to hit the middle and north side. Tomorrow, we will double the number of painted symbols. Then double them again the next right and so on. Each night we'll strike at a different time while continuing to expand the number of images painted.

"The Marshals are going to get seriously annoyed," one of the twins says.

"That's part of the plan," I admit.

"Cool!" his brother adds with a grin. "Anything that jerks the Marshals' chain is worth doing."

"Then let's go see how many Marshals we can annoy," Stef says. "We have to get you guys home before your curfews."

With that parting salvo Stef and the twins head toward the south side of the bridge. Then I turn to braid girl and ask, "What's your curfew?"

She shakes her head. "Gram told my mom we're at the movies.

As long as I'm back in two hours no one will be the wiser. If I'm late she'll cover for me."

She pulls out her phone to show me a picture of her and a woman with very short salt-and-pepper hair smiling in front of a movie theater marquee. The time stamp in the corner says the photo was taken five minutes ago. "It's always good to have an alibi." She shoves her phone into her back pocket, ties her braids into a pony-tail at the nape of her neck, and gives me a cocky smile. "Just wait until you hear what else we've come up with. I can tell you all about it while we do this."

As we walk to the L and ride the train several stops north, I learn the girl's name is Amber. She's two years younger than I am and in hushed tones tells me she found the truth by stumbling across her grandmother's old textbooks while playing in their basement when she was seven. "So your entire family knows about—everything."

"My grandmother and I do. My parents . . ." Amber scrunches her nose. "They believe that this country is on the right track and that anyone who says different is just trying to cause trouble. They turned in my grandmother when I mentioned she still had books at her house. The Environmental Department gave her a choice— to willingly turn over her books to officers for recycling or to be arrested. If it weren't for me, I think she would have let them take her. Instead, she claimed she had forgotten all about the books and told my parents that she was relieved to have them out of the house. After that, I started searching for other people with books. I can pretend to my parents that I don't know what was in the books that were taken from my grandmother, but I can't lie to myself."

I don't spot any military boots as we pass through the L sta-tion. We then head to an ice cream store located next to a Celebrate

Chicago store filled with T-shirts, trinkets, and screens displaying breathtaking images of the city's most popular sites. I glance at the photo Rose sent to me earlier, then push open the ice cream shop doors.

A guitar riff blares as we step inside.

"Wait here," I tell Amber. I weave through the tables to the counter where three employees are dressed in red-and-white-striped shirts with the name of the shop embroidered on the pockets. Each of them is busy scooping ice cream and scanning payment from customers' personal screens. I glance at the picture Rose sent me on my own screen, then make a beeline for the guy with two diamond studs winking from his eyebrow at the very far side of the counter. He's currently scooping pink ice cream for a young girl and her mom. His wide smile gives him a movie-star-handsome look. It doesn't surprise me that Rose had once dated him.

"Rose Webster left something for me?" I shout over the music. The guy nods. He reaches down and pulls out a duffle. Without any other acknowledgment, he drops the duffle atop the counter, and returns to work. I hoist the bag onto my shoulder and head for the exit. Once Amber and I are outside, I pull two backpacks out of the bag, hand one to Amber, and say, "Time to get to work. We can stick together for the first few until you get the hang of it."

"We can do more if we split up," she says. "That's the whole reason you asked for help, right?"

She's right, which sucks.

"I promise I won't get caught," she says. I know she can't really make that vow. Neither can I.

Taking a deep breath, I pull a transit card from my pocket and hand it to her along with instructions about which neighborhoods to center her efforts in. "Fast is better than good," I advise.

"I plan on being both because I am not going to let them win."

I smile. Neither am I.

For the next two hours I dart in and out of alleys, hide behind dumpsters, and scale fire escapes, leaving a trail of paintings and several angry shouts for the police behind me. When I finally head home, I spot several people pointing at a painting on a bus stop sign done in a hand that isn't mine.

The next day, Stef and eight others join in. By Sunday night, there are fifteen of us. On Monday, everyone at *Gloss* is buzzing about pictures they've been sent or have taken of marks around the city that resemble the e-zine's distinctive new logo. The staff is torn between being horrified at the damage to the design of city walls and buildings and signs, and energized. And this time the Marshals don't stand outside the door—they come in.

I hold my breath until Rose walks by my team's corner design room and smiles to let me know everything is still okay. I work long after Mrs. Meacham and the others go home, planting forbidden words in the text of advertising images that Rose has passed to me. Mrs. Webster doesn't need them, yet. It's still too soon. But I want them all to be ready just in the event I am not here to create them later.

If that is the case—well, then Mrs. Webster will have *Gloss*'s summer design intern to blame for the words that are published.

I start with words like "diverse" and "vulnerable." Words that I remember Atlas having me look up in a bound, paper dictionary weeks ago. They are words I have often thought about since that day. They aren't overtly controversial like the words I will disclose in images that will be published in later issues—words like "verify" and "revolution." But I think I finally understand why they were taken from us.

"Vulnerable"—people who require more time and attention. Like the homeless that the City Pride Department claimed no longer needed to live on the streets, and the elderly who would have known the forbidden words that others could not look up.

And "diversity"—a word to celebrate differences when the government wants only what is the same. Sameness makes people comfortable. It discourages discussion. Most of all, it represses change.

My mother changed and she died.

Change pushed my father to drink.

I'm not sure what changing will do to me, but when I leave the tablet with the finished designs in the bottom drawer of Rose's desk, I know that tonight I am going to discover whether I am brave enough to find out.

Defying my father took stubbornness. Outrunning the Marshals as they scoured the streets looking for anyone with a spray-paint can required determination and fast feet. But the next . . .

"We need to talk about this," Atlas insists as we walk down the alley in the haze of the cloud-covered moonlight and faint gold glow of the streetlamps up ahead.

An hour ago, Dewey watched from the doorway as I made my preparations for the night's work. He wordlessly nodded when I placed my Merriam Adams identification in the center of the table and he handed me the ones created for MaryAnn Jefferson. Merriam, the intern from *Gloss*, already left a message with her office about a family emergency. There is even a record of a train ticket purchased in that name. If things go well, she'll be back fetching coffee in a day or two. Mrs. Webster will know how to handle whatever questions come if Merriam doesn't return at all.

"You can wait another day," Atlas says again, as if I wasn't paying attention before. "We still have time to find my dad and Isaac and come up with another way to get information about the Unity Centers they were taken to."

"We don't," I say, running a hand through my newly darkened hair. "The paintings are getting people to talk. The fake online accounts the twins and the others have created to gush about *Gloss* are starting to come online. Momentum is building. If we don't have the answers people will ask for when they ask for them, it will all fall apart."

The logo—the paintings showing up throughout the city, but unreported by the news—have lit a spark. People are asking a question—the right question. *What does it mean?* But to turn the spark into something more, we need more. We need fuel to create a blaze government lies can't put out.

"We only have one chance to get this right. If we don't break through the wall of lies at the exact moment people are listening, we might lose them." The end of the alley comes closer and I slow my steps.

Since the moment I put stylus to screen and began sketching image after image, looking for the one that would launch a new fight, I knew I would have to take this step. Dewey and I planned for it even as Atlas worked to find another way. The fact that he is here speaks louder than all his protest. If he truly believed it wasn't necessary, he would have tried harder to keep me home tonight. He wouldn't be standing with me—where I need him to be—now.

I stop and stare at the exit to the alley.

A black sedan cruises down the street. A triumphant, patriotic-sounding boy-band tune is carried on the night air—probably from the public screens.

Atlas turns and looks at me, and when I look into his face the wall I have constructed around my fear trembles.

I don't want to be here.

I want to go back to months ago—when I didn't know the word "verify." When my mother was alive. My father didn't drink.

I think about the night my mother left the house and never returned. How annoyed I was when I wanted to talk about ideas for an art class project and she didn't have the time. She tried to hug me, but I turned my back on her. I can still feel her fingers on my shoulder and hear her voice say, "You'll be fine. I promise."

Then she walked out the door and went in search of the same truth I'm looking for now. She had to know there was a chance she wouldn't return, but she went anyway. I will do the same.

"Meri." Atlas gently lifts my chin so I am looking him in the eyes when he says, "I should be the one doing this."

I shake my head and take a deep breath. Neither quiets the churning inside. "You have a harder job than I do. You have to save me," I say, taking his hand in mine. With my other hand, I pull out the phone I have been using, press it into his hands. Then, before I give in to the fear I am pretending not to feel, I take several steps backward toward the street. "I trust you. Now you have to trust me."

"Meri..."

I leave the alley and step onto the sidewalk without allowing myself to look back, taking comfort in the feel of the small tracking and recording device I picked up from Dewey's friend pressing against my heel as I walk. But, I can picture Atlas behind me—frustrated and angry, stalking to the motorbike he has parked in a spot on the street and watching as I pass a man in military boots. The man is leaning against a recycling can.

I understand how Atlas feels—watching me go—helpless to do more than stand on the sidelines. Weeks ago, he asked *me* to trust *him* to face the Marshals on his own. Leaving him to confront the danger alone was one of the hardest things I'd ever had to do. Today, the tables have turned and it is harder still to put one foot in front of the other knowing what is about to happen. But I am determined to confront this choice with the same strength he demonstrated on Navy Pier. Atlas did what was necessary and he survived. I will do what must be done and hope the ending will be the same.

I focus on my anger—let it burn away my fear. I will do this for Atlas's father, and my mother, and Rose's brother, and all the people in this city who don't understand that they are in the dark. And I need do this for myself.

I unzip my backpack.

Maybe it would be easier if I could live with the lie, I think.

I shake the bag. Metal rattles inside.

But I can't.

I pretend to trip. The backpack gapes open and two cans of spray paint fly through the air. The first bounces on the concrete with a metallic clang.

Heads turn.

The bright pink cap separates from the other paint can as it crashes to the ground. The cap flies one way. The can rolls to the edge of the sidewalk and off the curb onto the street.

Blood roars in my ear.

Someone reaches down to pick up one of the paint cans, and behind him a man in a dark blue suit jacket locks eyes with me.

Marshal!

His steps are fast and fluid. Icy terror streaks down my spine. I take a step back—two. Then, holding tight to the backpack strap, I turn and run.

"Hey!" someone shouts.

"Stop! Police!" is barked behind me.

He's not the police—at least not the kind people think he is. But the heads snapping in my direction as my feet pound the concrete don't know what I know.

Hands reach out for me. A boy in a red baseball cap not much older than I am steps in my path. I dart to the side of him, but a tall, very large man in a football jersey blocks that path and reaches out to grab me.

I stumble back and spin. Panic propels me away from the bulky man's grasp and smack into the arms of the Marshal.

I scream for help as I try to pull away, but his grip is too tight. He shoves me to my knees, then wrestles my hands behind my back. No one helps me. The metal handcuffs clicking together echo louder in my head than the shouting people on the street or the cars honking or the Marshal thanking football-jersey man and the boy in the baseball cap for their assistance.

This is what was supposed to happen.

I have to stay strong.

Observers move back as a dark vehicle pulls up at the curb. The sedan has gold rims.

I try to take deep breaths and tell myself not to fight. It will only make things worse for me and for Atlas, who is watching this entire scene. He has to believe I will be okay.

Three sets of Marshal boots step onto the curb. One Marshal has my bag. The other two yank me to my feet and drag me to the back seat of the car where another Marshal waits. There is the faint flowery scent of perfume.

The car doors slam shut.

We start to move.

They're supposed to think I'm afraid.

I open my mouth to scream as an arm snakes around my neck and steals my breath until everything goes black.

SEVEN

I blink my eyes open.

Everything spins in and out of focus. It takes all my effort to keep my eyes from closing and to not give in to the languorous pull of sleep.

Something isn't right.

My brain is fuzzy—like there is a smear on my drawing tablet, making it hard to clearly see what is beneath. My mouth is impossibly dry—like I've been eating cotton that has sucked up every drop of moisture. The not-quite-white sheets feel scratchy against my cheek, which doesn't make sense. Nothing about the bed and the room I'm in makes sense. Not the glare of the bright white bars of light or the dull gray wall next to my bed.

Fighting against the strange heavy sensation, I sit upright and take in the row of narrow beds made up only with a sheet and a single, stingy pillow. A man with dark curly hair dressed in a torn, dirt-stained yellow button-down shirt stares at the black metal door to my right as if waiting for it to open. He has deep-set eyes and a hint of stubble that makes him appear both disheveled and dangerous.

I shift my legs over the edge of the bed. It squeaks in protest and the man turns his head. That's when I spot the large, sickly purple bruise blooming against the tan of his left cheekbone.

Fear bubbles. The fog clears and I remember.

I am in the custody of the Marshals now. My bag is gone, but I can still feel the device that's hidden behind the lining of my shoe.

My heart pounds as I instinctively look around the room for some way—any way—to escape.

But there are no windows to tell me whether I am on the top floor of a skyscraper or a basement deep underground. There is only the solid black metal door that I walk to on spongy legs.

I face the six beds lined up against the wall like soldiers and steel my shoulders and my soul for what is to come.

This was my choice.

The Marshals think they caught me in their trap. I set the stage and I walked onto it in order to play my part.

After my dad left, I spent days in Dewey's library looking for examples of the kind of information that would finally make people open their eyes and their minds to the truth. The real truth—not the one they have been conditioned to or personally prefer to believe.

While reading through the history books, there were several examples from the past that stuck with me.

The audio recordings that proved to our country that President Nixon was unfit for office. He resigned when the tapes were made public and he knew what people would hear him say.

The story of the Triangle Shirtwaist Factory in New York that in the early 1900s killed almost a hundred and fifty women and girls who had asked for better working conditions but instead were trapped in a fire that burned most of them alive and caused others to jump ten stories to their deaths. Laws were changed and unions were formed when the horrifying details of their deaths were printed in black and white for everyone to read.

And the one that haunts me more than the others—the first photographs and stories of the Nazi "death camps," which when published brought the horror of the mass murders to governments in countries around the world that were avoiding getting involved in the war.

Staying out of war was easy when it was abstract. It didn't feel real when it was happening to someone else. But those stories brought to life the innocent women, men, and children who were being killed en masse. No one wanted to believe it was happening, but once people saw the photos, they couldn't forget what they knew. They couldn't turn away from those images.

I'm here in this room to find the words that won't be ignored, sounds that will echo in people's brains, and images they will see even when they close their eyes. Atlas will have followed me to wherever this place is. He'll get me out before the battery life in the recording tracker runs out. Once he does, Mrs. Webster will publish it all. She'll show people the Unity Centers they didn't know existed and hopefully where the people go when the government makes them disappear. Rose said her father believed Isaac was still in the city. With any luck, I will find him here today. And Atlas and Dewey will help set both of us free.

My neck prickles. The man on the far bed is watching me with narrowed eyes and a half smile. I start to ask him why he's staring but before I can get out a word, he places a finger to his lips. The man shakes his head, points to the door, then motions for me to sit on the bed next to his.

I don't move.

The man rolls his eyes, puts his hands under his armpits, and moves his elbows up and down.

Really?

He's calling me chicken?

Still, I suppose he has a point. It's not like keeping my distance from a man who is as trapped as I am is going to make me any safer. If he wanted to hurt me he could have taken me out in my sleep.

He smiles when I walk across the room and take a seat on the bed directly across from him. From this close, he looks younger than I first thought—maybe a handful of years older than I am. And the bruise on his face is more pronounced. So are the scrapes on his arms and neck. All the injuries look recent—as if he'd received them within the last twenty-four hours.

"As soon as they realize you're awake, they'll come for you like they did the others." His raspy whisper rakes across my nerves like a rusty nail. "They always have questions."

I press a hand to my stomach to calm the hollow churning—a gesture the man acknowledges with a deliberate glance and an exaggerated sigh.

"Others?" I ask. "What others?"

He shrugs, winces, and rubs his right shoulder as he says, "Three men older than me. Two women a *lot* older than you. I never got any of their names. I thought they were coming for me when the door opened the last time. Instead, they brought you. I guess they aren't in a hurry since they already know my answers to their questions."

"What questions—"

We both turn at the soft click of a lock. The handle rotates and the door swings open to reveal a woman with short, sleek honey-blond hair and darkly lined and shadowed eyes that Rose would applaud. She smooths the fabric of her fitted gray suit jacket and looks around the room.

"Good," she says as her eyes land on me. Her painted crimson lips curve into an unfriendly smile. "You're finally awake. You certainly took your time."

"As if I had a choice. It's not like I drugged myself," I snap, before I can think about how stupid it is to fight with my captors.

The man on the bed lets out a low chuckle. The woman's smile grows even as her eyes narrow. "You don't want to make this harder than it has to be."

The Marshal and the man on the bed lock eyes. When the man looks down at the floor, the woman's grin grows wider and she turns her attention back to me. "You. Get up. You have questions to answer."

"Good luck," the man says when I stand on shaky legs. "It was nice having company."

"Don't worry, Wallace," the blond woman says. "You'll be spending lots of time together soon."

Behind me, I hear Wallace's low voice whisper, "I guess they already know your answers, too."

The blond woman steps out of the way and lets me pass into a brightly lit hallway. The seamless white of the floors, walls, and ceiling is interrupted only by a line of five closed black metal doors on one side of the hallway and four on the right. There is a silver water fountain immediately to my left. Just looking at it makes me realize how thirsty I am.

The door clicks shut behind the blond Marshal. I wait for her to lead me away, but instead she turns toward the door with a huff. "They said they fixed this thing," she mutters, and starts pressing buttons on the keypad above the lock. Her back is to me. I glance both ways down the hall.

The Marshal casts a quick glance at me, then jerks her eyes forward and I realize what she's doing. She's waiting—hoping that I'll run.

With the bruises on Wallace's face clear in my mind, I fold my hands in front of me and ask, "Can I get a drink?"

She nods and I take two slow steps forward and press the button. The water barely trickles from the spout and I only have enough time to wet my lips and get a few stingy drops into my mouth before the Marshal snaps, "Enough. Follow me."

I follow her down the hallway and around a corner to an elevator. The Marshal presses her index finger on a glowing panel that scans her print. The panel turns green and the doors ding open. Had I tried to run, I wouldn't have gotten far.

The Marshal presses the button for the bottom floor and I glance at the red illuminated number above the sliding doors. The building has four stories. The room I had been held in was on the top.

As the elevator starts moving, I rehearse everything Dewey and I put in place for MaryAnn Jefferson—whose identification I carry with me. The high school she attended in Wisconsin. The reason she came to Chicago. Even the date she filed her application for *Gloss*—one that is on file but was rejected, if they have chosen to look. All the information is designed to make it look as if I am new to the city—without any attachments to the Stewards or any other group the Marshals are looking for. She is—I am—swept up in the excitement of the new *Gloss* logo and the danger of putting her own mark on the city. This will get me held, but probably not disappeared permanently. MaryAnn Jefferson is nobody—connected to no one.

Because I am busy reminding myself of MaryAnn's details, I don't notice the elevator stopping until the doors open. The smell hits me first. A thick antiseptic scent I associate with hospitals and Nurse Hayes's office at school. Underneath that is the musty dampness of body odor and the pungent scent of waste.

The Marshal steps in front of me so all I can see is the rough concrete floors and the dim lighting. Then she steps out of the elevator with an order for me to follow and I suddenly can't breathe.

When I was seven, I went to a friend's house to see their new puppy. When we were done playing with the fluffy black-and-brown dog that tripped over its own feet and loved licking faces and it was time for me to be driven home, the mother picked up the pup and locked it in a cage. The cage was supposed to help train the puppy. And I suppose it did. But I will never forget how the pup pushed its nose against the bars and whimpered as we walked out the door. I remember thinking that putting animals in cages was the worst thing ever.

I was wrong.

Because these cages are full of people.

In the center of a cavernous, concrete parking garage space are silver metal bars. Hundreds of them stretching from the floor to just above the ceiling. More bars box off the top. The design is not quite the same as the ones from the archives of the City Pride Department—the ones that I "borrowed" Rose's brother's summer job security official badge to gain access to and caused Isaac to be taken away. Or maybe they only seem different because there are people huddled inside.

"Move!" The Marshal grabs my arms and yanks me out of the elevator. Her fingers dig deep into my skin, trying to force my feet forward, but if there is pain I can't feel it and my legs are as heavy as stone. Because now that the shock is subsiding I can see there is more than one cage—there are lots of them, all connected, creating separate kennel-like spaces. And they are *full* of people.

Gray haired and wrinkled.

Slightly older than me.

Some around the age of my father.

It's hard to tell how many people there are in total. Some are curled up on the cement floor, wrapped in thin silver blankets, sleeping or pretending to be. Others stare aimlessly as they grip the bars. One woman is yelling at me—no, at the Marshal—that she doesn't belong here. That this is a mistake. She has no idea why she's being held here and she wants to go home to her children.

"Please, don't do this to my children!"

For a moment, I don't see the woman's anguished face. I see my mother. Tired. Glassy eyed. Hair tangled.

Whatever I thought I was prepared to see, it wasn't this. And something hits me. By bringing someone here—by allowing someone to see this—the government has already decided that person will never be set free. If they were, it would ruin them. It would expose them for the evil that they were. Because the truth would get out. And no one could possibly accept it.

If it weren't for the tracker in my shoe and the rescue Atlas and Dewey have planned, I'm not sure I could keep walking. Why would they bring someone like MaryAnn here? It doesn't make sense.

"Move," the Marshal barks, and yanks me away from the faces in the cages. I have to go with her or fall. Heart pounding—stomach churning from the smell and the fear that is growing colder with every passing second—I put one foot in front of the other.

From the shadows of the cages, eyes—hollow—hot—hopeless—follow me as I pass several darkly uniformed guards to a wide opening in the concrete wall on the far side of the damp garage. Metal rattles. A man screams for help. But as we round the corner, it's the chilling shriek of pain immediately followed by a wail of tears that strips me of my remaining courage.

Behind a concrete wall partition are curtained areas—all lined up in a row. There is a desk in the first with a computer and several glowing screens. An official in a navy-blue uniform with silver embellishments on the collar and the cuffs sits behind the computer. A restrained man in a bulky, dark coat sits hunched on the other side of the desk. A curtain halfway down the aisle shifts to the side and a Marshal leads a weeping woman out of that space. The crying woman is holding the side of her head and screaming for a lawyer who she has to know will never come.

A tall, broad-shouldered official at the end of the row turns our way. "Melissa, bring your subject to area two."

The red-lipped Marshal next to me grabs my arm. She pulls me down the blue runner that is spread out along the row of stations and I remind myself that Atlas will use the signal from the tracker in my shoe to find this place—to free me. The Marshal yanks the second curtain to the side and shoves me toward a chair facing a desk like the one I just passed.

My foot catches on the stained rug. I crack my knee against the front of the desk, but grab the top to catch myself before I fall. I stand there, hands flat on the edge, looking across the expanse of the hard, smooth black surface at a man with a narrow, perfectly trimmed white mustache who is studying a handheld screen as if I am not even here.

"Sit," the man instructs.

Marshal Melissa grabs my shoulders and pushes me into the chair. My knee throbs in tempo with my pounding heart as I wait.

The man looks up and gives a tight smile. "This will go easier if you do as you are told."

I swallow down my panic and force myself to stick to the script. *Be confused. Non threatening. Scared.* The last is the easiest since I am terrified. "I don't understand. Where am I? What happened to me? Was I drugged? Are you the police?"

"The police deal with crimes," the man replies. "We deal with problems."

"I don't understand," I say, hoping the truth—that I do understand all too well—isn't visible in my eyes. "If this is about the paint, I can explain. It wasn't anything bad. I wasn't hurting anyone. They could have asked me about it and I would have told them whatever they wanted to know."

"Sadly, that isn't good enough." He picks up my government student ID that Dewey had created through the Steward network for just this moment. "MaryAnn Jefferson. You should have stayed in Wisconsin when your parents died. If you had, then this all wouldn't be necessary."

"I don't understand what *this* is. Please!"

"The city worked hard to create an environment where everyone can feel safe and takes great pains to instruct those who do things that disrupt those efforts. This is the first step in that instruction."

"But—"

"Miss Jefferson, you were caught with spray paint. The paint matches the colors that have been illegally used to deface public spaces throughout the city. While you are sure to have your reasons, discussing it with me won't do you any good. I'm simply here to start your processing."

He's not interested in learning why I was caught with the paint or whether I knew more about the logos throughout the city? But, I—MaryAnn—don't have anything to do with all those logos. She hasn't even spray-painted one yet! She shouldn't be here! Does he simply not care?

He places the screen down on the desk in front of him and says, "Have you made friends at the hotel you have been staying in or with anyone in the city who should be contacted as your instruction continues? Maybe someone who knew what you were doing tonight?"

"What? No." I shake my head. "I don't know anyone in the city, yet. I . . ."

"Good," he says, pushing a button on the screen he lays flat on the desk in front of him. "That makes things easier and it completes this step." He looks over my shoulder at Marshal Melissa. "Get the rest done quickly or she'll miss today's transport and have to wait until next week."

'Transport?" My heart skips. Transport tonight? No. "Where are you taking me? I didn't do anything wrong. Please. If you just talk to me, you'll see that."

"I told you, I am only here to start your processing," the man says with a sigh. "You will be transported to a place where you can receive the instruction necessary to keep you from greater disruptive acts. I promise, it will all go easier if you do what Melissa tells you. The goal is for us to help you learn. The last thing we want is for you to get hurt."

"If I could only . . ."

"Get up," Melissa snaps, and pulls me from my seat as I look back at the white-mustached man and say, "Please. Let me stay. At least until I talk to someone else."

We had counted on me being here for more than a few hours. I need to buy Dewey and Atlas more time to find me and for me to have the chance to take images of what is happening here. People need to see this for themselves.

The man looks into my eyes and there is no malice whatsoever in his expression when he says, "You may not believe it now, but this is for the best."

The Marshal marches me down the aisle, stops in front of a light gray curtain marked with the number four, and tugs it back.

"Have a seat," a female official at a workbench at the back of the space says, and she waves her hand at a padded chair in the center, which is flanked by two other uniformed officials. The chair reminds me of one a dentist would use—only my dentist's chair was never equipped with leather straps.

Oh God. No.

I take a step back, and am blocked by Melissa the Marshal, who shoves me down into the gray padded seat and holds me in place. Someone—I don't know who—grabs my arm and everything happens so fast.

I try to sit up and pull free, but there are too many people fastening the straps. Still I try to fight. My foot connects hard with a leg. There is a yelp, but there is no satisfaction from that as a strap loops around my left wrist and is pulled tight. Strong hands hold down my legs. Their grip is like a vise. None of the training Atlas and Dewey put me through helps. I fight back the scream clawing up, desperate to break free as another strap fastens my legs, then my ankles.

"This will hurt," a uniformed officer says clinically. Out of the corner of my eye, I can tell she is holding a heavy metal tool. "If you promise to stay completely still, I can make it hurt less. It's your choice."

My choice?

I ball my hands into fists. My heart pounds loud in my ears. I flinch as the uniformed woman beside me gathers my hair and shoves it under my head. There is a prick in my arm. I yelp from the sharp stab of the needle.

"Almost done," the woman whispers into my ear. I can't see her. But I can feel her fingers as she touches the top of my earlobe. "Ready . . . set . . ."

I scream and buck against the restraints, trying to get away from the waves of agony that echo from my ear down my body. My stomach heaves as the wave of pain swallows my will to fight.

A tingly coolness of something wet against my ear soothes away the sharpest edges of pain. "Hang in there," the woman says, patting my shoulder. "Almost done."

I can only whimper in response.

Tears burn when someone prods my ears. I whimper again at the sting of something heavy pushing against the wound. Then there is a click. The hands let go, but the heaviness in the center of the aching remains. A trickle of warm runs down the side of my neck as someone passes some kind of electronic instrument to the official who is working on me. There are a series of beeps and the official says, "You can release her now."

Through the haze of tears and pain, I register the fastenings being loosened. The Marshal pulls me out of the seat and the world tilts. My stomach churns. Something oily and hot snakes up my throat as one of the women from the station speaks to me, but the words swim out of reach. Something about pain medication kicking in soon and being fine as long as I don't try to pull it out.

Pull what out?

My legs are uncertain as I follow the Marshal out of the space and down the dirty blue runner toward another opening in the concrete wall. Slowly, I lift my hand to gently touch my ear. There is something metal and plastic that wasn't there before. But it takes until I catch my reflection in the polished chrome plate of a light sconce that I can tell what has been done to me.

My head spins. I blink several times, desperate to understand what I'm seeing. It looks like an ear cuff—one of those things that wraps around the outside of the earlobe, only instead of being able to clip it on and off, this one is riveted through the center of my upper ear. The edge of the cuff is deep red, but it is the markings on the front that makes me gag and fills my stomach with slick horror.

A series of black and white lines.

The device in my ear is a barcode.

I've been tagged.

EIGHT

That's not me, I think as I stare at the barcode. *This can't be happening to me.*

I want this to be a terrible nightmare that I'll wake from. But the pain isn't imagined. Neither is the line of blood that has trickled down my neck.

This isn't a dream. It's real.

A heartbreaking wail rips through the air.

And it isn't just happening to me.

"If you rip it out, they'll just put a different one on you—and that one won't be nearly as pleasant," Marshal Melissa says from behind me. "Now let's go."

Rip it out? My stomach roils at the thought of pulling out the ear cuff. My legs are uncertain as I shuffle next to Melissa down another cold, damp concrete corridor. There's a line of doors to our left. A large Marshal with close-cropped brown hair is standing nearby. He looks bored despite the weeping leaking from behind one of the doors.

Marshal Melissa opens the middle door and motions for me to enter. "You'll find a change of clothes on the table. You're to put what you're wearing now in one of the bins next to the door."

I step into the threshold of the doorway and hesitate. "What happens to the clothes I'm wearing now? What do you do with them?"

She cocks her head to the side. "Why does it matter?"

It shouldn't. All the clothes I cared about or fit my personality were packed up and carted away by the government weeks ago. But it does matter, which is why I say, "It matters because they're mine."

For a second the smug look she's been wearing falters. There is a glimmer of something human in her eyes. Then she straightens her shoulders and says, "And now they aren't, so you'd better get changed."

She closes the door with a bang behind me and I stand, numb, in the small room with the same concrete floor and unpainted walls as the rest of the parking garage. The muffled sniffling of the woman next door bleeds through the pale gray drywall as I sink to the cold, unforgiving floor and gulp back my own tears. If I cry, I might not be able to stop, and I have to stay strong. I can't give in to my fear.

I knew there was a risk in taking this step. I did it anyway. I told Atlas the risk was worth it. That the truth mattered enough to do whatever was necessary to make people open their eyes to it. But the reality of the cages—the barcode riveted in my ear—the weeping woman next door . . .

Stop!

I swipe at the stray tears that sneaked past my resolve and push to my feet. Freaking out will only make things worse. Atlas and Dewey will look for me, but that doesn't mean I can just assume they will be able to stop the transport and set me free. I have to think. Observe every detail. Keep myself steady until I get out.

A single stingy light bulb swings over a square metal table with three items of clothing folded atop it and a pair of cheap, elastic booties like people wear in hospitals. I won't be able to wear my shoes out of here.

Slowly, I remove my sneakers and feel inside the lining of the left one to check the carefully constructed pocket where the tracking device with its tiny built-in camera is located. It's round, slightly larger than a quarter, and four times as thick. Small enough to hide uncomfortably in my shoe, but too large to use where people might notice.

Taking a deep breath, I slip the device out of its hiding place, turn the pinhole lens toward me, and press the camera button. That done, I have to find a place to stash the device in my new clothing or everything I've risked was for nothing.

The provided short-sleeve shirt is lightweight and looks if it was accidentally washed with a stray red sock, which gives the pale gray fabric a slightly pink cast.

Carefully, I pull my black shirt over my injured ear, use it to dab at the blood on the side of my face, and ease on the new top that is far too long and twice as wide. Which gives me an idea. I gather the access fabric and tie it at my waist, then slip the device into the thick knot. It's not ideal, but after a couple of attempts I am able to move around with confidence that it can't be seen and won't accidentally fall out.

I pull on pants made of the same depressing color with a thick elastic waistband and wide cuffs at the bottom that I have to turn up to keep from tripping. Sitting down, I slide my feet into the thin-soled booties, then pick up the final item on the table. It's a thin, slick black hooded jacket with Velcro and plastic snap fasteners. The lining of the jacket is a fuzzy material that I assume must make the garment warm in addition to waterproof. Something I'm grateful for in the musty chill.

The coat stretches to my mid-thigh. I cuff the wrists so my hands are exposed, but leave the front unfastened so the knot of my shirt can be accessed easily. Now that I'm completely dressed, I fold the shirt, jeans, and shoes I was wearing and walk toward the bins that flank the door. I flip open the lid of the first. The container is almost full. So is the second. I clutch my own clothes to my chest and open the next two. Both are packed with ripped jeans, collared dress shirts, high-heeled boots, and silk ties. I dig into the last one and find cargo shorts, high-top sneakers, and sports jerseys of both the Chicago Cubs and the White Sox, as well as expensive suit jackets piled on top of faded, hole-ridden T-shirts that stink from a lack of laundering. But it is the vibrant teal-and-lemon-yellow shirt I pull out of the pile that almost brings me to my knees. It is the same size shirt I would have worn when I was in fifth or sixth grade. *Maybe even younger*, I think as I run my fingers across the sparkly silver lettering across the front that spells out: "Believe!"

A scream builds inside me. There are dozens of items of clothing . . . maybe hundreds, all packed into these containers. And this is just one room. The woman who I can no longer hear sniffling was in another. Each of the items represents a person. The quality of the clothing from one item to the next is wildly different. The people who wore them must be as well, yet they were all forced to leave these pieces of themselves behind to be collected by people who don't care who they are or why these things mattered.

Hands shaking, I fold the girl's colorful shirt and place it gently atop the haphazard pile of wrinkled garments. Then I slide the camera out of its hiding place and use it again.

"Hurry up!"

Quickly, I secure the recording tracker into the knot and set my own clothing atop the sparkly T-shirt. Then I close the bins and walk through the door, taking the memory of that girl with me.

The medication I was told would kick in has dulled the pain from its original agonizing fire to a dull ache by the time Marshal Melissa and her bright red smile escort me down the cement corridor. Our footfalls on concrete mix with the sounds of clanging metal, hopeless weeping, and the slamming of what I believe are car doors, until once again we are back to the large cages I first saw when I was led off the elevator and into this waking nightmare.

More uniformed officials than I remember seeing before are peering into the cages or punching buttons on their handheld screens. A bunch hover over a table on the far side—beyond the cages. Three trucks are parked behind the cages—near what appear to be loading dock doors. The vehicles are parked with their rear sides to me, so I can't see any distinctive markings. But they remind me of the moving trucks I have seen all my life—with the back doors open, ready for the loading to begin.

An older official points to a cage at the end and instructs Marshal Melissa to "Put her in there. We'll start loading up the trucks soon."

"Good." Marshal Melissa nods and grabs my arm. "I want to be home in time to do breakfast with the kids before they go to camp."

Believe. I repeat the word from the girl's glittered shirt to myself as Melissa swipes her ID card on the lock pad and opens the iron-bar door. *I will record these images and get out of here,* I tell myself as the Marshal shoves me and I stumble inside.

The door shuts behind me and my determination shudders at the hollow, metallic clang. I place my hands on the cold steel bars and grip them tight as I watch Melissa jangle the door to confirm it is locked. Melissa doesn't spare me another glance before she strides away.

She doesn't care that I am a person she helped tag and put in a cage. What does she tell herself in order to make this okay? To make it possible for her to go home to the children she just told someone she was going to meet for breakfast? How can anyone willingly be a part of this?

I wait until Melissa disappears from view before I release my grip on the bars and fumble under the coat for the knot at my waist.

Believe, I remind myself as I confront the space that is my new, horrible reality. *I can do this.*

"Get the supplies loaded up, then start with holding pen number one," a slightly distorted male voice calls through a loudspeaker. "Less than two hours until the end of curfew, so let's get moving."

It's sometime after four in the morning. I had no idea how little sense of time I had until now. Knowing just that small fact makes me feel more tethered to the person I was before the Marshals pulled me off the street. I hold on to that feeling and study the others being held with me all the while pressing the camera button on the device. I hope the lens can capture what I am seeing even as I attempt to keep it hidden from view.

There are over a dozen people scattered throughout the

rectangular cage that I'm standing in. Another thirty or forty people are imprisoned in the other connected cells. Maybe more. It's hard to tell in the dim light.

The smell and the state of attire of the people in my cell make it clear some of them have been here for some time. The man who checked me in seemed to suggest that if I wasn't transported today, it could be a while until I was moved. If it has been weeks since the last transport, Isaac could still be here. Maybe Atticus, too.

Adjusting my shirt, I slide the device back into hiding, then pull my jacket tight around me.

"Move! Move! Move! These trucks have to be out of the city before the sun comes up."

Uniformed officials pick up the pace carrying boxes into to the trucks and I walk deeper into the cage, trying to look at every face that I pass. When Atlas and I were arguing about my choice to get captured, Dewey told him I would have a better chance of staying under the radar. He had a list of reasons—but Atlas's resemblance to his father was at the top. The few photographs of Atticus I had seen told me he was right.

I straighten my shoulders and take a deep breath of the rancid-tasting air. So many of the people in the cages sit alone on the hard cement. Some are curled atop their black jackets or are wrapped in aluminum foil–looking blankets. Eyes follow me. None have Isaac's sharp cheekbones and deep-set eyes.

I step around smears of rotting food and keep walking toward a curtained-off area in the back corner of the cell where two men stand, backs to me. Their heads are bent close together. As I approach, one with unkempt red hair, a scraggly beard, and a build like a slightly out-of-shape football player glances over his shoulder and snarls, "What the hell do you think you're doing?"

I go still as the other man turns to face me. He has a long scar running down the length of his forearm. His oily black hair is slicked back into a ponytail, which gives me clear view of the ripped, partially scabbed-over skin at the top of his right lobe. The metal barcode cuff is embedded in the left.

"She's a new bird," Ponytail Guy says. "Not worth getting bent over." He glances toward a uniformed official strolling by the bars.

The red-bearded guy takes a deliberate step in my direction. "She should know better than to listen to other people's conversation."

"I wasn't," I say.

"I'm supposed to believe you?" The red-haired man advances. I step back and glance around. A few of the others in the cell are watching. Most, however, keep their heads turned away, but the tension in the way they sit or stand says they are aware of what is happening and if I'm attacked, they will not do anything to stop it.

"Transport one is ready for loading!"

The two men in front of me swing their heads toward the trucks as several uniformed officials approach a cell on the far side of the garage. There are rattles and metallic clangs as an official opens the door to one of the other cages and shouts for everyone inside to get moving.

The order draws pleas from those inside.

"I haven't done anything."

"Please."

"I won't tell anyone."

"My mother needs me."

The officials don't speak to anyone as they herd the dozen or so people in their dirty, washed-out pink-gray matching outfits and black jackets out of the cell. Some keep pleading—saying the names of their wives or mothers or father or children. One woman screams. Most move like they are sleepwalking as they are prodded and pushed onto a ramp and up into the first truck.

"The girl is a nobody," Ponytail says to his friend. "Forget her. The guards will be coming for us soon."

The red-bearded guy points a dirty finger at me. "Stay the hell away from us, or you'll learn what we did to three of the officers that brought us in here."

The two walk back to their spot by the fence. Ponytail forgets about me, but Red Beard's glares make me shiver with a new kind of fear. I'd assumed that everyone inside the bars was like me—that they had been put here because they knew the truths the government was trying to hide. That the danger I needed to be on guard against was from those not in the cages.

Stupid.

I'd forgotten that just because I think something is true, doesn't make it real. I can't forget that lesson again. Not if I want to get through this.

Red Beard and Ponytail watch the loading of the trucks. I move to a different section of the cage and press myself against the bars, squinting into the dim spaces for Isaac or any signs of the girl who once owned the shirt with the sparkles and the positive message.

"Get group two ready," the loudspeaker voice calls.

Uniformed officials scurry to the next cell.

Metal clangs when the door opens.

There are more shouts this time—not just from the people in that cell, but from the others who are soon to have their numbers come up. Voices yelling for lawyers or to call their families or screaming that this is a mistake. There's even one I hear above the din who's shouting about the mayor.

I listen for Isaac's voice and move down along the bars when I spot someone with his build. The hood of his jacket is pulled up so I can't see his face. If only he turned. . . .

"Move!" A uniformed official backhands the man. The hood falls back, revealing blond hair as the man goes down to one knee.

Not Isaac.

I keep scanning the faces of the people who marched out of the cages. Then the next cell is opened. More people are led to the ramps and up onto the trucks.

Everyone in my cage is on their feet now. Some join me: faces pressed against the cold bars, watching as others like us are urged forward. The ramp for one truck is removed. The back doors are slammed shut. Then our cage door rattles open and a dozen uniformed officials stream in.

I'm shoved and bumped and step on something that squishes under my thin bootie. When I reach the door, I glance around for somewhere to run even though I know there is nowhere for me to go. There are too many uniformed officials and the one standing off to the side, at least ten strides from the others, is holding a gun.

My heart strains in my chest. I put one foot in front of the other, taking shallow breaths of stale air while desperately trying to push aside the waves of fear. *Pay attention to every detail. Look for Isaac and Atticus. Trust the tracker will help Atlas find me as long as I don't do anything stupid to attract attention.*

Believe.

"You'll answer my questions now!" A deep, booming voice cuts through the terror. I know that voice. "I'm here on behalf of the mayor."

I pull up the hood of my jacket and look around for the man who belongs to the voice who could make this terrifying situation even worse. He knows I am not MaryAnn Jefferson, disruptive Wisconsin student. He can tell the Marshals who my mother was—and that I have worked with the Stewards. They'll know I am someone who can tell them where the Lyceum is hidden and what the Stewards know. They might not care about MaryAnn and her secrets, but they will care about mine.

"The mayor has questions he needs answers to about the prisoners held here."

"Subjects." The official looks up from his tablet. "They are referred to as subjects."

"Fine. The mayor needs a list of all the subjects who have come through this facility, and I want to speak with . . ."

"Get moving!" An official shoves me.

I lurch forward and ram into the back of the man in line in front of me. He stumbles. I gag at the intense odor as we both tumble to the ground. My knee cracks against the concrete. Pain sings up my leg. The man who went down with me groans.

"What are you doing? Get up!"

A uniformed official yanks me to my feet. My hood slips. I pull it back up to cover my face as the familiar booming voice snaps, "You!"

A man in a deep gray suit grabs my arms and pulls me out of line.

"What do you think you're doing?" an official shouts as the line of my cellmates go around me. "Mayor or no mayor, we have to get these subjects on transport and out of the city before curfew ends."

"You have your orders to follow and I have mine. My orders

involve her. And she's not going anywhere."

No way out, I think as I look up into the face of the man in the suit who long ago helped me ride a bike—Rose and Isaac's father—Marcum Webster.

NINE

"Please, let me go," I whisper.

"Is there a problem with this subject?" A bald official appears beside Mr. Webster.

"You could say that." Mr. Webster's hand tightens on my arm. His dark eyes that I have seen crinkle with laughter are stony now as he stares down at me. "Do you know who this girl is? We have been—"

A woman's scream cuts off whatever Mr. Webster was going to reveal and I turn toward the sound as the ponytailed man snaps the neck of a female official from behind. Her slack body sinks to the ground as the red-bearded man jabs something into another official's stomach. Red Beard shoves his victim into three other officials and makes a break for the front of the trucks as all hell breaks loose.

The men disappear from my sight. The bald official shouts, "Go to full lockdown!" and then races into the fray.

A whooping alarm sounds. Lights go from dim to blazing white.

Some of the "subjects" who had yet to board the trucks attempt to flee even though they have to know there is nowhere for them to go. There are screams. Desperate shouts. The man I tripped on bolts in the direction of the elevators and is tackled to the ground by an official who punches him over and over again until he goes to the floor. A nearby woman is shoved face-first against the cage bars.

Another group of officials stream out of the elevators and Mr. Webster grabs my arm and yanks me behind a table.

"Please, Mr. Webster. They think I'm a girl named MaryAnn. Don't tell them who I really am." If he doesn't reveal my real identity, the officials here won't take steps to learn what I know. They won't be able to force me to betray the people I care about.

A gunshot cracks beyond the trucks. Another.

Mr. Webster flinches at the sound of the gunfire, then shakes his head. "The city has to be protected. You are going to help the Marshals do that. You see what can happen if they go hard on you. If you cooperate . . ."

"Do you know what the word 'verify' means?" I ask, looking back to where several officials are dragging a man into view. The man's face and red beard are streaked with blood from the gunshot hole in the center of his forehead.

"Do you know why it scares them enough to do that?" I point at officials unceremoniously dumping Red Beard's limp body next to a cage. "Or this?" I point to the barcode riveted into my ear, hoping to see some regret in Mr. Webster's face.

His expression is like stone.

The whooping alarm is cut.

Two officials drag another body away while the others once again herd subjects into the trucks.

"Mr. Webster, do you know what the truth is?" I ask desperately as the bald official steps over a body and walks in our direction, two other officials following in his wake.

"I know we can never go back to the way things were," Mr. Webster says, tightening his grip on my arm.

"There's always a few who think they can get away." The official stops beside Mr. Webster and wipes his hands on his pants. "It makes for a calmer transport if we remove the instigators on this end, but it tends to throw off the schedule. We need to get this subject boarded with the rest so the trucks can leave. Take her to truck number three."

"Actually—" Mr. Webster's fingers dig into my wrist when I step toward the waiting officials. "This one is going to come with—"

"Isaac," I blurt. Mr. Webster goes still. His deep-set eyes burrow into mine.

"No one is talking to you," the official snaps.

"I'm sorry," I say quickly, searching for the right words. Hoping I don't get this wrong. "Before you came back, he wanted to know how I ended up here. I'm here because of a boy named Isaac."

A horn honks.

"Let's go!"

A female official waves her arms over her head at the back of the only truck that still has its doors open. Nervous faces—some dirty or streaked with blood—peer out from the shadows. I don't want to climb in with them, but if Mr. Webster takes me to the Marshals, Atlas and Dewey will never get to me and I'm not sure I will be able to stay strong enough not to break. If I do—any hope we have to change things will be lost. Everything my mother gave her life for . . .

"You *don't* know about him, do you?" I ask.

Mr. Webster shakes his head. Tears spring to his eyes. "You're here because of him. Do you think . . . you'll see this Isaac again?" Mr. Webster asks, ignoring the official who is insisting that I be loaded into the truck—now.

"That's what I'm trying to do," I answer carefully, hoping he sees the truth—the plea in my eyes. Whatever I will face going into the truck cannot be as bad as what will happen if Mr. Webster reveals who I really am or if they find the device hidden in the knot of my shirt.

"Are we clear?" a uniformed official standing by the trucks shouts.

"We have to roll." The bald official lets out a frustrated sigh. "Since you think this one is so important, her transport can wait. Just put whatever is left of her back into one of the cages when you're finished."

The bald official turns back to the trucks and waves them on. Tears burn the back of my eyes.

"Wait." Mr. Webster frowns and shakes his head. "I've gotten all the answers the mayor is looking for today. If we need more I'll ask another one of your subjects." His eyes meet mine. There is anger and maybe I'm imagining it, but I also see hope. "Send her with the others."

He squeezes my arm, then slowly takes three steps back for the bald official to take charge of me. The man snaps at me to hurry and leads me to the ramp of the still-open truck—away from Mr. Webster and the threat of discovery.

A female official at the bottom of the ramp pulls out a handheld scanner. She waves the black device in front of my injured ear. When it beeps, she looks down at the screen and nods. "She's logged. Get up there with the others."

I climb the tarnished metal incline toward the others already packed into the cab that looks even smaller now that I approach. The minute I step onto the truck, officials pull the ramp away. I catch sight of Rose's father in the distance, staring at me with an expression I can't begin to name. Then the doors close. First one. Then the other—plunging everything into darkness. The engine rumbles to life. The cab walls and floor vibrate. Then the truck lurches forward.

Tears I fight against and am powerless to stop slip down my cheek. I wrap my arms around my waist, then lean against the back corner of the cab and close my eyes. Not to block out what is happening around me. I can't. It's impossible to ignore the weeping, the gasps, and rattle of metal. I can't risk taking pictures without the GPS recorder being seen and trusting all these people with that dangerous secret. So instead, I do what I always do when I feel alone or afraid—I draw.

I imagine the strokes I would use to create rough texture of the desk where I was told I would be transported. How to make the S-shaped contour of the grayish-beige chair with the dark brown straps where I was tagged as if I was not even human. I try to recall the exact pattern of sparkly color that peeked out in the bin with the discarded starched collared shirts, ripped denim shorts, and plain black pants. I may not have a camera to collect the images, but if I am able to work on a tablet again—no, when. When I draw on a tablet again, I will be able to re-create every detail. Every sharp line of the connected cages and hollow, betrayed look in the eyes of the people behind those bars will ring true.

The floor beneath me shudders. I bang my shoulder against the truck's wall and jerk my eyes open. There are thuds and shrieks from the others as the truck swerves sending bodies tumbling. I grab the wall and shift my balance to keep upright as the truck veers sharply again.

Then everything settles down as if nothing happened.

I rub my shoulder and scan the interior of the truck. Thin threads of golden sunlight that sneak through the top and bottom seams of the door chase away some of the darkness. There are at least twenty of us in this truck going to who only knows where. The lack of stops and starts implies we're driving on an expressway. Without knowing the time we have been traveling or the direction we're going, it's impossible to guess where they're taking us or what will happen when we get there.

If they were just going to kill us, there would be no point in loading us onto these trucks. Keeping us alive—transporting us on roads that others travel—is a risk they wouldn't take if we were simply going to end up like Red Beard and Ponytail. At least, that is what I hope.

"If you're going to go to sleep again, I would advise sitting down." The vaguely familiar whisper rings like a bell as the man I met in that hospital-like room—Wallace, I think the Marshal called him—steps out of the shadows.

His dark curly hair is more unruly than it was before. The bruise on his cheek more pronounced. The dried blood and barcode cuff on his ear are the greatest differences from our first meeting. The curiosity and slightly mocking look in his brown eyes, however, is exactly the same.

Several heads turn at the sound of our voices where there has been nothing but silence.

"I wasn't sleeping," I say quietly.

"Your eyes were closed."

"Do you know many people who sleep standing up?"

"No." He checks his balance as the truck hits a bump. "But there's always a first time for everything. I was hoping to be impressed."

"Sorry to disappoint," I shoot back. "I didn't realize I was putting on a show."

"I'm Wallace," he says with a grimace. "If you want me to like you, you'll never call me Wally. And you are?"

"MaryAnn." I give him the name the Marshals think belongs to me, then add, "But I prefer Mary. How did you get here?"

"The same way you did, I would imagine." He shrugs and leans his head back against the door. "Through the parking garage and up the ramp."

"I didn't see you in the cages." As far as I could tell, the officials didn't lock anyone else up after me.

"They just finished putting this thing in my ear by the time they began loading the trucks." He frowns and touches the edge of his ear. "I guess I should be grateful I missed hanging out in the holding zones. They didn't look like much fun. Not that this is any better." He holds out a small bottle of water. "Thirsty?"

I glance at the others, then back at the bottle—yearning to wash the stale taste of the drugs and the scents of the cages from my mouth. "Where did you get that?"

"There's a box of supplies stacked in the back."

"There's more?" I ask.

"You might want to go easy on how much you drink." He looks down at the bottle. "We don't have a bathroom."

I laugh. It's not really funny, but I can't help it. I've been drugged, tagged, seen men killed, and am now a prisoner in this truck to who knows what hell—and he's worried about where I'm going to pee.

He cocks his head to the side, which makes me laugh harder. Heads turn—eyes widened at the happy sound, and my laughter fades like smoke.

"I was worried about everyone else," I explain, taking the bottle. Careful not to spill, I uncrack the seal. "I didn't want to drink if there wasn't enough for everyone."

He studies me as I put the bottle to my lips and take a small sip. The fresh liquid slides down my throat and I let out a sigh. I allow myself just one more swig—because now he's gotten me thinking about the lack of bathrooms—before putting the cap back on.

The walls rattle. Wedged in between the sounds of the truck are whispers from the others in the cab. Maybe it was my crazy laughter that made them realize there weren't any officials around. Or maybe they just couldn't take the fear-filled silence any longer. Whatever the reason, I'm glad for the quiet chatter, which makes me feel a little less alone.

I twist the bottle between my fingers and study the inside of the truck as if it is an assignment from one of my art classes. It's challenging to decide what colors make up the slivers of white and gold and slightly burnished lines of light that edge the doors, and sneak through pinprick holes in the wood-lined floor. I consider what the best angle would be to capture the woman who has braved opening one of the boxes of supplies or the brown, tan, white, dirt-streaked, bloody, or clean hands of all the people who reach out for the bottles and small packages of food she passes to them.

"I grabbed a couple of granola bars if you want one," Wallace says as I set the small bottle on the ground between my feet. A gray-haired man with stubble on his chin and cheeks takes an angry bite of the bar he has unwrapped. The hood of his jacket frames his face.

Eyes edged with thick black brows dart around the deep gray shadows inside the truck. When he spots me watching him, he quickly looks away.

"Would you like me to leave you alone?" Wallace asks.

"What?" I pull my thoughts from the image I am sketching into my memory.

"It's okay if you don't want to talk." He starts to shove his hands into his pants pockets, realizes the baggy government-issued garments don't have them and throws up his arms in annoyance. "No pockets? That's it. I quit."

"I don't think that's allowed, "I say. The truck hits another bump. "But feel free to try and let us know how it goes."

His slightly bruised lips curve. "Maybe we can form a union and demand better clothing."

"I can think of a few other things I'd complain about first," I say. "Like those bathrooms. Those would be high on my list of demands."

"I'll make a list," he quips. His smile fades as he steps closer and lowers his voice. "Hey. You didn't ask what it meant."

I freeze. "What?"

"Union. You know the word—not the version everyone uses. You know the other meaning."

Oh God.

My heart skips in my chest. I know about unions because I read about the Triangle Shirtwaist Factory fire. Unions are an idea the government stamped out generations ago. It's a concept I'm not supposed to know.

"I don't know what meaning you're talking about. A union is people coming together—like when they get married." I stare unflinchingly at him, hoping he believes me.

He doesn't. His eyebrows arch. Doubt colors his face. But he doesn't call me a liar. Instead, he unfolds his jacket and pulls out a granola bar he has stashed inside.

"You should eat. The food will help counteract whatever side effects you're experiencing from the drugs they gave you."

Between the bumpy ride, the smell of bodies, and the unknown path in front of me, I have zero interest in food. But I take the package because he's right about needing to eat. Besides, if I am eating, Wallace won't expect me to talk. Until I understand more about what I am facing, I have to watch what I say. To everyone.

I slide down the wall and sit on the floor with my back resting in the corner. I take my time unwrapping the packaging. Wallace sits beside me, watching as I eat the granola bar in small, careful bites. When I'm done, I fold the wrapper into a small square and set it next to the water. Wallace passes me another, which is good because now that I've started eating, I realize I'm famished. The next bar does little to fill the hole in my stomach. I consider filling it with more water, but I decide against it—just in case.

Wallace says nothing as he sits beside me. The truck sways and jumps. Eventually it slows and comes to a stop. When the engine goes silent, everyone scrambles to their feet and moves toward the door.

"Don't bother." Wallace puts a hand on my arm when I start to get up. "They aren't opening the doors. We're just refueling."

The doors don't open. We hear voices. Car doors slamming. And then Wallace is right. The engine starts and the truck begins moving again.

"How did you know?" I ask when people shuffle back to their seats.

"The gasoline." Wallace shrugs and leans his head back against the door. "I could smell it."

This time I'm the one who's being lied to. The question is—why?

I find myself mentally sketching Wallace's face. The mop of curls that drape over his slightly tanned forehead. His lanky build. Studying the way he cocks his head to the side and how his eyes narrow when he watches those inside the truck eats up the miles to—wherever we are traveling.

The temperature in the cab increases with every uncomfortably passing minute. The air becomes thick—sticky—tangible. Sweat dribbles down my neck and soaks into my clothing. I peel my jacket off first. Then roll up my pant legs and my shirtsleeves and take small sips of the water, which has turned the same temperature as the stew-like air.

Someone—a woman with a voice sharp and efficient as a carving knife—takes charge of moving the boxes of supplies to create a small space where people can relieve themselves in the empty bottles. Soon, the warm smell of urine makes my stomach lurch and my head swim. I vow not to relieve myself in one of the tiny containers. Maybe it's stupid, but I can't bring myself to do that. Especially not surrounded by all these people.

Wallace leans close to me and whispers, "Don't worry. We're almost there."

I blink. "Where?"

"I'm guessing they're taking us to the farm. If I'm right, we have to be getting close." Wallace peers out the crack in between the doors. He shifts several times, then slams his fist against the metal and sits back down. "I can't see a damn thing."

"The farm?" I whisper.

"There are two places the government takes subjects for instruction—the farm is the closest to Chicago. If they were taking us to Nevada they would have used larger trucks and made sure there was a portable toilet on board."

The truck slows. Everyone inside the cab quiets. The rattling of the walls grows louder as the truck hits bump after bump. I'm glad I'm sitting against the wall, especially when the truck takes a sharp turn. An older man standing near the middle of the truck loses his footing while stacked boxes slide into people seated nearby. Then, after what seems like an eternity, the truck slows and finally stops.

We hold our breath.

There are footsteps.

Shouts.

Wallace stands, and I scramble to my feet to stand behind him.

Locks click.

Metal grates against metal and the doors swing open.

I squint against the sudden burst of light and gratefully breathe the hot, fresh, clean-smelling air.

The first things I see when my eyes adjust are charcoal clouds in a hazy blue-gray sky. On the ground, officials dressed in the same uniforms as the ones from the Unity Center in Chicago drag a ramp up to the truck and fasten it to the edge. But I barely glance at those things as I look at what lies beyond the trucks.

First are the buildings. Large warehouse-looking facilities at the edge of a gravel road and more, smaller buildings beyond those.

Everywhere else are fields.

Row after row. Acre after acre. Lines of green.

Wallace was right. This *is* a farm.

"Out of the trucks! Women to the right. Men to the left. Move!"

I grab Wallace and pull him to the side of the truck cab while the others swarm forward.

"How did you know this is where they were taking us?" I ask. "Have you been here before?"

"No," Wallace says as the numbers inside the truck winnow. "I've only heard stories."

"From who?" I ask. "How could you know this place existed?"

"I thought you'd already guessed." He gives me a curious smile. "I know because I'm a Marshal."

TEN

"You're a Marshal?" That can't be. After all—he's here. In this truck. With all of us. How could I have been talking to someone who has ripped people from their lives, thrown them in cages, and shipped them off—simply for refusing to believe whatever the government tells them?

"I should probably use the past tense, all things considered." He touches the barcode at his ear, grimaces, and sighs.

"I don't understand."

Thunder rumbles.

"How I got here?" he asks.

"You two," an official yells. "Move!"

"We have to go." Wallace pulls my hand from his arm. "Do what the officials ask. Don't attract attention. As long as you blend in and do what they say, you'll be fine. Come on."

He heads out and I have no choice but to shrug on my coat and follow.

The wind catches my hair and tugs at my sweaty clothes as I walk down the shaky metal ramp. Thunder rumbles again as an official shouts for me to head after the others who are being led through an open gate. Red lights blink from atop the two gateposts. Stretching between posts, a large wrought-iron sign over the gate reads: The Great American Farm. And suddenly, I have a good sense of where I am.

We've been taken to somewhere in Iowa, Missouri, or Nebraska. It could be any of the three. The national agricultural site is expansive—encompassing thousands of acres from all three states. But now that I realize where we are, I'm even more confused.

Everyone in the country knows something about the Great American Farm. It would be hard not to, considering the news specials that run at least three or four times a year and grocery store displays that proudly announce what vegetables, meats, and fruits came fresh from its fields and barns. I even had to write a paper on this place when I was in fourth or fifth grade—it was a Thanksgiving assignment, I think. Something the teacher made us write so we would appreciate the food our families served over the holiday. Every article I found online mentioned that the farm was the largest of its kind in the world—created after companies from other countries tried bullying farmers into selling their harvests to them for prices far lower than was possible. When our farmers refused, the foreign companies pressured them by refusing to buy their products at all. Suddenly, farmers were left without the money they needed to support their families and farms.

There were foreclosures. Bankruptcies. Dozens of suicides. The collapse of the industry and the panic that followed was compared to the stock market crash of the early twentieth century. All because of companies from other countries who were upset they weren't allowed to cheat us.

That's why the Great American Farm was founded. First the government helped farmers by giving them grants. When it was clear the money was not a permanent solution, the country purchased struggling farms and created a new agricultural model designed to streamline the country's food supply so that everything we needed came solely from within the boundaries of the fifty-one states. Many of the farmers who sold their land were happy to be hired by the government to help lay the foundation for the Great American Farm and assist with the everyday work. The best agricultural experts collaborated with architects and engineers. Hothouse environments for popular imported vegetables and fruits were created. Barns, food processing centers, cottages, and dormitories for paid and volunteer workers were built. I've seen dozens of those workers interviewed on the news specials.

Now I wonder if any of that is real. If there were other reasons foreign countries didn't pay our prices or whether the farmers truly wanted to sell. Maybe their lands were simply taken—like what happened to the Native Americans.

I spot Wallace at the back of the line, his hair being tossed by the gusting wind. Despite the confident way he spoke in the truck, out here in the gray light, he looks defensive. Scared. An official holding some kind of long black rod suddenly changes direction and heads toward Wallace. Without warning, the official cracks the rod against the back of Wallace's legs. Wallace stumbles and the official pulls his arm back to strike again.

A broad-shouldered female official riding a Segway rolls in front of my view and shouts for us to start moving. I hope there will be bathrooms where we're going, I think, because now that I'm no longer in the truck, I really have to pee.

Lightning slashes white across the sky.

Under the grumble of thunder there is a yelp of pain.

I don't look. I clench my fists, put one foot in front of the other, and keep my eyes on the back of the person in front of me. *I don't care if Wallace is being beaten,* I tell myself with each step. *He's a Marshal. He deserves it.*

Gravel crunches beneath our feet. The thin booties provide little protection, making each step more challenging than the last. A drop of rain spatters on the ground. Another. Then just like that, the skies open.

Growing up, I hated when I got caught in the rain. My wet clothing and hair made me feel heavy and awkward and I looked a lot like a drowned rat. Today, I fasten my jacket tight around me to keep the small tracking recorder safe, and then revel in the deluge from the sky. Of having the sweat and blood, and the smells of the cages and the truck that seeped into my clothes and hair, washed away.

I look up at the clouds, run my hands over my face, and then turn to glance behind me. The trucks that brought us are turning around and driving back down the road—leaving us in their dust.

"Ow!" I grab at my stinging arm as the official pulls back the black rod she is holding and prepares to strike again.

"I told you to run."

Rain pounding, arm stinging, bladder ready to burst, I hurry behind the others toward a narrow, white-and-blue warehouse-style building at the end of the gravel road. The roof is lined with shiny, black rectangular solar panels. The same roof is on an identical structure on the other side of the road that the men are being herded into. News reports say most of the farm—from the barns and dorms to the electronic cars used on the property—runs on sustainable energy. While the government must be at least partly lying to the public about this place, the energy part clearly is true. We are led inside and instructed to sit.

Inside the building, everything is colored in a shade of gray. The floors. The overhead rafters. The windowless walls. Even the chairs that run in two back-to-back rows down the center of the long space. Long industrial lights break up the color palette. The starkness of their white illumination gives everything a washed-out appearance.

I take my place in the last seat. Directly behind me is a much older woman with gray hair, narrow black glasses, and a wheezing cough.

Rain drums on the roof.

Thunder echoes.

A compact official with jet-black hair pulled tight off her face and a pronounced chin pounds a black rod on the ground to get our attention. But the room doesn't go completely silent as all around us the *plunk, plunk, plunk* of water drips off our clothes and onto the concrete.

"Welcome to the Great American Farm. I am Lead Instructor Burnett and you are currently in the orientation and processing center." The woman uses long, purposeful strides to move to the other end of the line of chairs. "Our Instructors are tasked with preparing you to work at the farm. Everyone who comes here contributes to the safety and prosperity of the country, which is why we are happy to welcome you—our newest volunteers."

"I didn't volunteer to work at the Great American Farm," a

brown-skinned woman with blond-streaked hair says quietly.

"Neither did I," another halting voice says.

I shift uncomfortably in my chair. Some of my friends talked about maybe volunteering at the farm since volunteering could help them pay off their student loans. Hundreds of doctors and teachers and even carpenters and mechanics have worked off the money they owed for their education beyond high school by working here. My father's coworkers had done it. Even one of my mother's friends made the choice. After a year or two, or sometimes three if the debt was really high, the government forgave the debt and the volunteer could leave the Great American Farm as a true patriot freed of their financial hardship.

Enlisting in the military gave the same benefits, but most of the students at my high school considered working in fields or tending to horses and cows far better options than push-ups and marksmanship drills. There were even a few, whose families would have no problem paying for college, who talked about spending time as a volunteer just to give back.

Volunteering for the farm was never something I'd considered. My parents told me they would pay for whatever education I chose after I was done with high school, which meant I was lucky enough not to have to think about how to pay off any debt—and dirt and manual labor weren't my thing.

"Your disruptive actions volunteered you," Instructor Burnett's words crack like a whip.

I clamp my legs tight together as Instructor Burnett walks down my side of the line—tapping her long black metal rod against the side of her thigh. "The Great American Farm celebrates the country's unity. You have been identified and brought here because you have exhibited behaviors that put our country's unity at risk. Some of you have deliberately tried to circumvent or corrupt computer systems put in place for your protection. Others defaced public property or have chosen to cause unease by sleeping on the streets. One of you even aided criminals by impeding the officers sent to detain them."

"I haven't done any of those things," a light-haired woman two seats down says earnestly. Her wide blue eyes are red rimmed, but lit with a desperate hope.

Instructor Burnett reaches into her pocket. She pulls out a hand scanner and approaches the woman who spoke out. The scanner beeps. As Instructor Burnett holds the machine up to read the screen, I glance at her feet.

The other officials wear plain brown work boots. Instructor Burnett has the black military running ones.

"Rachael Corn." Instructor Burnett glances at the light-haired woman. "You hoarded paper books instead of taking them to a recycling center and encouraged others to selfishly do the same."

The light-haired woman in front of Instructor Burnett shakes her head. "That's my name," she says quietly. "But that's not me. I'm not selfish. I organize recycling drives. I told the man at the other place that there was a mistake. Someone made a terrible mistake, and he wouldn't listen. But what you said proves I'm not supposed to be here. Just ask my husband, David. He works for the City Pride Department. We know important people. They can all tell you this is a misunderstanding. They'll tell you I should be allowed to go home. I want to go home!"

I lean forward to get a better look at the woman who's growing louder and more insistent with every word. Slightly dirt-streaked round cheeks. High forehead. Pale, blotchy ivory skin. Slight wrinkles under the eyes and around the mouth that Rose could eas-ily make disappear with her magic makeup touch. When she isn't tired and wet, the woman probably passes for late forties. In this harsh white light without any enhancements to ease the years, Rachael Corn looked at least two decades older, which probably meant her husband was around the same age.

Corn. The last name sounds familiar. I rack my brain, trying to call up the image to go with the name. Was he part of one of the design teams my mother worked with over the years. Could we have attended some of the same grand openings and awards ceremonies together? If so, I can't recall.

"Contact David," the woman insists in a more confident tone. She sits up straight in her chair and smiles. "You really don't want the people we know to learn about this mistake or that you were warned you made it and did nothing to remedy the situation. If you call my husband now, I promise I won't tell anyone about this mix-up. I don't need an apology from your supervisor and I won't demand anyone get fired. I just want to go home."

"You want me to ask your husband whether you belong here?" Instructor Burnett glances down at the scanner screen again and shakes her head. "It seems it was one David Corn who filed the report that caused you to become one of our volunteers."

"No." Rachael shakes her head. Her eyes go dull and wide. "That can't be." She grabs the hand of the woman next to her and squeezes it tight.

The black rod whips in front of Rachael's face, narrowly missing her nose, and clangs against the concrete next to her feet. Rachael lets out one last squeak, then falls into terrified silence.

Instructor Burnett waits to make sure she stays that way, then continues, "Regardless of what you wish to believe, you are all here because of your disruptive choices. Choices that have threatened to take us backward to a time when there were mass shootings. When gangs terrorized the streets in cities and towns around the country."

"How does *not recycling books* encourage violence?" I'm so focused on how badly I have to use the bathroom that the words just slip out.

All eyes swing toward me as Instructor Burnett strolls to my end of the line. The scanner hovers over my ear and beeps. Instructor Burnett flicks a drop of water off of the scanner and recites, "MaryAnn Jefferson—caught defacing public property. A violation of the American Pride Beautification Act."

Several seated women gasp. Whatever they did to get brought here was clearly not the same as my offense.

Slowly, I lift my chin. "I wasn't caught defacing property. A can of spray paint fell out of my bag. For that, I was arrested, shoved into a car against my will, and drugged."

The official slowly shifts her gaze from the screen to me. "Were you planning to use that paint to deface public property?"

I ignore the drip running along my cheek and take a deep breath. "I didn't do anything wrong. I can't say what I was planning. Neither can you."

She scoffs. "Do you think that explanation helps your cause?"

"I was taken against my will and brought here," I say calmly, despite my racing heart. "I think the facts about why you did that matter, don't you?"

The woman behind me chuckles. I remember Wallace's warning to avoid drawing attention. Suddenly, I wish I could take my words back.

Instructor Burnett's eyes narrow as she studies me.

Finally, she says, "I will certainly be making a note of this conversation. Do you have anything else to add?"

"I'd like to use the bathroom," I say.

Several women down the row nod in agreement.

Instructor Burnett taps the rod one last time, then slowly starts walking again. "Bathrooms will be available when you move to the next room. The more cooperative you are, the sooner you will have the opportunity to use them. Do you understand?"

Several of the other Instructors smile.

Not a single one of us sitting in our lines says a word.

"Good." Instructor Burnett gives an approving smile. "Some of you might be teachable after all."

Her eyes slide in my direction, as if after my words she isn't so certain about me. "You have been granted the opportunity here at the Great American Farm to make amends for the disruptive choices you have made in the past and to learn the error of your actions. Here you will be taught the value of putting the unity and safety of your country above your other interests. At this farm you will have a chance to contribute to the food supply our country relies upon. The harvests here are essential to our economy and the Instructors will do their part to make sure you are dedicated to your work."

She stands again at the front of the line of chairs and looks at Rachael, who has tears silently streaming down her cheeks. "You will obey your Instructors without question. You will do your work without complaint. Anyone disobeying an order from an Instructor will be punished. We do not wish to punish you, but actions have consequences," Instructor Burnett continues. "It is our job to make sure that is a lesson you don't forget again. We take that job very seriously."

An Instructor standing along the wall holding a long black flexible rod that reminds me of a riding crop smiles at the official next to her. My stomach curls at the glee in the woman's eyes.

"Anyone with ideas about trying to leave before completing your instruction would be wise to leave those thoughts here," Instructor Burnett says sharply. "A number of measures have been put in place to ensure you cannot leave the boundaries of the farm without completing your time here. You have all been fitted with one of those measures."

Slowly, I touch the edge of the cuff riveted into my ear. A few others do the same and Instructor Burnett nods.

After a beat, she continues, "The boundaries to the Great American Farm are at times unmarked, but do not make the mistake of believing they are not real. Your ear markers each have been installed with an education protocol chip. The minute you came through the gates of the farm, that chip was activated. Any attempt to deactivate the chip will send an alert to the farm's Instructors. If the chip is not deactivated when you cross the boundaries of the farm, the education program will be triggered. You will be designated unteachable. A drug will be released into your system by the program protocol and you will die."

ELEVEN

Rachael lets out a horrified gasp. Someone whimpers. The woman beside me lets out a hushed "No." Two—a woman maybe my mother's age with hints of white streaking down her auburn hair, and another in her early twenties—nod as if this is completely expected. I try to memorize their faces.

The ear cuff isn't just a tag.

The barcode is not simply a method of tracking who we are, what we have done, and where we go. It's a leash designed to prevent any attempt to flee. If I try to escape I will die. If I don't try, everything we have done with *Gloss* and all the risks Rose and her mother and Stef's group are taking to help bring the truth to light will fail.

Instructor Burnett holds up a hand and waits until everyone goes silent. Finally, she says, "This information is not designed to scare you. It is merely a warning. You have been given a second chance. If you waste this one, another will not be given. Others have doubted my words. If you do, I assure you that you will fail as all before you have done. Cooperate. Contribute." She gives an almost motherly smile. "Prove that you are willing to continue to make this country great. Those who demonstrate their ability to do these things will earn their way back to the lives they left behind. In many ways, the choice of how long you work here at the farm is up to you."

The woman with the gray hair behind me snorts, then coughs.

Instructor Burnett looks at the coughing woman and then nods to the pairs of Instructors standing near the front of the room. Each pair has one Instructor with a scanner. The other is holding a long black switch. When the first three "subjects" on each side are scanned, the Instructors order them to head to the next room. Their exit is accompanied by the sound of the patter of the rain on the metal roof and the pounding of my heart.

Finally, the Instructors return and begin the process with the next six women. Scan them. Walk them to the gray double doors in the back of the room, then disappear inside it.

"I hate when it rains," one Instructor standing near the exit says just loud enough for me to make out her words. "It takes longer to clean up after we're finished processing them."

"Yeah, but they don't smell as bad when they've been wetted down first." The other one laughs. "Do you remember the group that came in from Chicago last week? Ugh. A little mopping is a small price to pay for not feeling like I have to throw up."

"That's what happens when they wait almost a month in between transports."

My heart jumps. If it took a month for the last transport from Chicago to arrive, Isaac would have been a part of that group. The Great American Farm is massive. Several hundred thousand acres of barns and fields and barracks and outbuildings and processing centers. The odds of me finding any one person are long. But if Isaac arrived recently, there's a chance he could still be at this training facility. If not, at the very least, someone here could know if he's okay or where he was sent.

"Last group," Instructor Burnett announces. When the Instructor with the scanner gets to me, I notice a streak of blood on the back of her hand. She grabs my ear, pulls it toward her, and the world swims in front of my eyes.

The fresh flash of pain rolls all the way down to my stomach. I hold my breath and pray for the agony to end.

Finally, there's a beep, and the Instructor lets go.

I blink back tears as I fall in line behind the woman with the gray hair who laughed at the idea of ever being allowed to leave. Then I shuffle with the other through the double doors into a white tiled bathroom.

Never have I been so glad to see a toilet stall in my life.

"First things first," Instructor Burnett says as she pulls the doors shut behind us. "You all need to get clean. Leave your coats in the bin by the door. They will be returned later. Undress in one of the stalls. Leave your shirts, pants, and shoes on the floor. Take one of the towels and a bar of soap from the cabinet over the toilet. You will then proceed to the next room where you will have five minutes to shower."

The others start to vanish into the small cubicles that line the room, but the gray-haired woman stares at Instructor Burnett and asks, "You want us to shower?" Horror colors her voice and it only takes me a second to realize why. "Are there going to be Instructors in there monitoring us?"

"Instructors are not the ones who need washing," Instructor

Burnett replies, watching the woman intently. "They will be waiting for you through the next set of doors once you are done."

Color drains from the gray-haired woman's face. She stands motionless as Instructor Burnett pulls a small personal tablet out of her pocket and taps the screen. One of the other Instructors—the one holding the long switch—advances, eyes focused on her target. Not sure what else to do, I step forward and bump into the gray-haired woman as if by accident.

The gray-haired woman stumbles. I stammer an apology that I don't mean and am relieved the gentle jolt seems to have done the trick. The gray-haired woman gets moving. As she shuffles toward a cubical without another word, the Instructor with the riding crop retreats, and I quickly head into a bathroom stall. I yank the metal door closed behind me, grateful to have reached the toilet in time.

When I finish peeing, I wrap my arms around myself and squeeze my eyes too tight for tears to fall. When I leave this little box, I have to take a shower.

If I hadn't read Dewey's history books, I wouldn't find that prospect terrifying. But I have. I know what was left out of the electronic versions of history textbooks that I used in school. Based on her reaction, I'm betting the gray-haired woman does, too.

The Holocaust. Nazi Germany. World War II.

I force myself to get moving. I can't lose control or I might not survive long enough for Atlas to track me down. So, I take stock of the small stall I'm in. There don't appear to be any screens or cameras in the ceiling high above. Nor are there any located inside the stall that consists of three silver metal walls, a slightly dented door, and a metal shelf two feet above the toilet, which is stocked with a stack of stained white towels and a small pyramid of lime-green bars of soap. There is a law against US government cameras being used in public spaces and a holiday that commemorates the day the last of the cameras were removed. That kind of monitoring had become a symbol of the divide between citizens and the government, and the removal indicated the new partnership that had been embarked upon.

Dewey said the government couldn't risk using cameras to track down dissidents like the Stewards because cameras indicated a lack of trust. That was the reason why those monitoring devices were made illegal dozens of years ago. If the government resorted to those tactics and got caught, it would not only be against the law, but also a loud signal that they were not telling the truth. People could ignore their doubts or suspicion, but learning the government felt the need to monitor them could shake public faith enough to cause trouble. Instead, the government quietly passed laws allowing them to increase the monitoring of online devices, social media posts, and phones—all in the name of national safety.

"Most people don't worry about what they can't see. Especially when they don't want to give up the devices they are using," Dewey explained when he warned me to watch for cameras once the Marshals took me into custody.

So, even though I can't see any signs of monitoring devices, I am once again careful to keep my own camera out of sight when I undress.

With my jacket providing cover, I unknot my shirt and slide free the recording tracker. Despite walking in the rain, the device is dry. Which is great, only now where do I put it?

Instructor Burnett yells to hurry up.

Damn it!

I pull off my shirt—ouch—pants, and booties, and set them on the metal shelf. Then use the hand I have the device in to clutch the towel I wrap around me. Grabbing a bar of soap, I take a deep breath and go out to join the others.

The gray-haired woman emerges from around her stall moments later. Her steps are stiff. Her hazel eyes spark with anger as the door in front of us swings open and we are told to go inside.

I concentrate on putting one foot in front of the other—trying not to remember the pages I read about people who were alive when they walked into the showers, but when it was over were taken to an incinerator. The room has white tile and drains on floors that are glistening wet. The same tile covers the walls. A row of shower-heads on one wall. Low, gray benches line the other side.

"You will have five minutes to get yourselves clean," an Instructor announces before disappearing out the door, and closing it behind her. There is a loud click of the lock tumbling into place.

The gray-haired woman stands still as a stone—staring at the showerheads. The others look at each other as if trying to decide what to do next.

There is a short, low buzzing sound, then suddenly the showerheads begin to spray. The gray-haired woman backs away. I squat near one of the drains and run my fingers through the liquid running toward one of the drains. Then I sniff at my wet hand to be certain.

"It's just water," I whisper over my shoulder. "This is a normal shower." At least as normal as anything right now can get.

The gray-haired woman's lips tremble slightly. Then she straightens her shoulders and nods. If the others were concerned about what was coming out of the showerheads, they don't show it. Most have already removed their stained white towels and have stepped into the spraying water to get clean.

Carefully, I fold my towel, tuck the GPS recorder inside, and place it on the far end of one of the benches. Then I follow the gray-haired woman to the other side of the room.

After years of showering in the girls' locker room at school, I'm used to frustrating lukewarm water and getting clean as fast as humanly possible. And like high school, I don't watch the others in the shower with me. Instead, I keep my eyes focused on the tiled floor as I scrub. The soap has a minty, antiseptic smell and barely lathers, but I don't care. I wash, rinse off, and head for my towel just as another woman with a short cap of dark hair is making a beeline for it.

I dart forward and reach for the towel at the same time the other woman grabs and tugs.

"This is mine." I pull hard enough to almost take the other woman off her feet. The thin fabric comes free from her hands, but when the woman regains her balance she reaches for the towel, again.

"Give it to me!" the woman snarls, lunging toward me.

I turn toward the side and hug the towel to my chest hoping the device doesn't slide free.

"There are other towels," I say desperately when the woman latches on to the fabric with a viselike grip. "Please let go!" If we are still fighting over a stupid towel when the Instructors open the doors, they are going to wonder why. Time is ticking away; the woman isn't giving up and I don't know what to do.

"Excuse me, but isn't this yours?"

The woman fighting me for the towel looks blankly at the gray-haired lady who tapped her on the shoulder and is now holding out a perfectly folded, albeit horribly stained, towel.

"Here." The gray-haired woman gently pries the other woman's fingers from my towel and hands her the other one. "They'll be opening the doors soon. You'll want to dry off."

The dark-haired woman shoots me a nasty look, but takes the other towel and shuffles away. I let out a sigh of relief.

"Thanks," I say, feeling into the folds of the fabric for the round device. I palm it as the gray-haired woman reaches for her own towel. "I wasn't sure how to reason with . . ."

She lifts her arms to towel off her hair and I see it. A few inches under her armpit hidden from plain sight. Less than an inch high or wide. The three dark black lines on each side that create almost a V. Wavy lines at the top—like licks of flames—in the center of which is an S. The same image Atlas has tattooed on his arm. The one I used to create the new *Gloss* logo. This woman standing in front of me is a Steward.

I lower my voice enough so the others won't be able to hear over the sound of the water still streaming out of the showerheads on the other side of the room and ask, "Could you verify your name for me?"

The woman gives me a sharp look. "You're not old enough to . . ." She frowns, glances around, and quietly says, "It doesn't matter. I'm Dana. Do you . . ."

A low, hornlike alarm sounds. The showers' spray grows weaker and weaker. When there are only a few drips coming out of the silver fixtures, the doors at the far side of the room swing open.

"Your time is up," an Instructor announces from the exit.

"We'll talk later," Dana promises before heading for the door.

Quickly, I palm the GPS recorder. Then, wrapping the towel around me, I follow the others into another tiled room. This one is cold and smaller than the other. On one wall are shelves filled with undergarments and the same ugly pink-gray clothing that we wore on the trucks. On the other are row after row of shoes. Tennis shoes in a variety of colors. Brown moccasins. Tan work boots. All in various states of wear and tear.

"Hurry up."

I shiver as I dry myself off as best as possible, then rummage through the clothing to find a support tank, underwear that looks newer than the others, and a shirt and pants that appear to be close to my size. Then using my locker room skills, I change my underwear under the damp towel. It's probably stupid to be concerned about changing in front of a bunch of women I don't know after we just showered in the same room, but I do it anyway.

The pants are too short. The shirt is narrow, but long enough that I think it can be tied into a useful knot. I sift through the shoes on the rickety, scarred wooden shelves until I find a slightly-too-big pair of broken-in powder-blue high-tops with slightly frayed laces in my size. Gently, I run my hand over the round patch that has started to pull away from the canvas fabric.

"There are some newer ones over there." Dana points to the other side of the shelving unit. "I can help you look."

"These are fine," I say. Then, hunched over to make sure no one can see, I slide the GPS recorder in between the canvas and the lining of the beaten-up right shoe.

Like Dana, the other women in our group have gravitated to shoes with the least amount of scuffs and scars. A few months ago, I might have cared enough to do the same. I have a different set of priorities now.

The dressing room opens. An Instructor shoves a coat at each one of us with orders not to get wet again, and we are led outside.

The air is heavy and warm.

Rain falls in a light mist, which is probably something they'll insist we appreciate because rain helps things grow. Right now the sounds of the rumbling thunder combined with the crunch of gravel beneath my feet and the slightly green-yellow tint to the sky give this walk to the unknown a horror-movie quality that I find more than a little unsettling.

Despite the stickiness of the air, I shrug on the jacket, which is at least two sizes too big. Ugh! There is a mildewy floral smell that reminds me of my grandmother's funeral.

"Keep moving." An Instructor snaps one of the riding crops in my direction.

I pick up the pace. But when the Instructor turns away I slow my steps and look around again, trying to figure out exactly where I am and what the best way out of here might be.

There are a dozen or more buildings in the area. To the west, I see more structures. Winding clouds of smoke puff into the sky from a number of chimneys. To the east is a covered walkway like this one that leads to the same, massive building we're walking toward. Where there aren't buildings there are fields of rich black soil and deep green growth that seem to go on forever. Getting out of here on foot—if I can find a way to get the ear cuff off without triggering their poison—won't be easy.

The tempting scent of spices and baked bead waft from the large barn as does the faint strains of drums and maybe a base guitar. I walk faster toward the smells of food, and I'm not the only one. After almost a day with nothing but fear, determination, and granola bars to fuel me, I am running on empty.

The source of the music becomes obvious when we step into the dimly lit, wide-open structure. Over a dozen enormous screens like the ones outside my school and displayed on buildings throughout Chicago are set up along the top of the expansive room. Some are playing closed-captioned newscasts from cities around the country. Videos of the Boys of America song "Together We Are Free" blare from the others. I spot the familiar faces of the Chicago Channel 2 anchors smiling from one in the back corner. They are showing a video of people at the beach—some riding bikes, others on the sand or standing at the edge of the glistening lake.

My breath catches in my throat. I was standing just there only hours ago.

It feels like a lifetime from here, where Instructors line the room in their blue uniforms. Where they threaten with their long metal rods and riding crops. Where the music is too loud for anyone to speak more than a few words without being drowned out by lyrics that speak of unity and strength and freedom. Where there are rows and rows of benches and long white tables—all filled with people dressed in the same ill-fitting clothing. A few watch the screens with desperate eyes. Others look down at the table. There are occasional glances at our group as we are led to the tables nearest to the entrance.

I scan the crowd looking for brown eyes that are quick to brighten with laughter, and the handsome face that captures the attention of almost every girl at our school.

Please, let Isaac be here.

Someone bumps me and I walk down the center aisle, past benches filled with people who I recognize from the cages in Chicago or the truck I was transported on. I spot Wallace sitting on the end. His face is mostly hidden by the black hood as if he is blocking out everything around him. I should ignore him. He's a Marshal. That alone tells me he can't be trusted. Still, he knew we were coming here. If he knew that, maybe he also knows a way for me to get out.

As I walk by his table, I step on the edge of one of my shoelaces with my other foot and make a show of kneeling down to retie it.

"What are you doing?" An Instructor grabs me by the shoulder as I give the laces one more yank. "Get up!"

"My shoelace came undone." I point down. "I just need to finish tying it."

The Instructor rolls her eyes and lets out a loud, frustrated sigh. "Finish up and join the others." She leads my group of women to a bench several rows down and orders everyone to sit.

"Wallace?" I hiss as a new song starts to play. "I need to talk to you."

"Later," he says, never looking down at me. "Meet me at the fence."

The fence. I have no idea what that means, but I'll figure it out.

A shadow looms over me as I pull the laces into a bow and scurry toward my place next to Dana at our designated table. Once I am seated, Instructor Burnett and a dark-bearded official climb the steps to a small wooden dais.

Someone cuts the sound system. "Red, White, and Blue for You" fades out leaving behind the haunting echo of the patter of rain overhead.

Instructor Burnett taps on a microphone. "Rise."

Benches scrape across the gray wood-planked floor and we all get to our feet.

The screen directly behind the two instructors displays the image of an American flag. The other feeds display white words marching across a black backdrop. I skim the words, blink, and start reading them again as the bearded Instructor leans into the microphone and announces, "Begin."

Everyone who was here before today places their hands over their hearts and in loud voices recites the words that move across the screens.

I swear that I will be a faithful citizen. That I will celebrate our country's greatness and take pride in our shared accomplishments. And that I will always be obedient to the laws and my duly elected leaders, and put my country's interest above my own.

A few women around me join into the recitation halfway through. When an Instructor approaches me with his riding crop raised, I move my mouth, but not a single word passes my lips.

When the strange oath is finished, the bearded official says, "Each day you stand here gets you closer to fulfilling that promise. To our new subjects . . ." He glances at our group of tables. "You will say these words every day until they are part of you. You will work here until you believe. We will see that you live by these words."

He sharply places his hand over his heart, then in the same crisp movement puts his hand down at his side like a salute. The others around the room repeat the movement and take a seat. I look around the room and do the same.

"What the hell was that?" Dana whispers.

I don't know if she is talking to me or herself, but I don't have a chance to respond before the screens flicker. Most return to their previous programming of muted newscasts and loud, flashy pop-music presentations that make it impossible to talk without shouting. But one screen on every wall continues to display the words of the recited oath—a constant reminder of what they intend to teach us here.

"Do they really think they can convince us we don't know what we know?" Dana asks.

I glance around the room. Most of the ones who were here before today are sitting quietly at their tables. A few lean close to each other as they exchange words. But there are several others intently staring up at the screens with the white words of the oath, moving their mouths, silently repeating the words over and over again.

Large tureens of some kind of stew and long, thin loaves of bread brought to the ends of each table pull my attention. The older men and women serving the food are wearing what I have come to think of as the "farm uniform" as they ladle stew into small wooden bowls. They then tear hunks of bread and place them atop the stew before passing them down the table. The hollowness in my stomach is more pronounced with every bowl I pass until finally mine arrives.

There are no spoons or forks or utensils of any kind. So I pick up my bowl like the others in the room and sip. If I were in Chicago, the last thing I would want is hot soup on a warm, sticky day. But here, I gobble down the carrots and potatoes and mop up every drop of the almost paste-like brown goop with the bread as if it is the best thing I've ever eaten. It's not, but when I'm finished far too quickly, I'm sorry there isn't more. I find myself reading the words on the screen to keep myself from grabbing Dana's bowl out of her hand.

A horn blows. The screens go black and benches scrape the floor as everyone gets to their feet and starts filing toward the doors in the back.

"Women to the left," a loudspeaker voice announces. "Men to the right."

I rise with the others, fall in step, and that's when a tall, lanky man up ahead catches my eye. The smooth gait—the set of his shoulders makes my heart leap.

Isaac!

"Excuse me," I say, shoving my way forward through the mass exodus of bodies trying not to lose sight of the back of Isaac's head. "Please. Let me through."

I elbow people to the side and ignore their grunts of annoyance and pain and the shouts over the loudspeaker to "settle down." I don't listen. Instead, I duck around a large, lumbering man and grab hold of Isaac's arm. He turns, looks down at me, and—

There is nothing familiar about the face that is at least a decade older than Rose's brother.

"You're not him."

"What do you think you're doing?" The man tugs his arm away as others behind him push their way forward.

"I'm sorry." I let go and look down at my empty hand. "I . . . I thought you were someone else."

"I wish." The guy follows the exodus through the right door.

I really thought . . .

A weight settles in my chest. It wasn't him.

"Hey, you can't just stand there," a woman hisses as she grabs my arm and pulls me along into the line headed to the left. "You have to keep moving or they'll make an example of you."

A few women in the line nod.

"I thought he was a friend of mine," I explain. "He went missing and was brought here last week, I think. From Chicago. Maybe you know him?" We step through the wide door and start down a hallway with narrow windows. "His name is Isaac. He's almost eighteen. He's six feet tall with dark skin and short dark hair. He wouldn't have known why he was taken and . . ." I bump into the woman in front of me who has stopped walking.

"Isaac. Did his father work with the mayor?"

"Yes." My breath catches. What are the odds that there is another boy that age here whose father worked at City Hall? It has to be him. "Is he here? Can you tell me where to find him?"

Her hazel eyes shimmer and everything inside me goes still. "I'm sorry to tell you this, honey, but the Isaac I met is dead."

TWELVE

My fault.

My fault.

My fault.

"You have to get up."

Hands grab at me. Shake me. Someone steps on my hand and I lift my head.

How did I get on the floor?

"They're coming." The words mix with a dull buzzing inside my head. My stomach heaves. "You have to move."

Someone helps balance me as I push away from the concrete floor and get to my feet.

"Move!" the woman snaps. "If you don't they'll punish you. Would your friend have wanted that?"

No. He'd think that was giving up. Giving in because I know it's my fault he had been taken here in the first place. He never let anyone on his team give up when they felt beaten or useless. "You're giving up if you don't step up," he would say. I whisper it to myself and put one heavy foot in front of the other.

The hallway swims in and out of focus, but I keep walking through the door and into a room filled with women of all ages and dozens and dozens of bunk beds.

"Over here." The woman who still has a strong grip on my arm leads me to a bunk bed about halfway down a row. "This is mine. You can take the top bunk."

"I told Jennifer she could have it," someone complains.

"Now you can tell Jennifer that it's taken." The woman sits on the bed next to a flattened pillow and waits for me to do the same. For the first time, I focus on her face. Not a woman's face. A teen-age girl with light tanned skin and curly brown hair with streaks of yellow threaded through it. There is also an angry-looking scab just over her right eye. "I'm Liz. Are you going to throw up?"

I put a hand on my uncertain stomach and shake my head.

"Good. They won't feed us again until morning. The nights suck hard enough without being hungry. I'm sorry about your friend."

Hot, bitter tears build.

"I never talked to him," Liz says. "Never had the chance."

"Do you know what happened? How he . . ." I should be able to say the word, but I can't squeeze it past my throat.

"I just know that he tried to stop someone else from getting a les-son and the Instructors decided to drag him away, instead. When I first got here, I was warned that it's always worse if you fight back." Her tone is clinical even as her hands are balled into tight fists. "Isaac must not have gotten that warning, or he didn't listen to it. That was two days ago."

Two days. When Mr. Webster saw me at the Unity Center, he

still believed Isaac was alive. Has he been told about Isaac's death since then? Has he broken the news to Rose and Mrs. Webster? I doubt whatever Rose and her mother are told will be the truth. It will be up to me to pass that on once I find a way out of here. If Mr. Webster doesn't reveal my real identity first....

A horn blast sounds.

"I've gotta go." Liz reaches under her pillow and pulls out . . . something that she shoves in the elastic of her pants. "I've got crap duty. You can use the top bunk, but don't just sit there all night. It'll send the wrong signal. You don't want anyone to report that you're weak. Just remember to leave your jacket on the bed when you aren't around so people know it's taken."

"Wait," I say as she starts to leave. "I heard someone mention something called 'the fence.' Do you know what that is?"

"It's through there." She points to a wide opening in the wall between two sets of bunk beds. "I shouldn't need to tell you this, but—be careful. The Instructors aren't the only ones who can hurt you here."

Liz weaves her way through the maze of beds and disappears out the door. When she's gone, I drop my head into my hands and picture Isaac.

The way he grinned when he zoomed his bike past us and made Rose shout that she was going to tell their parents.

How his nose crinkled when he studied the basketball hoop from the free-throw line at one of the games Rose guilted me into going to.

And the way he took Rose's hand in his and held on tight when she told me their parents were getting a divorce.

He shouldn't have died. It was my fault he ended up here. My stupid choices that pulled him into situations he knew nothing about. If it weren't for me, the officials who run this system wouldn't have taken his life like they took my mom's and so many others. How many have died so they could keep the truth from coming out? How many more will die if no one stops them?

Steeling myself, I wipe my tears with the edge of my shirt. I don't have time for tears. If I just sit here and cry, Isaac's death won't matter. And it will. It has to. The only way that's going to happen is if I document what I see, find a way to safely remove the cuff from my ear, and get out of this horror show.

I shrug off my jacket, and throw it across the top bunk to mark it as mine. Then I squeeze through the tight space in between the beds and take stock of the room.

It's quiet. Dozens of women crammed into this tight space. Barely any of them are speaking. Most lie on their beds—sleeping, or pretending to be. A few make their way to what I think is the bathroom. One or two head toward the door that Liz pointed out to me. I wish I could take out the recording device and capture this image, but I can't take the risk of someone noticing. Instead, I memorize every detail as I weave through the tight spaces between the rows of black metal bunk beds each made up of a single off-white sheet and ungenerous pillow to the hallway Liz had shown me.

Wet hay and gravel crunch under my feet when I step from the long concrete hall into an open-air space. If this were a normal farm, I imagine the area would be expansive enough to exercise horses. In this farm, the area doesn't hold four-legged animals. Here, people sit against the walls, or talk as they walk in twos and threes around the space like inmates in some kind of prison movie. One older woman runs laps around the perimeter as if training for a marathon. There are no Instructors on the ground with us. Instead, there are a dozen of them situated on balconies ten feet above us, giving them a perfect view of everything happening.

But while the people catch my attention, it is the line of matte-black steel slats, a few inches in between each, that rise from the floor to a dozen feet in the air and divide the area into two sections that holds it. Women on this side. Men on the other. The top of each slat is cut to a sharp point like some kind of medieval torture device, making it both imposing and grim. I can't imagine any way that a person could scale the flat, smooth metal bars, but the spiked tops would certainly keep them from safely climbing to the other side. Which I am guessing is the point.

This is the fence. Now to find Wallace.

An eerie fog hangs over the courtyard as I walk past several groups of women toward the fence. A few women are quietly talking with some of the men through the slats. One older lady has reached between one of the narrow openings in the metal barrier and is holding tight to a younger man's hands. There are more men in their side of the arena. Several are throwing some kind of ball. The cover of it looks like it was made out of a pillowcase.

I run my hand along one of the slats of smooth, cold metal and peer through the six-inch spaces between them. Finally, I spot a man seated on the ground at the far end of the arena who holds up his hand when he sees me turn his way.

I cross to the other side of the courtyard, lower myself onto the wet hay and gasp as I look through the slats. Dried blood stains Wallace's shirt. A crimson-stained bandage covers one side of his neck. Wallace gives me a tentative smile and for a flash of a second I see Isaac looking back at me from the other side of the slats—bruised and beaten.

"It looks worse than it is," Wallace assures me.

"What happened?" I ask, forcing the image of Isaac to the side.

"Someone overheard us talking in the truck. When they realized I used to work for the government . . ." He closes his eyes and leans his head against the brick wall. "Turns out being a Marshal means that everyone in this place has a reason to hate me."

"Why *are* you here?" I ask.

Wallace studies me through the slats. "You didn't ask what a Marshal is. You know what they are. What I was."

Another mistake. The right words can change lives, but so can the wrong ones. This time I don't make denials. I just pull my knees up against my chest and wait.

Wallace shrugs. "You're smart. I wouldn't trust me, either."

"Right now I don't trust anything," I say. "But you knew where we were going and you seem to know what to expect now that we're here. That means you know more than I do."

"And knowledge is power. Right? If it wasn't, I wouldn't be here right now." He surveys the arena. I do the same. One of the men playing "ball" is watching us with narrowed eyes. When he sees me looking at him he turns his head away, but the two women speaking with the men at the fence continue to cast furtive glances our way. Or maybe I'm just paranoid after Liz's warning.

"Do you know why you're here?" I ask.

Wallace shifts so he is directly facing me. "I started asking the wrong questions."

"What kind of questions?"

He frowns and looks at the ground. "Both my parents are police officers. My entire life I've been grateful that things are safer in Chicago—in this entire country—than they used to be. I decided I wanted to help keep things safe—like my parents. My dad helped me train. When I applied for the academy, I was accepted immediately and graduated first in my class."

Wallace looks up. "Right before graduation, I was given an opportunity to continue my training with a special law enforcement unit. A group of investigators who were quietly commissioned to work in cities around the country after the FBI was disbanded. You couldn't apply to the unit. My dad told me he'd tried. You had to be chosen for the Marshals. I was chosen."

I hate the glow of pride in Wallace's voice because I understand it. For most of my life, I wanted not only to be as good as my mom, but to eventually be better. To do greater things for the city. It was part of what drove me as an artist and made me determined to succeed even when I was certain my mother thought I would fail.

"So you said yes."

"Of course I did." He grins. "I mean, the Marshals were elite. They tracked down and detained terrorists. They do the most important work of any law enforcement agency in the country."

"If it's so important, why doesn't anyone know about them?" I ask. "Why not tell people how great the Marshals are?"

"We can't. Not without giving the terrorists what they want— the chance to create uncertainty and fear. People deserve to feel safe." Wallace shrugs. "At least that's what they told us during my extra year of training. I studied city schematics and was lectured on crimes that weren't reported on the news. I learned about places like the one you were brought to when the Marshals took you into protective custody."

"Protective custody?" I say the words back to him, but mine are sharpened with sarcasm. "I was kidnapped, drugged, and had a barcode embedded in my ear—against my will. Does any of that sound protective to you?"

I wanted him to realize his choice of words mattered. His phrase made the process sound gentle. Anyone who heard those words spoken would certainly believe the government acted out of concern for my well-being. They painted a picture of kindness and empathy directly over the inhumanity of the ear tags and cages or this arena with the spike-topped fence and the host of guards.

Like the book Dewey showed me on the history of slavery in America. The words drew a picture of the unspeakable things humans convinced themselves was okay because of a difference in skin color. Slavery was mentioned in my schoolbooks, but nothing prepared me for the descriptions of the families ripped apart and sold to different owners or the beatings and abusive treatment. When I looked back at the texts my teachers had us read, I noticed the word "worker" was frequently used in place of the word "slave." With a change of that one word suddenly an entire history of pain and dehumanization is softened into something less shameful.

Wallace's eyes narrow. "We were trained to call it protective custody."

"Have you drugged people when they tried to call for help?"

"My job—"

"Did you lie to their families about what happened to them?"

"The less people know, the safer they are. Publicity would only encourage others who want to appear on the news to cause disruptions!" Wallace jumps to his feet and stalks away. I stand as well and notice that more eyes have turned our way. The men playing ball have stopped and are watching Wallace pace in a circle while running a hand through his unruly curls.

Finally, he takes several deep breaths and walks back. "I'm sorry. It's hard to think that . . ." He shakes his head. "You probably can't understand, but we all believed everything they said."

That's something I do understand. I wanted to deny everything Atlas told me—everything that I read in the books the Stewards had kept from being destroyed. Had it not been for my mother's death, I doubt I would have ever questioned what I had been told to believe. After all—it was working for me.

But Marshals murdered my mother. Marshals are the reason Isaac had been brought here, beaten, and killed. Just because I understand why Wallace believed in the Marshals' mission doesn't make any of it right.

"You still haven't told me why you're here."

"There was a girl," he says quietly as a gentle misting rain begins to fall.

Of course. I roll my eyes.

"Not like that," he snaps, then lowers his voice. "She was twelve. Two months ago, my partner and I were ordered to pick up her father. He was part of the terrorist group that's been operating in the shadows for years—or what I was told was a terrorist group. Protocol is to get the subject isolated from family or acquaintances before we take them into protecti—"

He glances sharply at me and shakes his head. "The man picked up his daughter from school and was walking her home when we were told to take the two of them. They said she was a part of it. That he had already enlisted his daughter in his mission and that she was recruiting her friends with the group's propaganda. You've read the real history, so you know—the same way young children were recruited to be suicide bombers before we shut our borders and weeded out that kind of destruction. So we moved in to capture them both. I was in charge of taking her."

He turns so I can't see his face. I can barely make out his words when he continues, "He knew who we were when he saw us. I was putting her in the car when he went down like all the others we tried to take in. I can still hear her scream. His daughter was in front of him and he killed himself so we couldn't bring him in. But she thought we had killed him."

They did. He might have used the deadman's switch or some other method to kill himself, but they were the ones that pushed him to do it.

Others in the courtyard make their way to the entrance. I hold my ground as Wallace continues, "The girl didn't know why her father died. She didn't seem to know anything about what he was involved in. She was confused and scared and looked at us like we were crazy when we mentioned some of the terrorists' code words. They said she'd been trained to tell convincing lies when we brought her to the Unity Center and that she would help us locate the rest of the terrorists." He crosses his arms and shrugs. "I moved on to the next assignment, but I couldn't forget that girl. She didn't know anything. We should have never taken her."

It makes me think of the sparkly T-shirt I saw in the Unity Center bin. Obviously, it wasn't this girl's . . . but I can't shake the image from my mind.

"I'd never doubted the information we'd been given before. But this time . . ." He rests his forehead against one of the steel slats. "I started asking questions. I thought it was important to learn if an error was made so we didn't make the same mistake the next time. They told me there was no mistake. The girl confessed her crimes and was sent here to help gain a sense of civic pride. My partner said to let it go."

Two of the women walking around the courtyard have come closer. Neither of them is looking at us. Still, I keep my voice low and ask, "You didn't let it go?"

"I should have." He sighs. "I went to the funeral for the father, instead. To be honest, I'm still not sure what I thought I was going to find. What I didn't think I'd see were two caskets—father and daughter—who were supposedly struck by a car whose brakes had stopped working. My bosses said she had been transported here to the farm. They lied. And I started wondering what else they were lying about. That's what I was trying to find out. I snuck books out of a recycling center and read things I'd never heard about before."

"Like what?" I lean against the slats.

His eyes flick to me. "Things like the unions. Like words I never knew existed, listed on a piece of paper our field office worked to get off the streets."

He was talking about the pages that my mother, Atlas's father, and Dewey created. The papers that I helped some of the Stewards distribute to people on the streets of Chicago trying to show them the truth. We thought that no one had paid attention or cared enough to do anything with the information they read.

Wallace had read it, though. Maybe it *had* meant something.

"You know something about those papers?" Wallace gives me a sharp look as I consider what to say.

He was a Marshal, but now he's here—tagged, just like me and everyone else in this place. If I want to get out of here, I need all the help I can get. And yet . . .

"No," I lie.

"Are you sure?" Wallace asks. "Because—"

A low, grating horn blasts three times. The woman who was running changes direction. A gray-bearded man gives the makeshift ball one last toss, and those who were still walking or sitting in the courtyard turn and head for their respective entrances.

"We have to go," he says, pushing away from the bars. "Meet back here tomorrow?"

I watch the women hurrying inside, and nod.

"Remember—avoid unwanted attention from the Instructors. Keep a low profile if you can. If they don't pay you any special attention you'll have a better chance."

"A better chance at what?"

"Surviving."

"Wait," I call before he can walk away. "What was her name?"

"What?"

"What was the girl's name?" I ask.

"Her name?" He frowns as Instructors from above shout for us to get inside. "Her name was Anne."

The rain falls harder as he walks away from the fence and I turn and do the same.

After my mother died, I spent the days and nights after school in my room because being around other people—seeing them laugh—watching them do normal things—was like salt on a wound.

Rose hated that I was alone so much. She called and texted and pushed me to go out with a group of our friends to the movies or hang out at her house after school. She never wanted me to go home until my father was there—so I wouldn't face an empty house or draw in my mother's studio by myself. Rose didn't know about the bottles my father thought he could hide from me or the uncertain sound of his footsteps on the stairs that I couldn't ignore no matter how much I turned up my music and willed them away.

"Alone" didn't mean lonely. When I was alone, I could shut out the world. I could lose myself in colors and shapes and textures and use them to place a dam between me and the things I didn't want to acknowledge. Alone was better when you didn't want to feel. Seeing people was like holding up a mirror to the pain, and instead of the one image of hurt and sadness—there were two.

Tonight, there is no alone.

Liz has not yet returned to the dorm. I dry off as quickly as I can in the gray, chipped-tiled bathroom with towels stingier than the ones in my high school locker room, then search for my bed even as others around me talk in groups of twos and threes. No one has thrown my coat onto the floor, so I climb up onto that bunk, pull the sheet over me, and ignore the building panic as I carefully remove the GPS recorder from my shoe.

Dozens of women move quietly through the room—lying on the bunks—whispering in corners. I shift the sheet and capture the image of Dana sitting on a pallet haphazardly placed on the ground not far from the bathroom. I take another of a woman curled up in a corner staring hopelessly at the ceiling. A horn blasts again quickly followed by a low, hollowed-out metallic sound. The room goes completely black for several long seconds before the exit signs over the doorways hum to life and cast parts of the room in a pale, sickly green.

Mood lighting. Just perfect.

I huddle under my sheet as those who have not found their beds navigate the dark by the meager glow and eventually settle. My eyes are gritty. A film of fatigue wraps around me. I'm not sure how well the recorder will capture images in the dark, but I take several pictures anyway before stashing the device back in my shoe. Then I close my eyes and try to find the emptiness in between breaths where I can stop myself from thinking. But there is no emptiness here, because there are people.

Shifting in their beds.

Whispering.

Whimpering.

The quiet sounds of someone weeping in the darkness.

Then from somewhere nearby, there is singing.

A folk song. My music teacher from elementary school would probably recognize it, but the unfamiliar notes sung in the low, throaty voice lends the song an otherworldly quality. Everyone goes quiet as the stanzas float through the darkness.

> *My heart will be true*
> *My heart will be strong*
> *Through the darkness of the darkest night*
> *That keeps stretching for far too long*
> *My heart will be true*
> *My heart will be strong*
> *Though the seas churn with anger and rage with might*
> *My heart will be true. I will not lose sight*
> *When the mountains are steep and impossible to scale,*
> *My heart will be strong, I must not fail.*
> *There is beauty in trying when there is no end in sight*
> *I must keep on walking if I want to find the light.*
> *When the monsters at night make me cower in my bed.*
> *When all my foolish dreams and false hopes have long fled.*
> *You will know I still love you when you hear this, my song.*
> *My heart will be true.*
> *My heart will be strong.*

I pull the thin sheet over my head, but I still hear every word she sings and the tears others shed. I want to yell at her to stop because she's just making it worse, but that would draw attention so I shut my eyes tight and wait for the song to end.

Her voice cracks on the final phrase. Finally, the sounds of muffled weeping are all that is left when the song is gone. After several minutes, those fade and I uncover my face and stare into the darkness, trying to keep fear and doubt over all I had done at bay.

Maybe I should have stayed safe in Chicago. Maybe Atlas was right about not needing a better truth to tell in order for people to pay attention. Maybe I should have listened to my father and gone with him to try to forget everything I know to be true. To forget what my mother died for.

Stop. I swallow hard against the tears.

This was my idea. My choice.

It had to be me who got captured. Dewey and Atlas were both longstanding members of the Stewards. And Atlas had the tattoo on his arm. The Marshals would have recognized it and tried to force him to give up the location of the Stewards' Lyceum. Not to mention, he was more skilled at fighting the Marshals. He would have a better chance of getting someone away from them than I would. And both of them would be considered a greater threat by the Marshals than a girl with a couple of spray cans whose government identification and cover story made them believe she was new to the city.

There is no changing past decisions. I can either become what Instructor Burnett and the other Instructors want me to be or I can keep fighting.

They wanted me to take an oath. Fine.

"I swear," I whisper into the flat pillow. "I will be a faithful citizen. That I will get out of this place. That I will put my country's interest above my own and set the truth about our country free."

Over twenty-four hours has passed since I allowed the Marshals to capture me. I've learned where the people who have disappeared have gone. That's the answer we were looking for and I've found it. I've taken photographs that people need to see. Since there is no way to know where Atlas is or if he has figured out how to get me out of this place, I have to start figuring out how to do it myself.

THIRTEEN

The blast of a horn jerks me awake and I almost fall off the edge of the narrow bed trying to sit up. By the time I blink away the haze of sleep everyone else is already sliding out of their beds to get ready for whatever the Instructors are planning.

There are no toothbrushes in the bathroom. No one else standing at the trough of sinks in the bathroom appears to care about the lack as they splash water on their hands and faces and hurry out to make room for the next person to wash. I use my finger to rub the worst of the stale, cottony film from my mouth and am headed back into the dorm room when the next horn sounds. I spot Dana in line and lift my hand to get her attention. She sees me. I know she does, but she doesn't acknowledge the greeting.

"Friend of yours?" Liz appears at my side. Her hair is wet and her cheeks are shiny pink.

"Not exactly," I say as Dana whispers something to the woman next to her. They both give me a strange look, then turn away. "Maybe not at all."

"Don't feel bad. People do all sorts of things they normally wouldn't just because they're here." The doors at the front of the room clang open and the line of women starts to move.

Liz grabs my arm and pulls me into the line. "You don't want to be one of the last to leave the dorm or they might run out of food before they get to you and you'll end up hungry."

"Really?" I look back at the tired faces of the women shuffling behind me.

"Don't worry about anyone else," Liz says. "You think that sounds mean."

"A little," I admit.

"That's because it is. It's also practical," she explains. "Trust me. I was in the holding cells for three weeks. I've been here at the farm for almost two. I learned the hard way—do what you have to in order to survive, and screw the rest."

"Then why help me?" I ask.

"You look like you might be useful. I want you to owe me." She glances at me and I wait for the smile that will say she is joking. It never comes.

She pulls her hair back with a piece of ripped fabric as we shuffle through the hallway and back into the humid dining hall. The screens above flicker. I look for the Chicago news feed as I'm handed a tray, then follow the line around the edge of the room to a line of carts. We are given a bowl of what looks like oatmeal, a small red apple, and a glass of water.

I follow Liz to one of the tables and shovel the vaguely warm, congealed food into my mouth, not caring about the lack of flavor. As I eat, I watch the stories from back home march across the screen. Without the sound, I only have a vague sense of what most of the news spots are covering. There is something about the L, a heat advisory at the beaches, and the final days of Celebration of America that started three weeks ago on the Fourth of July and will be ending this week. My father used to love the patriotic festivities. Every year, he scoured the schedules to pick out the best parades, concerts, and fireworks displays for us all to attend. The best ones always happened in the first week, but there were other events that we enjoyed during the extended celebration. And all of it was made even better by the decorations Mom's department created for places like City Hall.

Last year, Mom refused to go to any of the events. Other years she'd pack coolers of food and drinks to bring to the parades and made popcorn for us to eat while we watched the fireworks. Last year, she stayed inside her studio and painted while Dad and I went off to enjoy the fun. I should have understood that something had changed. Would I be here now if I had asked her what was happening? If she had tried to explain, would I have understood why it was important? Would I have even listened?

I almost drop my apple as the image of the *Gloss* office building appears behind the male news anchor. The caption says "Unusual surge in popularity for Chicago's very own e-zine" but the announcer isn't giving his typically plastic smile as he reads the story for the viewing audience.

I start to stand and Liz yanks me back down. "What are you doing?" she whispers.

"Sorry," I say, looking back up at the screen, but the image has changed to the logo of the Chicago Cubs with the headline about a record-setting strikeout game. "I was just surprised by something."

"I don't care if a snake slithered up your pants. You stay seated until they tell you to get up," she whispers. "If the Instructors start looking at you, they might notice me. If you want to survive this place you have to keep it together. I plan on getting out of here some-day. Do you?"

The music fades and the screens change to once again display the oath that was said yesterday.

"Yes," I answer, as Instructor Burnett appears on the dais and we all rise to our feet. "I'm going to get out of this place."

"Then play along and blend in. It's the only way you'll ever get your chance."

Instructor Burnett puts her hand over her heart. She waits until we all mimic her, then the oath begins. Liz says the words in a loud, clear voice and shoots an annoyed look my way when I move my mouth, but don't give voice to a single word. Maybe the best way to survive is to go along with the program. To do what they say. To pre-tend to believe what they believe. But everything I've read says that is how the road that brought us here began. People pretending what is happening is okay. Willing to let things slide because it is easier than rocking the boat and risk sinking with it. Maybe it is smarter to lie low for as long as the battery in the GPS recorder lasts and hope Atlas finds a way to get me out of here—to become something I have been fighting against in order to survive.

When the oath ends, I take my time lowering my hand, so it isn't as obvious that I am not executing the strange salute that Instructor Burnett and the others perform. Finally, Instructor Burnett says, "Adhere to your oath and be proud of the work you do for the good of our country. Each day is one day closer to being redeemed. I wish you a productive day."

There are only the doors at the front and the two that lead to the dorms in the back. Each is flanked by Instructors. If I could get the ear cuff off without alerting anyone, I doubt I could escape from this building without getting captured. There has to be another way and I have to find it.

"Don't be in too much of a hurry," Liz says as I start to follow a group heading for the exits. "If it isn't raining, it's better to be in the middle of the line. The ones in the front end up working the fields farthest away. They're the last ones to get water when the Instructors remember to give it to us. The back of the line typically ends up working in the gravel pit near the mine."

"There's a mine?" I ask quietly as I follow Liz's lead and hang back to let others move in front of us in line. "What for? Coal isn't used in the US anymore." It was one of the facts touted by science teachers every Earth Day.

"How can you still believe that *anything* you learned is true? If you're that naive, maybe I don't want you to owe me," she says as we step somewhere into the middle of the line. She waits until we pass an Instructor holding a metal rod raised—ready to strike—then explains, "The mine isn't operational. It's just used to store stuff. At least that's what it looked like the one time I was there. I don't plan on going back."

They sky is still dark when they march us out into the humid air. The partial moon still glows white against the black night. The dim gold-and-pink shimmer only at the edge of the horizon, hinting that sunlight is on the way as we trudge single file down a dirt road that runs beside a bunch of buildings. Instructors travel on the road beside us in small, roofless golf carts. A few others wield their black metal rods and riding crops from electronic Segways—the kind that groups use when they are taking the Michigan Avenue tour of Chicago. Several groups at the front are directed by Instructors to head for a series of structures. The rest of us are told to keep moving.

As we walk, Liz quietly identifies the buildings some of the other subjects are heading toward. Some, like red-and-white wood chicken and cow barns, I could have figured out on my own. I try to remember the others as she mentions them, in case they are important.

The white buildings behind the dorms and the arena are the kitchens.

Storage is in the wood and stone buildings just beyond those.

And the small blue windowless building with the green roof, far in the distance, away from all the others, houses both the infirmary and the morgue.

"No one that's gone to the infirmary has come back during my time here, so don't do anything stupid."

Good safety tip, I think as the sky grows brighter and we keep walking. The cool damp of the early morning disappears as the sun rises higher. Sweat drips down my back. After what seems like forever, teams of Instructors break us up into groups—six of us for every two Instructors.

Liz and I stick together in a group with a much older woman and three men. The men all are at least twenty years older than me and all need to shave. The tallest of them stares at the Instructors with a small smile as they give us instructions for pulling off the top of the vibrant green corn stalks.

"It's too early for tasseling," the tallest man says.

The male Instructor turns his head. "Did you say something?"

"My grandfather was a farmer. It's too early for . . ."

A metal rod cracks against the back of the man's knees, sending him to the wet ground where the female Instructor whips the rod down on his back. I was watching the male Instructor, so I never saw her move.

The man on the ground pushes up and slowly climbs to his feet, still wearing the same small smile he had before he went down.

"Your concern for the country's food supply is to be encouraged. Talking out of turn is not," the male Instructor says before the female can strike again. "Planting started earlier in this section of the farm. Tasseling the other fields will begin in a week or two, so this is a skill you will need to learn well."

Once they run us through the process twice, we are led into the muddy row in between cornstalks and told to start.

Grab the stalk with one hand. Then get a firm grip of the top of the plant with the other. Bend the top section down. Pull the top off without damaging the rest of the stalk. Then move on to the next.

Grab.

Bend.

Pull.

Grab.

Bend.

Pull.

The Instructors watch, rods in hand, as we repeat the process over and over. The sun grows brighter and hotter. My shoes sink into the thick, sticky mud. The backs of the sneakers rub against the my heels and my shoes almost come off when I yank them free in order to move from one stalk to the next.

I have no idea how long it takes to finish the first row. Sweat trickles down my forehead like a faucet with the handle not quite tightened. In between stalks I wipe my forehead against my sleeves. Minutes later, I need to do it again.

On the way to the next row, I spot several men in other groups who have taken off their shirts and women who have removed their pants and wrapped the fabric around their heads like hats to combat the heat. Remembering that I have a support tank on, I start to pull my own shirt off, only to hear a loud whistle from down the row. I look over at Liz who shakes her head. "Don't," she mouths.

Her sweat-coated clothing clings to her, but as hot as she must be, Liz hasn't so much as rolled up a hem. Neither has the woman working farther down the row. Since they have been here longer, I keep my shirt on and get back to work.

My mouth is dry.

Grab.

Bend.

Pull.

A dull ache throbs at the base of my skull.

Each stalk takes me a bit longer to get ahold of the plant with my sweaty, sore hands. Each step takes an extra few seconds to travel and when suddenly there is a breeze, I stop altogether and lift my face to the stingy swirl of air. The leaves rustle and under it all I hear voices chanting.

I step into the stalks, close my eyes, and try to make out what they are saying. The sounds of the corn drown out most of it. But every few seconds I catch a word or two.

"... faithful ... greatness ... accomplishments ... elected leaders ... above my own."

"Again!" a faint voice calls, and the chanting starts over with the words "I swear."

The oath. The Instructors in the rows next to ours are having people repeat the oath while they work. I wish the GPS recorder could capture audio. If so—

"No stopping!" demands a male voice.

I jump back into the row and see the male Instructor stepping out from the small yellow canopy tent at the end of the line. The tent is one of many that have been erected at the ends of the rows since the sun reached the peak of the sky. We work in the direct sun. The Instructors get refreshments in the shade. As the Instructor comes back down the row, he flicks his metal rod to extend it and I quickly reach for the next stalk.

The minutes seep together in a haze of sweat and heat and fatigue. The breezes that I relished soon feel like the enemy—taunting with the hope of relief before quickly taking it away.

We are herded to the next row and I understand why Liz warned me against removing my clothing. The back of one of the men in our group glows an angry shade of red as we spread out to resume our task.

With each stalk, my mouth grows drier. To distract myself, I contemplate escape plans in case Atlas can't get inside the farm and is waiting beyond the fence. My being relocated from Chicago before being rescued was never part of the plan, but I know that won't stop Atlas from finding me. After we agreed that I would allow the Marshals to capture me, Atlas took me to North Avenue Beach. Moonlight danced on the gently lapping waves as we walked across the sand. When we reached the water's edge, Atlas said, "My dad used to bring me here a lot when I was a little kid. We spent so much time underground that he wanted me to have a special place that on difficult days would remind me why this country is worth fighting for."

"It's beautiful," I told him.

His strong fingers found mine. "I wanted to bring you here—to see you in this place," he said, leaning close. "You need to know that to me you're part of what I'm fighting for. No matter what happens, I won't let them have you."

I picture the way Atlas looked in the moonlight. The warmth in his eyes. I can almost hear the sound of the water.

Stupid! Thinking about the lake reminds me of my thirst. The Instructors have water. I've seen subjects come by to exchange the Instructors' empty canteens for new. If the Instructors wanted to give us water, they could.

Since no water appears to be coming anytime soon, I paint a picture of Lake Michigan in my mind and try to imagine myself there as I work. The water is dozens of shades of layered blue as the sun reflects off the surface. The people at the water's edge, standing in the low, white-tipped waves as they roll onto the shore. The ripples along the top from the wind that skims along the surface. Cool. Wet. Refreshing.

A strangled whimper pulls me back from my useless imagination. I turn and see the older woman in our group stagger forward, sway, and then crumple to the ground.

"Help!" I whisper, my throat too dry to shout as I hurry down the row to the woman who is lying still as stone.

She's breathing, I think as I kneel next to her on the cool, moist ground. I can see the rise and fall of her chest as I roll her gently onto her back. Under the streaks of dirt and sweat her face is flushed; her lips dry and cracked.

"Get back!"

I scramble to my feet and retreat several steps as the male Instructor hops on his Segway and rides down the row toward the unconscious woman.

"Do you need help?" our female Instructor calls from the tent. "I can page Operations that we have an unresponsive."

"No need." He comes to a stop, uncaps his canteen, and pours a stream of water onto the fallen woman's face.

What a waste of water.

Horror and humiliation wash over me. The Instructor dumps another stream of water onto the woman and she starts to sputter. Her eyes flutter. She slowly licks the water off her lips. Pouring water on her face instead of putting the canteen to her lips and encouraging her to drink was cruel. Instead of recognizing that immediately, I saw the trickle of liquid and wished I could have it.

The woman struggles to sit. When she finally manages to stay upright, the male Instructor looks back to where the other one is still watching and laughs. "She's fine. See?" He drops the canteen to the ground. The cap pops off when it lands with a thud beside the woman. Water sloshes onto the still-damp ground and I have to fight the urge to dart forward and snatch it as the woman on the ground picks up the canteen and places the opening to her lips.

"We might as well get them all water since they've stopped, anyway," he yells. "They'll reach the quota faster if they aren't falling down on the job."

When the female Instructor nods I want to shout with relief.

"You have five minutes to walk to that tent, get water from the cooler, and return to work. I'd suggest you don't waste it." He glances over his shoulder, then slides his attention to me. "You can help her up," he says quietly. "But she needs to walk to the tent on her own. And she still has to get herself back to the dining hall. Do you understand?"

No. Not really, but I pretend I do and nod. Satisfied, the male Instructor steps off his Segway, takes the canteen and shouts for the others to hurry. Once he's gone, I squat beside the woman.

Liz and the sunburned man walk by us and head toward the canopy where water waits.

"Thank you," the woman whispers with a smile when I help her ease to her knees.

The fallen woman's gratitude makes me cringe because I'm aware of every heartbeat—every second that it takes for her to clutch my arm and teeter to her feet. I want to be a nice person. She has every reason to move slowly and it isn't taking all that long. Not really. But if she doesn't let go of my arm in another ten seconds, I am not sure I will be able to keep myself from yanking away so I don't miss out on getting a drink, even if it means sending her back to the ground.

Just because I want to be nice doesn't mean that I am.

But she doesn't have to know that, because she lets go of my arm and gives me several shaky nods. "Go get water. You need it."

Ugh. Well, I can't just leave her now without feeling like a complete jerk. "You need water, too."

"I'll catch my breath first." She takes a hesitant step forward. Sways. I put my hand on her shoulder to steady her. "You go before the time is up. You've done enough. Please."

I'm torn. Finally, I offer a compromise. "I'll go get water. Then, when we start tasseling again, I'll work faster so you don't have to do as much."

She pats my arm and glances down the row. The female Instructor is approaching—not on her Segway, but with long, determined strides as she reaches into a long dark gray bag that is hanging from her shoulder. I freeze when she pulls her hand out of the bag and is holding a black handgun.

"Go. Go now." The woman gives me a shove. When I turn, the

female Instructor has her gun raised. I start walking as she runs and brace myself for when the gun swings to me. It doesn't. Instead, she rushes past, shoves the older woman back to the ground, and keeps running.

"I don't see him!" the female Instructor screams as she scans the field. I glance back at the canopy where Liz and the sunburned man are huddled in the shade, holding their water while the other Instructor waves his arms and shouts.

An alarm whoops. People yell above the sirens. Through the stalks I see another Instructor zooming on his machine deeper into the field and I realize what's wrong. The fifth member of our work group—the man who told the Instructors it was too early to take the tassels from the corn—has disappeared. When the older woman fell to the ground, the man must have spotted his opening. With the Instructors' attention on us he took the opportunity to escape.

At least a dozen heads bob over the shoulder-high corn as the Instructors race down the rows. How long a head start does he have? If he can get away, then maybe . . .

The crack of a gunshot echoes over the sirens. Another.

The alarm stops.

The cornstalks whisper in the breeze.

"I got him," calls a voice in the distance, and I expel the hope I was harboring with my breath.

I get water from the cooler under the canopy and slowly drink the entire bottle. Five minutes is long over, but our male Instructor doesn't stop me when I reach for a second bottle and drain it. When I'm done, I don't wait for his orders—I walk back to the spot where I was standing when the woman collapsed and, without being instructed, I return to work.

Six Instructors carry the man's body through the corn. He must have found a spot he thought he could hide in, because he hadn't gotten very far. Either that or he wasn't very fast.

I'm true to my word and pull tassels faster than before so our Instructors won't notice the older woman's pace has slowed until it is almost nonexistent. I work while trying not to think about the man who attempted to escape. But as much as I try, I can't keep the echo of the gunshots from replaying over and over in my head.

I don't know what time it is when a horn sounds and the Instructors shout that we are done for the day. The older woman is still upright when we begin the walk back to the dorms. She moves slowly, but she is moving. She's stronger than she looks.

"He shouldn't have tried to escape," I hear someone whisper as we make our way along the dirt path beside the fields toward the buildings in the distance.

A sunburned stoop-shouldered man in front of me adds, "They warned him. They warned all of us."

As if that made what happened okay?

"No one knows his name," I say, looking down at my hands that are red and raw and covered with at least a dozen small, thin cuts lined with dried blood.

"That would make him real," Liz answers quietly, before picking up her pace—as if she can move faster than the memory.

The trek back to the dining hall seems twice as long as it did this morning. No one is moving quickly. Several subjects stumble as they walk. Two collapse on the dirt and don't make an attempt to get back to their feet. We are ordered to step around them. I'm glad to see the woman from my group makes it to the dorms. When we arrive our barcodes are scanned. We are given a change of clothing and thirty minutes to shower before we are to go to dinner. Thirty minutes exactly.

How do they expect us to tell the time when there aren't any clocks?

When it is my turn to shower, I don't care that the water is barely warm or that the soap is rough and stings my palms. I'm grateful for both.

Grateful.

I actually felt grateful. Just for a second, but still. How insane is that?

Once we start filing into the dining hall there is no more talk of the man who died. There is barely talk at all as the screens flicker and the music blares. I don't know what is most horrific, I think, walking single file to the table we are directed to—a man being murdered for wanting to leave this place, the way others blamed him for his own death, or the way they are quick to act as if it never happened.

They should all know better.

Wallace sits at another table. He subtly raises his hand when he sees me. Even though I still don't know what I think of him, I do the same. Then I try to mimic the others by looking up at the screens while I wait for food. Like the Instructors want me to do.

"How long does it take?" I ask Liz.

"What?"

"To act as if any of this is normal?"

"It's never normal. We just know it's the way things are here." Liz glances around and leans close. "I overheard the Instructors on duty. This isn't going to be the normal for much longer. Recruiters are coming."

"Recruiters?" I repeat.

Heads swivel toward us.

"Do you know how to be quiet?" Liz hisses. She shakes her head and waits for the others to direct their attention back to the screens or to whatever conversations they were having. Then she says, "Recruiters are in charge of choosing who works at which areas in the farm. They move us from here to our permanent level of Great American Farming in order to make room for the next group of subjects to arrive."

"We're going to be moved?" I whisper as we rise for Instructor Burnett.

She nods.

"How long?" I ask as the oath appears on the screen.

"What?" Liz asks, with her eyes directed forward.

"How long until the Recruiters arrive?"

"Tomorrow. The day after. Soon."

An Instructor slams a rod on our table. I jerk my eyes to Instructor Burnett and pretend to pay attention as my mind races.

Being moved means I'll end up deeper into the farm—farther away from the boundaries. Farther from where Atlas is likely to be waiting. With only two days of battery life left before the tracker stops signaling. Maybe if I'm lucky, Rose's father will try to intercede, but if he couldn't save his son, I don't think he will be able to save me. The only thing I am certain of is that I can't let the Recruiters move me deeper into the farm. I have to be out of here by the time the Recruiters come if my mission is going to have any chance of success.

We finish our less-than-satisfying dinner and trudge back to the dorms. I shift under the covers, reposition the GPS recorder in my right sock, and retie my shoe. Then I pretend to sleep in my bunk while I wait for the lights to go out. When it does, the singing starts. Then the weeping. Then finally, silence.

In the quiet, I ease myself over the edge of the bed, lower myself onto the floor, and weave through the bunks to the bathroom.

There are no mirrors here. Maybe they don't want us looking at ourselves. If we did we might remember our humanity. We might wonder how the country we love could put us in a place like this. Or maybe they don't want to risk someone breaking the glass and using it as a weapon or a tool.

The bathroom stall doors, however, are dented silver metal, which offers a reflection of sorts. So I sit on the last toilet and lift my hair to examine the ear cuff, because there has to be a way to remove it without triggering its poison.

The barcode still turns my stomach. I embrace the anger as I run my fingers along the device to see if I can figure out how to get it off. The rectangular barcode is embedded to a kind of disc. That disc sits atop the plastic piece, which is wrapped around my ear. There is another disc on the other side. I can only assume the front and back discs are held together by some kind of snap or pin, but no matter what I try, I can't get my fingernails under the seam to pull them apart.

Did the man trying to escape today figure out a way to remove the device or did he just plan on tearing it off his ear and hoping for the best? I hear the sound of someone else shuffling into the bathroom. The faucet runs as I consider my dilemma. The device doesn't have an easy way for me to remove it, but it also doesn't appear high-tech. For it to have a trigger that dispenses a poison when it passes through some kind of electronic fence like Instructor Burnett described, wouldn't it have to be more . . . sophisticated?

Trust, but verify.

The words I first read weeks ago—painted by my mother's hand in a secret room for the Stewards—pop into my head. Then, the idea of verifying anything I was told about my country was completely foreign. Now I should know better than to just believe what I was told. If the government needs this farm to succeed in order for the country to thrive, would they really outfit everyone with a device that could accidentally kill workers if it malfunctioned?

Maybe.

Or maybe the reason so many Instructors hunted down the man who disappeared into the cornfield is because they had to. Because if he made it to the boundary he could escape—and live.

Do I want to risk my life on the chance that they lied about the capabilities of the devices?

I don't have an answer to that question when I look at the reflection of the device one last time. Shaking my head, I push open the door, step out of the stall, and nod at the woman who is still at the faucet washing her hands. I look down at my own hands as I head back into the dorm.

I'm almost to my bunk when a small group of women step out of the hallway that leads to the outdoor courtyard. I register Dana's face in the green glow of the Exit sign and footsteps rushing toward me a second before a hand slaps over my mouth and I am grabbed from behind.

FOURTEEN

"Let me go!" I scream against the hand that is clamped over my mouth, but no one listens. Fingers dig into my arms. I thrash from side to side and kick as hard as I can. My foot connects with flesh. Someone yelps and I'm jerked off my feet and dragged back into the pitch-black hall.

"What's going on?"

"What are you doing to her?"

"Stay out of this!"

"Let go of me!" I scream, when the hand holding my mouth slips. I bite down on the fingers that fight to silence me and writhe against the arms that pin mine.

The attack for no reason—the absence of light—the lack of help coming from the women in their beds who were awakened from the sounds of my struggles, add to the fear and my desperate fight to get away.

"Shut up!" Something cold and hard presses against my throat. "Shut the hell up right now."

I freeze and blink against the blinding darkness, wishing I could at least see my attackers' faces. I can't see the weapon they are holding on me, either, but I imagine the worst and fight the urge to scream for help again. There are women down the hall in their beds who know this is happening. They haven't come to my aid.

Liz. She has to know I am being held—terrified. More screams won't move her or the others. They've made their choice. I'm on my own.

Nails dig into my ankles. The person holding my arms shifts grips and I remember something Atlas told me once when we were training. I allow my body to go completely limp. Suddenly, I'm dead weight.

"Crap!"

The person holding my arms loses her hold and drops me. My upper back cracks against the concrete floor. Pain sings through my shoulders as I roll onto my side and yank my legs from my attacker's grip.

I'm free and now I'm glad for dark. I get to my feet, feel for the wall as they ask each other if anyone has found me, and with my fingers grazing the concrete as a guide—I run.

"She's running toward the courtyard. Don't let her get away."

As if there is any chance that could happen.

I burst out of the pitch-black hallway into the courtyard that's lit by the partial moon and impossibly bright stars. Under any other circumstances, I would stop everything and study the white crystal-like lights dotting the dusty black sky, but the footsteps pounding the concrete behind me keep me moving.

Hay crunches beneath my feet. No one is stationed in the balconies. No Instructors are watching. Nobody is here to stop whoever is running behind me.

The fire escape–style ladders I spot at the edge of the balconies are too high for me to jump up and reach them. The ground under the hay is concrete. The walls are stone. The fence is steel.

I'm trapped.

A woman appears at the entrance. Then two others.

"Over there!" A broad-shouldered woman points as another woman, one I recognize, appears beside her. Dana.

The four start toward me. Four of them. One of me.

I stumble back against the fence, glancing from side to side desperate to find any method of escape. One woman with a round face and thin, shoulder-length dark hair limps. She is hanging back a bit, but the other three advance with determined, terrifyingly deliberate steps.

"Dana," I say, doing my best to keep my voice calm and even—as if soothing a growling animal. "Why are you doing this?"

"We know what you are."

"What does that mean?" My back bumps up against the metal slats.

"What did you tell him?" Dana demands, moving toward me, hands balled into fists raised in front of her—poised to fight.

"Tell who? I honestly don't have a clue what you are talking about."

The broad-shouldered woman runs at me and I dart to the side, only to have my path blocked by a dark-skinned woman with wide-rimmed glasses. With the fence behind me and the four closing in on all sides, I'm in serious trouble.

"You were talking to him," snaps the broad-shouldered woman. "We saw you. Did you rat out Dana? Are they looking for the rest of us?"

"The rest of . . ." I look down the fence line to where the woman with glasses is creeping closer. Why do they think I would turn them in? For what? Unless . . . unless they are Stewards, too. "You've got this wrong. Wallace isn't—"

Dana lunges. I duck, but not before her fist grazes my shoulder. I spin and shove her back into the broad-shouldered lady. I don't want to hurt her. I don't want to hurt any of them. We're on the same side! I just have to figure out how to convince them of that.

The tall, broad-shouldered woman catches Dana. While Dana regains her balance, I back up against the fence again and say, "I didn't tell Wallace anything. I listened to his story. He told me how he ended up here—a prisoner, like us. He started asking questions his bosses didn't want him to ask. He's proof people *can* change their minds if we tell them what's happening."

"You expect us to believe that?" Dana's quiet, controlled voice is more terrifying than any scream. "We know there are people promising better treatment to snitches who give them information to use against our friends back home."

"Maybe the Instructors have promised people things," I say. It made sense. And maybe they are using other "subjects" to pass along the offers. Prisoners would trust others far more rapidly if they appeared to be in the same situation as themselves. "But I haven't been promised anything."

"If she talked, they would have already come for you," the woman with the glasses says. "We don't have much time. The one I bribed only promised to keep the other Instructors out of here until bed check."

There is movement in the shadows by the women's entrance to the courtyard. People have come down the hallway from the dorms and are hovering at the edge of the arena—listening. Watching. Keeping me from saying all the things that might convince Dana and her friends that I'm not a threat. Any mention of the Stewards or Atticus or the Lyceum will only make things worse—not just for us but for those back in Chicago who have thus far avoided the Marshals. All I can do is stare Dana dead in the eyes and hope she can hear and see the truth when I insist, "I'm not what you think. We are on the same side."

Dana takes a step forward and I place my hands on the slats behind me. "I wish that were true," she says. "But we can't take the chance. Make it fast."

The woman with glasses moves first. I lean into the metal slats like I'm cowering. Then I lift my leg and kick the woman square in the stomach. When she doubles over, I dart around her to give myself some space to operate. Only I'm not fast enough. Glasses recovers quicker than I thought she would. She sticks her foot out, hooks it around mine, and sends me stumbling to the ground.

I glance behind me. The others are advancing and the woman I kicked is acting as if she was never hit.

"Don't ever question whether you are going to hurt someone," Atlas told me during our first fighting lesson, when I kept pulling every punch because I hated the idea of hitting him. "The minute you worry about whether you should hurt them is the minute you lose the fight."

Dana is part of the Stewards. The other women seem to be as well. But right now we aren't on the same side. I have to survive tonight.

The glasses woman rushes at me. I roll away so the foot the woman stomps down just misses me as I scramble to my feet. Instead of running away, I bolt in her direction and pitch a fistful of hay at her face. She instinctively raises her hands so she doesn't notice my kick until my foot connects with her knee with a sickening crunch. She screams and crumples to the ground. The limping woman moves to help her while Dana and the broad-shouldered woman charge.

Two against one. Both are taller than I am. Dana doesn't appear all that strong, but she also didn't look like someone who would ambush a sixteen-year-old girl on her way to bed, so first impressions aren't exactly useful. Atlas said the best way to win a one-on-one fight was to inflict the best damage, not necessarily the most. His advice when fighting more than one person was less complicated. It was more along the lines of—run.

I bolt along the fence toward the other side of the courtyard, then glance at the women behind me. The broad-shouldered one with her long legs is only a few feet away. Dana isn't all that much farther. And there are at least a dozen more women at the back of the courtyard now—watching.

My foot slips on hay. I grab the fence to prevent myself from going down. It is a second or two before I recover, but that's all it takes. An arm is suddenly around my throat pulling tight and I can't breathe.

My heart strains in my chest.

I pull desperately at her hands, but the squeezing doesn't stop.

I'm not going to die!

I dig my fingers deep into the woman's arm and yank down. Her arm moves an inch. Maybe two. Enough for me to gasp for air and regroup. I rise up onto my tiptoes. When she tightens her grip to choke me again, I stomp down on her foot, twist out of her grip, and ram right into a wall.

Not a wall. A fist that cracks hard against my cheek.

Light flashes behind my eyes. I stumble and lift my arms to block the next punch, which throws Dana off-balance. Before she can recover, I smash the heel of my hand up into her face. There's a satisfying crunch as she yelps and covers her nose with her hands. I step back and ram into another wall that isn't a wall. This one clamps fingers around my wrists.

Oh God. I scream as she twists my arms and pins them behind my back. I kick, but hit nothing. I buck and twist and fight, but I can't get free.

A fist rams into my stomach and my legs buckle. I gasp for air and even though I see the next punch coming, there is nothing I can do to stop it from landing. I double over, lungs burning, but am yanked back upright so when the next punches are thrown, they strike me in the chest—the face—my arms.

My legs are kicked out from under me. I crash to the ground, wrench my arms free, and tuck tight into a ball, using my arms to protect my face and body from the kicks and slaps and tearing of my hair that I want to stop. I want it all to stop.

There are whimpers. Mine. Theirs? Voices shouting, "Stop!" Or maybe "Help!" I can't tell.

Then suddenly the blows just stop. I huddle on the ground, everything throbbing, waiting for the attack to start again. Blood pounds loud in my ears, so it takes a second for me to hear that the women are talking.

"The Instructors will be coming. You three—get cleaned up so they can't tell you were here." Dana's voice carries over the roaring in my ears. "I'll finish the rest."

I groan and lift my head as Dana squats beside me. Streaks of blood run down her face. Her nose looks like it might be broken. Her eyes meet mine and something sharp and cold presses into the side of my neck. I roll to the left, but not quick enough and I cry out from the fresh slice of pain.

"Get away from her!"

Liz.

Her voice cuts through the din of shouts both male and female. Some of the men must have heard the noise and came out to watch the show.

I wait for Dana to cut me again. Instead, there's a scuffle somewhere behind me. I push up from the hay, blink, trying to clear the haze of pain, and see several women holding a now-struggling Dana.

One of my rescuers is the older woman from today . . . the one who collapsed in the field.

My other attackers are gone. They must have joined the women who came out to look at the fight or have gone back inside to avoid being caught.

It's over.

I sag with relief. Everything hurts. My face. Stomach. Legs. Chest. The pain explodes as the fear of immediate danger fades. But I'm still alive and—

"The Instructors are coming!"

"Let me go!" Dana thrashes side to side trying to get free, but the women hold fast. "You don't understand!" she screams.

"Yes, we do." Liz holds up a small piece of scrap metal with a thin, bloody-looking edge at the top. It's the makeshift weapon Dana used to cut me. Had she gotten her hands on a real knife, I would be dead. Dana would have killed me—not to save herself, although she would have done that, too, but to protect the Stewards she thought

I would betray. After all, what was one life compared to protecting the work that will change the future for everyone?

"Liz." I press my hand to the side of my neck that is slick with blood and struggle to sit. "Let her go."

"Move!" someone in the distance shouts.

"Back to bed!"

"The Instructors! They're in the dorms!" a voice calls from nearby.

Which means it's only a matter of minutes before the Instructors get to us here.

"Let them go. Please."

"You can't mean it." Liz drops beside me. "They could come after any of us—they could come after me next."

"You have to let them go." I wish there was time to explain. Dana wants me dead, but we are still on the same side.

"But—"

"It's important." Everything is on fire. The world around me swims.

Through the haze, I see Liz nod and the others release their grip. Dana stumbles, falls, then gets back up before running out of my view.

"Clear a path!"

The sounds of Instructors are getting closer.

"They're going to make you tell them who did this," Liz says with a gentle hand on my shoulder.

"Too dark." The words are thick in my mouth. "No one could see. Can you tell everyone that?"

"Why save them?"

"They'll owe me a favor," I say.

A reluctant smile tugs at her lips. "This better be worth it. If they think I'm lying, I'll end up in the infirmary with you—or worse."

"Trust me." I brush her arm. "It is."

"Don't die or I'll be seriously pissed." She slides the sharpened piece of metal into the folds of her shirt, springs to her feet. "I'll see you at recruiting."

Not if I can help it.

She bolts toward the women clogging the exit—which have intentionally or not slowed the appearance of the Instructors. Knowing I won't have much more time, I swipe at the blood trickling from the gash on my neck and smear the wet, sticky warmth across my face and the front of my shirt—to make it look like I am hurt worse. I'm beaten and sore and bleeding. In any sane world, that would be enough to be sent for medical attention. This place is anything but sane. From the way Liz talked about the infirmary earlier, only people with the worst injuries are sent there, and no one who goes ever comes back. While the idea of visiting a place that doubles as a morgue is a risk, it's one that will get me out of this building and a potential step closer to escape. So, I smear more blood on my forehead and on the backs of my hands as the lights from the sides of the arena start to shine.

I collapse onto the hay with my back to the entrance and go still.

"Over there!"

"Get inside!"

"I said move!"

There are shouts and sounds of scuffling. I keep my eyes closed as heavy footsteps crunching the hay approach.

"There's a lot of blood, but she's alive."

"Good. Help me get a cart to take her to the infirmary," a nasal voice snaps. "If the girl's going to die I'd rather she do it there. At least then we won't have to deal with getting her to the pit."

The footsteps crunch away. I allow myself to open my eyes for a second. That's when I see him.

The familiar lanky shape, curly hair, and intense stare that I woke up to in the Unity Center. He's on the far side of the area standing next to the entrance to the men's dorms. He takes a step away from the wall and cocks his head to the side, but the sound of crunching footsteps has me closing my eyes so I can't tell whether he saw that I was awake or not.

Someone hauls me up. I groan when they dump me in the back of what I think is a golf cart and strap me down. It's not until the cart jerks forward that I'm brave enough to look, just in time to see Wallace nod to me and smile.

The golf cart is a new kind of hell.

The driver hits every rock and bump. Each is like another blow from Dana's fist. Tears sting and I grit my teeth and focus on the positive sight of the brightly lit dorm building shrinking in the distance. Liz promised to not reveal the identity of my attackers. I don't know if she is owed that many favors, but I hope for Dana's sake that she is. Otherwise, there is a chance she and her friends are being carted away right now. If so, I find myself hoping she has another sharp metal object she can turn into a deadman's switch as well as the courage to use it.

I should feel bad that Dana might have to make that kind of choice—between her own life and the lives of all the Stewards she was trying to protect.

I don't.

Between the sounds of the motor and the crunch of gravel, it's hard to make out what the Instructors are saying. From the pieces I do hear, they were aware of the attack planned on me tonight and did nothing to stop it. Now someone will smooth things over with Instructor Burnett like it has been done before and they'll get the extra leave they were promised.

"I'm going to the beach," one Instructor announces.

"You should talk to my friend. They know a guy who does a black market run with his boat from the coast of Texas to a resort in Mexico. I went last year. The beaches were amazing and the food was beyond belief."

"That has to be expensive. I can barely afford a few days in Florida."

"I bet Recruiters will pay for information about this one. You know Davis will pay double if we give him a heads-up first."

"Davis makes my skin crawl."

"Yeah, but he comes through with the cash. The beaches aren't the only thing amazing in Mexico."

I miss what comes next as the cart hits a bump and I let out a yelp.

"Well, it sounds like she's alive. Let's hope she doesn't end up in the pit because now I really want to spend time on that beach."

The pit?

The Instructors don't explain the comment as the cart turns, slows, and comes to a stop.

"We know you're awake," one says, undoing the straps holding me to the cart.

Do I admit that I'm conscious or keep my eyes closed? Both options suck, but the possibility of the unknown pit prompts me to slowly open my eyes.

An Instructor stares down at me, hands on her narrow hips. The one standing just behind her is holding a gun.

"Can you walk?" the closer of the two asks. She has curly blond hair, wide, angelic eyes, and a soothing voice that just minutes ago was hoping I'd live so she could trade me for an illegal vacation.

"I think so," I whisper.

"Then let's go."

I swallow a sob as the blond Instructor hauls me to my feet.

The world tilts. My knees tremble. My legs are sore and weak, but somehow they hold. I grip the edge of the white golf cart and am relieved when I successfully take a step. It hurts, but I can do it.

My whole world becomes about putting one foot in front of the other and taking small, shallow breaths that don't set my lungs afire. With each step I take stock of my injuries.

My left knee is swollen. My cheek and chest weep, but the ache in my hip seems less painful now that I am moving. More impor-tant, the cut at the base of my neck seems to have stopped bleeding and nothing feels broken. It could be—and probably should be—so much worse, I think as I let go of my hold on the golf cart and limp toward the white front door that is illuminated by overhead flood-lights. I don't know if I could run—especially on gravel or uneven terrain—but if I saw an opening to escape now, I wouldn't hesitate to make the attempt. Maybe my attackers weren't as committed to hurting me as they wanted to believe they were. Either that or tight-ening up my muscles when I was on the ground really did keep those hits to my stomach from doing more damage. Tomorrow I might feel different, but for now I'm grateful.

"Can't she move any faster? I'd like to get some sleep tonight."

If the woman didn't have a gun, I'd give in to the impulse to flip her the bird. Instead, I slow my steps and moan dramatically. If they want faster, they can carry me.

Apparently, they don't need to get to bed quite that bad. The blonde opens the door and taps her foot as she waits for me. I get one good look at the outside of the windowless building—making note of the rack of wooden-handled shovels near the end of the building and the shadow of a hill in the distance beyond—before grabbing hold of the threshold and pulling myself inside.

They scan my ear cuff in a narrow reception area, then all but push me into a room with a line of empty, narrow gray cots and an older man in baggy mint-green scrubs who is waiting with a syringe in hand.

I hate that I can't fight off the syringe they slide into my arm and that I'm glad when they help me onto a bed. Their parting instructions are to get some sleep.

I don't want sleep. What I want is to find a way out of the farm. The window of opportunity will stay open for only so long before the Marshals go after Mrs. Webster and Rose, shut down *Gloss*, and capture Stef and Ari and the kids. I can't let any of them end up here—or worse.

But as much as I want to fight, whatever was in the syringe makes my limbs heavy. The pain slides away and I feel almost as if I'm floating when a man in scrubs arrives. He pokes and prods me and assures the Instructors they can report to Davis that I'm going to live.

"She needs stitches and might have a cracked rib. Check back tomorrow afternoon after I've had more time with her."

Feet shuffle. I hear a door open then close. The man in the scrubs hums to himself as he moves around the room.

"You sent for me?" A low voice reaches through the haze of sleep. I fight to pry open my eyes and blink to clear the film of fatigue and drugs.

"False alarm," the man in scrubs answers. He's standing with his back to me. "But I think you should sleep here tonight, just in case she takes a turn. No point in either of us going all the way to the barracks if there's a chance we'll have to come right back."

The other man steps out of view as the one in scrubs pulls keys out of his pocket and heads for the door. "I'm going to see if they have coffee brewing over at the barn. Use the screen to send me a message if there's a problem. She's all yours until I get back. Have fun."

Scrubs Man lets out a low laugh. He closes the door behind him. I hear the rattle of keys and I'm locked in this room at the mercy of whoever this person is.

Deliberate footsteps grow louder as they approach.

Fatigue and whatever drugs I was given refuse to be denied. Through the fog, dark blue pants streaked with dirt appear at my bedside. A dark blue shirt with silver buttons comes into view as the man sits on the edge of my bed.

A hand lifts the hem of my shirt. Fingers brush my arm.

"No," I whisper.

A face swims in front of mine. I see the smile. A glint in the eyes. Feel cool air on my stomach, and in my mind I scream as everything goes black.

FIFTEEN

"No!" The word is barely a whisper as I claw myself out of the sticky, thick void and I blink away nightmares of my mother's and Isaac's bloody, broken bodies.

My head throbs. Bright white lights beat down from above. I grit my teeth and struggle to push to my elbows. Swallowing does nothing to chase the bitter horror of the dreams or the barren dryness from my mouth.

The windowless room is empty save for the two lines of cots—none of them dressed with any kind of bedding. The walls are painted a jaunty lemon color that someone must have believed would come across as cheerful, but instead is strangely ominous.

I can't help wondering if Isaac died looking at these walls.

He died and I'm alive.

I squeeze my eyes tight against the unfairness of it—of everything—of the soreness that sings in my muscles with every movement, of the fear that I might never get out of this place.

"Stop," I scold as I shove to a seated position. Sitting here feeling sorry for myself only wastes time. And I doubt that is a commodity that I can afford to waste.

I take a deep, painful breath, swipe useless tears from my face, and notice that my hands are clean. So are the shirt and pants I'm now wearing.

I look down at my feet and let out a relieved burst of air. My shoes are the same old sneakers, my socks are stained with blood and dirt, and I can feel the GPS recorder pressing against the skin beneath both.

Slowly, I ease my stiff legs over the bed and lift my shirt to examine the bandage that someone wrapped around my chest. The fabric looks impossibly white next to the splotches of purple, sickly green, and yellow bruises that have spread over my stomach.

And that's when I remember.

The hands on my shirt. Fingers on my neck and face. Words whispered in a low voice too far away in the drugged darkness for me to understand.

Someone touched me. Undressed me. Washed me and . . . what else?

What else did the man do to me when I was drugged? What else happened to me?

I close my eyes only to snap them open again because when they are closed I can feel the path of the finger on my arm. Feel the cool water on my legs.

Hints of memories hover out of reach. Taunting. Terrifying.

Who touched me while I was unaware? Did I tell him no? I don't know.

I don't know.

What else don't I know?

Nothing happened, I tell myself. I want to believe that. I need to and yet . . .

A door slams. I hold my breath.

Heavy footsteps sound in the outer office. There is the distinctive jangle of keys.

They're coming.

That first thought makes my soul go cold with fear.

The next—*I won't let anyone touch me this time*—gets me moving.

Ignoring the aches, I shove to my feet and cross the white-and-gray-swirled tile. I stand next to a video screen that I can't pull off the wall. It's mounted in a heavy steel case beside the thick white door. There is nothing else that I can see that can be used as a weapon, but I don't intend to be a victim again.

A key slides into the lock. The handle turns.

I ball my hands into fists, and when the door swings open and a man in a uniform appears, I launch myself forward. I'm not as fast as I would like to be, but the man is holding a tray. He's unable to defend himself when I hit him from the side, pivot, and kick him square in the crotch.

The tray crashes to the ground. The man doubles over and wheezes for air as plastic cups and medical supplies roll across the floor. I skid on a patch of water. race toward him and shove him into the wall. When he lets out a satisfying "oof," I make a break for the door.

But not quick enough.

A hand grabs the back of my shirt. Desperate, I throw myself forward. The shift of my weight catches him off guard long enough for me to cock my fist, turn, and aim for his stomach.

"Damn it."

He twists to the side so my strike doesn't land as hard as I intended.

"Let go!" I stomp my heel down on his foot and grab at the other hand that has latched on to my arm. "Don't touch me."

"Meri! Stop!"

It takes several seconds for me to understand he's saying my real name. To place the voice. To stop fighting and turn. When I do, he takes off the hat pulled low on his forehead to give me a clear view of an impossibly familiar face.

"Isaac?"

There's a scar on his chin that wasn't there the last time I saw him. His eyes are rimmed with fatigue, and there is the horrible bar-code cuff embedded in his ear. But otherwise he's the same Isaac who I remember.

I shake my head. "You can't be here. You're dead."

"I'm not, and I'd like to keep it that way." He glances at the door. "If someone sees us like this they're going to ask questions neither of us want to answer. Can I let go or are you going to do something—you know—stupid?"

It's the edge in his voice that convinces me he's real—the same tone he always used on Rose and me when he thought we were acting immature or doing something that would embarrass him. Slowly, I lower my hands to my side.

My stomach lurches as he closes the door. The latch clicks into place, once again trapping me inside this room.

"Are you okay?" he asks, then shakes his head. "Sorry. Stupid question. We don't have time for stupid questions or for almost any questions at all. In under an hour the Instructors are due to take you to Recruiting. Which means we have to get you out of here, now. If Davis gets ahold of you . . ."

"Who is Davis? Why does he want me?"

"He's powerful." Isaac flips his hat onto the closest cot, then heads to another on the far side of the room. "Recruiters aren't just looking for people to work the farm. They're in charge of motivating the Instructors and administrators. Money works well. Competition and money combined work better."

"I don't understand."

"I don't know much about it. Just what I've overheard." He flips the cot onto its side and feels around the metal frame. "Stuff for Instructors to bet on, I think. I guess whatever you did last night got someone's attention." He turns. "The Meri I know wouldn't have survived a four-against-one fight."

"I'm not who I used to be." I shrug and wince at the flash of pain from my shoulder.

"I get that. Funny how learning your entire life is a lie can change a person."

Yeah, funny.

"Well, the Instructors who brought you here are interested in this new you." He turns back to the cot. "They get rewarded for finding good competition recruits. Even the Instructor who runs this place will get some kind of reward for getting you back on your feet and making you look presentable. Got it." He slides something free from the metal frame as I take a step back from the cots.

"Is he the one?" I ask.

"What?" Isaac fiddles with something else, then flips the cot back into its original position and turns. "Meri?" When I don't answer, he takes a slow step forward. "What's wrong with you?"

"Someone was left here with me. He . . ." I look down and twist the fabric of my clean shirt. How do I ask? "My clothes . . . He was told . . ."

Have fun.

I shake my head. "It's not important."

The answer won't change anything.

"Meri."

His fingers brush the top of my arm—just the barest of whispers—like the wings of a butterfly—but I jerk as if burned.

"Meri."

I force myself to look up into his eyes and cringe at the pity I find there.

"There wasn't some guy. It was me. I had to get you cleaned up—wrap your rib cage. You were a serious mess. I almost didn't realize who I was looking at. You're scanned in under a different name."

I take a breath. Two.

"You're the one that saw me? Without my clothes?" I look down at the shape of his hands. The size of them. The lack of calluses on the fingers that are currently holding a small, thin black box.

"Well, it's not like that was the first time," he jokes. "Remember when we all went camping and your tent collapsed?" He's trying to put me at ease. He's trying really hard.

"Rose still thinks you're the one that made it fall down," I say carefully.

"My sister isn't stupid." Then the joking disappears. "Do you know . . . is Rose okay? Is my mom? Do they know where I am? How I got here?"

"Your father told them you were taken by some criminal gang that targets government families. I told them the truth—about everything." His eyes go hard and flat at the mention of his father. I don't know what he has learned about the missing words and all the government has done in the name of "law and order" and "security," but Isaac clearly understands that his father helps the government do the terrible things they have done.

But according to Isaac there isn't time to talk about all those things. There isn't time for almost anything, but there has to be time for this. "I'm sorry." They're words I never believed I'd get the chance to say to him. "It was my fault the Marshals came for you. I took your badge and used it to get into the City Pride Department Archives. I'm the reason you're here. You should never have been pulled into this. It's my fault."

"You're right. It's your fault." Isaac stalks away. "If it wasn't for you, I would be home. I wouldn't have this crap in my ear or been treated like an animal."

I lift my chin and repeat, "I'm sorry."

"I don't care," he shoots back. "'Sorry' changes jack, but neither does you getting stuck here for the rest of your life. So you can either have a pity party, in which case I leave, or you suck it up and do what I tell you to in order to get out of here. I'm assuming you want to escape this place, right?" He glances down at my shoe, then back up at me.

He knows about the GPS recorder. He's the reason I still have it.

I have so many questions. Instead, I say, "Yeah. I want to get out of here. Do you know how we can do that?"

"We won't be leaving," he says bitterly. "You will. For this to work, no one here at the farm can suspect I'm involved."

"No." I shake my head. "No way. I'm not leaving you here." Not when I'm the reason he was sent here in the first place. How can I live with that?

"If I go with you now and they catch us, it will be bad for me, but worse for you. I was never supposed to be sent here in the first place. Someone screwed up by taking me to the *Unity Center*." Sarcasm drips from the words. "When the Marshals ran my address, they only looked at who lived there. It wasn't until after I was scanned and in a holding cell that they realized my father works for the mayor. By then it was too late for them to change their mind about holding me. I'd seen too much."

"Did you ever see a man our dads' age named Atticus?" I ask. "He would have been put into the cages a few days before you." If Isaac is alive, maybe Atticus made it, too. Maybe he is here somewhere.

Isaac frowns. "I don't remember that name. He wasn't in my transport and once I got to the farm there wasn't much time to meet people before I landed here. Is this Atticus the one who put you up to taking my identification?"

I shake my head. "No. My mother knew Atticus. I never met him. I was hoping—"

"I'll do my best to find him," Isaac offers.

Which makes me feel even worse. "I still don't understand why you think you can't leave with me."

"Because you're not important," he says matter-of-factly. "No offense."

"I—"

"Look, they know my father works for the mayor. The government can use me as an example of what can happen to anyone's families—even those working for the system—if they aren't careful. If you do deactivate the tag and escape, eventually they might give up looking for you, but they won't stop looking for me."

Guilt stabs deep. "I can't leave you. What will I tell Rose? Or your father? I saw him." My desperate words tumble on top of each other. "He's been trying to get you back. He was at the Unity Center demanding to know where they took you. Your dad saw me before they loaded me onto the transport. He could have revealed my real name and forced me to tell the Marshals about the people I'm working with. But he stayed quiet. He let me get on the truck because he wanted me to find you."

Isaac's eyes flash with anger, but his voice is cold and flat. "Tell my father if he wants to find me he can go to hell—because that's what this place is." He opens the black box. There is a thin silver scalpel resting inside. "I stashed it under that cot two days ago. Just in case . . ." He snaps the box closed and holds it out. "If you play this right, the Instructors will think they're looking for a scared, injured girl who has no idea where she is or how to get out. They'll underestimate you and you'll make them pay."

Slowly, I take the box. "I *will* get you out. People are going to know what's happening here and we're going to put a stop to it."

"I'm going to hold you to that. When I leave, go back to your cot and pretend to be asleep. Another aide will check on you soon. Once they leave, you're going to have to move fast."

I shift my weight and wince. Moving fast might be easier said than done. As best as Isaac can guess, the closest boundary is a four-lane road about twenty miles to the east. The chances of me making it there aren't great. But that's what I have to do.

"If you let them track your barcode they'll catch you long before you reach the boundary." He looks at the scalpel I'm holding, then back at me. "Promise me that you'll get rid of it at the first opportunity after you leave the infirmary."

Things are moving too fast. I can't think. He can't mean for me to use the knife on myse—

"Promise!"

"Okay," I say. "I'll try."

He shakes his head and glances at the door. "You can't just try, Meri. You owe me."

"I know, but Isaac, how could you know all this?"

His smile is grim. "I'm not the only one working here who doesn't belong."

He puts on the hat, picks the tray up off the ground, and hurries for the door. "Wait to remove the tag until you get out of the building. They'll send fewer officials to capture you if they believe they're tracking your barcode. You don't want your blood tipping them off."

My blood. Oh God.

Isaac opens the door and presses something into the locking mechanism. "When you get back to Chicago, tell my mom and sister . . ." His deep brown eyes meet mine.

He has long, thick lashes—just like Rose. I never noticed before—how they have the same eyes.

"Wait," I say, pulling off my shoe. I dig the GPS recorder out of my sock. Isaac doesn't look surprised when he sees me point the device at him and press the side button. "For your mom and Rose."

Isaac's eyes swim with tears, but none fall as he gives a small nod, then turns and heads out the door.

I'll pay him back, I think as the door closes. *I'll pay him all the way back.*

Isaac guessed I would have five minutes, maybe ten before the Instructor came to check on me. I take several of those minutes putting my shoe back on. Once the device is safely stashed beside my heel, I stretch out on the cot with Isaac's black box under my butt. Then with nothing else to do, I stare at the ceiling, taking shallow breaths as I wait.

My heart races at the rattle of keys. I close my eyes, will my muscles to relax, and let my mouth hang open just a little to make it appear as if I'm still unconscious. All the things I used to do to convince my mother I was asleep instead of sending late-night messages to Rose or sketching a new design.

The door closes. Footsteps shuffle. I shove the memory flashes of fingers on my arms—water dripping on my thigh—to the side and focus on my breathing. Slow. Controlled. But each breath I take feels shorter. Shallower. More painful than the last.

The footsteps stop.

Something kicks the cot, causing it to jiggle. I groan, but keep my eyes closed and relax my breathing again.

The footsteps move away. I wait for the door to open, but instead hear a series of beeps and a short buzzing.

"Yes?" a tinny female voice says.

"She's still unconscious."

"How long?"

"An hour? The drugs should be out of her system by then. If she doesn't get up on her own, the technician can give her something to wake up."

"Instructors will be here in thirty minutes. I trust she'll be awake."

There's a beep. More footsteps. Finally, the door opens and closes. I wait for the man to notice there wasn't the telltale click of the door latching shut and the lock being engaged.

I count to ten, then open my eyes. The man hasn't return to check the lock. That means it's time for me to move.

Small black case in hand, I get to my feet and cross to the exit. I wrap my fingers around the handle and take a deep, painful breath and open the door. The search for me will begin the minute the man returns to wake me up and realizes I'm gone. I have less than thirty minutes to get out of here. *No time to waste*, I think as I step into the windowless office area that Isaac promised would be unoccupied.

It is. I don't have much time, but I allow myself to take precious seconds to check inside the desk drawers, hoping to find some kind of instrument that will remove the barcode from my ear without blood.

There isn't one.

I shove aside the disappointment, grab a half-full bag of raisins, three loose Band-Aids, and a bright pink foundation compact.

No more stalling. I slip all my items into the raisin bag, walk to the door, and prepare to run for my life.

SIXTEEN

I step into the sticky heat. The sky is gray and filled with stretches of ominous clouds that obscure the exact location of the sun.

"Head for the hill. Once you reach the other side, you'll want to follow the creek," Isaac told me.

When Liz pointed out these buildings yesterday—how could it be that it was only yesterday?—I noticed the infirmary was isolated from the other structures in the area. Cornfields are to my right. Without Isaac's guidance, that's where I would head. Not to the terrifying expanse of overgrown grass to the left or the hill rising up in the distance. Grass covers most of it, but there is one section that is thick with bushes and trees. The closest building is painted in bright red and far enough away that I can't tell if the two Instructors standing outside with their backs to me are men or women. Four green carts like the one that brought me here are parked at a charging station close enough for the Instructors to reach in a matter of seconds.

If I get to the top of the hill, the Instructors won't be able to follow on those carts. They'll have to chase me on foot. But that's a big *if*.

One of the Instructors beings to pace. If I wait a few minutes, the two could decide to go inside. But if I don't go now, the Instructors coming for me might arrive and I will have forfeited this chance.

After what Isaac has done for me, there is only once choice for me to make.

"When you leave the building, walk. Don't run," was Isaac's advice. "Running will attract attention."

Maybe, but the base of the hill is well over a football field in length from where I stand now. Not making it to the trees at the top of the hill before those Instructors turn around will guarantee I get caught. Isaac's ass isn't on the line right now. Mine is. Which is why after taking several slow steps, I glance at the Instructors one more time, then run.

My battered legs burn.

Gravel crunches. I reach the grass past the building, grit my teeth, and run harder. The grass gets longer. Wilder. I don't look over my shoulder. It will only slow me down. Against the backdrop of swaying green, the pale pinkish-gray shirt and pants will stand out like a white light against a moonless night sky. No one is going to mistake me for a weed. But if I reach the trees halfway up the hill, the lack of sunlight and the shadows of the branches will at least give me some cover.

Fragrant wildflowers and prickly weeds snag my baggy clothes as if trying to hold me back. I want to shout with triumph when I reach the bottom of the hill and almost immediately realize I started celebrating too soon. While the incline is gentle at first, it grows steeper and harder to climb with every step.

I grit my teeth and will my legs to keep pumping as I trek through the grass. My chest strains against my bandaged rib cage. Each shallow breath is like inhaling glass, but I refuse to give in.

The tips of my shoes catch on the weeds. My legs tremble under the effort of staying upright and making the rapid climb. I tether my focus on the closest tree, lean forward and push myself to reach it.

The grass rustles and a startled rabbit shoots out of its hiding place. The trees grow nearer and I look for one wider than the rest and when I reach it slip behind its trunk. Breathing hard, I close my eyes and listen to the rustle of the leaves.

Birds chirp.

The wind gusts.

No alarms blare.

There are no shouts.

I brave a glance down the hill.

No one has arrived at the infirmary.

The Instructors that had been standing outside the red building have moved. One is gone. The other is getting into a dark green golf cart. No one seems to be aware that I am missing. Yet. If I am still wearing the ear cuff when they realize I'm gone . . .

The official in the cart speeds off. Once the vehicle is out of sight, I resume climbing the hill, moving deeper into the grove of trees that grows denser the closer I get to the top. My side throbs, but I don't slow my pace. Fear keeps me moving.

The hill flattens near the top, making it easier to navigate and I start to run again. When the hill slopes sharply in the other direction, I half climb, half slide down several feet of uneven terrain, then glance back to where I came from.

The infirmary and other buildings are no longer in sight. Since I can't see them from up here, I'm betting anyone outside those buildings can't see me. I head for a squat bush that is attempting to grow under the shadow of a much larger tree. Kneeling on the dirt next to it, I drop the bag I have been clutching and flex my hand. When my fingers aren't so stiff, I pull the compact out of the bag, flip it open, and wipe grime off the mirror with the bottom of my shirt. I wedge it into one side of the bush and now am eye-level with my reflection. Then I dig out the black case.

I stare at the scalpel for several long seconds. Slowly, I remove the blade from the box and spin the narrow, round handle between my fingers. The Marshals put the barcode in my ear against my will. They tagged me like an animal. I refuse to allow them to use it against me now.

I push my sweat-damp hair behind my ear and feel the ear cuff one more time, searching for a way to get it off without cutting through my ear or releasing the poison they say is inside.

Ow. I bend the side cartilage of my ear all the way forward so I can get a good look at the seam on the back to figure out how the two pieces are held together.

My hair slips back over my ear and I try again.

The cuff part that wraps around the lobe from the front to the back makes it impossible to see how the tag comes apart.

A siren sounds. My heart sputters. They know I'm gone. It won't be long before someone searches for my barcode location and comes this way.

I grab a broken branch off the ground and place it in between my teeth. Then, before I can lose my nerve, I lift the scalpel.

My hold on my ear slips. I wipe my sweaty fingers on my pants and get a firm grip on the side of my ear. Cutting inside to out is the fastest way, I tell myself as I fold and flatten my ear against my head.

Now or never. Before I can talk myself out of it, I bite down on the stick and jam the tip of the scalpel between the back fastener and my skin next to the post.

A scream claws up my chest into my throat. Blood drips. The scalpel slips and pops out from under the tag. My heart roars in my ears and I dig my teeth into the stick, shift the scalpel, and try again.

I dig the blade under the backing and the cuff. Just one quick movement, I tell myself. A little more pain and I'll be free.

Oh God! The pain flares impossibly hot and overwhelming. Blood drips faster in the mirror's reflection. I gag as pieces of the stick tickle the back of my tongue, and start to cough.

I scream against the branch again as the coughing jag causes the scalpel to dig deeper into my ear. My fingers are weak and brittle, but I don't drop the knife.

I shift my grip, take a deep breath, and brace myself to cut the rest of the way though and that's when I see it—the back of the ear cuff that held the metal post in place is dangling in the mirror's reflection.

The blade drops from my fingers that are slick with my blood. My stomach heaves and my hand trembles as I yank the barcode out of my blood-slicked ear and let it drop onto the dirt. Blood swells from the jagged hole along the side of my ear and trickles down my neck but I don't care.

Their tag is out and I'm alive.

Sirens whine in the distance. The sound urges me on as I wipe the blood off the knife and the compact, shove them back into the bag, then reach for the ear cuff. With the tag tight in my fist, I once again start down the incline.

The pitch of the ground is steep. My legs are liquid. Drips of crimson seep into the grass as I stagger away from the bush, lose my balance, and slide downward. I squelch the shriek of pain. Rocks and bushes scrape against me as I skid along the steep incline. Until finally—oof—my feet land on a large rock just before I reach the bottom and I come to a jarring stop.

If I was bruised before, I'm going to be Technicolor now. But my inadvertent slide was fast, and after three more steps, I reach more level ground.

Now to find the creek Isaac told me to follow.

I head through the trees down a far gentler slope than the one I just navigated. Between my jagged breathing and the crunch of twigs and leaves I no longer can hear the wail of the sirens.

When the trees thin I spot a low steel fence. In the distance beyond the fence is a cornfield with waist-high stalks. Just beyond the fence is the creek Isaac instructed me to find. It's three-feet wide and widens to the right as it flows into a concrete tunnel set into a hill.

My instructions were to "Follow the creek to the left" as it snakes through rockier ground around the base of the hill and disappears into more trees. But I can't help looking at the tunnel to the right as I climb over the fence to the other side.

Water trickles as I look down at the blood-streaked ear tag in the palm of my hand, consider my options, and head right. I wipe my hand against my bloody ear and place it on the narrow trunk of a young tree. A few feet beyond that, I smear a streak of crimson onto a low, bright green bush beyond it and paint the cheerful yellow dandelions at the bank of the creek. I take several steps, cock my arm back, and pray that I have good aim before letting the barcode fly. It skips off the water, then sinks a few feet inside the opening to the concrete tunnel.

Chase that. I turn on my heel and follow the creek in the other direction. If I'm lucky, the Instructors will waste time following the false trail I have left and give me more time to figure out how to get away.

I run along the narrowing bank of the water. The trees get thicker and . . .

I stop and listen. Voices shout somewhere above and sound like they are getting closer.

The creek narrows to barely a foot wide and disappears under a wide thicket of prickly, green leaves that are growing in mostly grassless, muddy ground. Since I can't afford to leave a trail of footsteps behind me, I step into the water and keep going.

The voices grow louder. I have to force myself to take careful, soundless steps through the water as my heart screams for me to run. When I reach the thicket, I clench the bag between my teeth and half crawl, half slither under the foliage through the narrow stream of water until I emerge on the other side wet and muddy and covered in little prickly thistles.

I lie there, a stingy trickle of water running against my cheek. Then, arms trembling, I shove myself out of the wet and onto my feet. This isn't like running the mile in phys ed where the teacher will let you stay after school to try again if you don't finish with a passing time. There are no do-overs today.

The ground evens out and the shouting gets louder. They're closing in.

I wince at each snap of a twig as I shove my way through the brush, looking for the building Isaac told me I'd find somewhere out here.

My leg muscles weep as the ground once again slopes upward.

I'm thankful it isn't very far before the foliage thins. I crest the hill and spot a black steel fence that surrounds a field of dirt and mud. A yellow machine—I think it's a backhoe—sits in the middle of the muddy field. Beyond the field and the fence is a slightly tilted gray wooden structure.

That has to be the building Isaac wanted me to find. The field looks too muddy to cross without leaving any tracks, but going around the perimeter will take too long.

It takes two tries to scale the low metal fence that thanks to my training would have normally required almost no effort to get over. The sun is still hidden. The air is hot and thick with the earthy, damp smell of dirt and decay as I hop from dry patch to dry patch, doing my best to stay out of the mud.

Sweat drips down my neck. My clothes are heavy with mud and water. I am halfway across the pasture when I realize the voices behind me have gotten closer. It's still faint, but I make out a woman shouting two words that make my heart go still.

". . . this way!"

They're close. There's no way I'll make it to the other end of the pasture before they push through the brush. The only option I have is to hide. I make a beeline to the backhoe. The closer I get, the less dry dirt there is to step on until there is only mud and puddles. I stick to the water-filled tread marks when possible and pray they don't see the places where I leave fresh treads.

My pursuers are louder still by the time I reach the small backhoe. Its wheels are thick, but not very tall. There isn't enough space for me to fit under the machine and the open cab with its exposed narrow seat doesn't offer any place for me to hide.

Now what?

I turn to the large shovel-like section that is suspended two feet off the ground and get an idea. The digging part of the machine is shaped kind of like a bucket with teeth. Albeit not a very big one. But there is just enough room inside the dirt-caked metal bin for me to climb in, fold myself into a tight ball, and hopefully be completely out of sight.

It isn't long before I hear three voices. They're still too far away for me to make out everything they're saying, but I can recognize a fight when I hear one.

". . . said to . . ."

"I'm telling you . . ."

". . . who cares . . . go back . . ."

"Going to check . . ."

Slowly, I shift my head a fraction of an inch and peer through two of the digger's teeth so I can see pieces of the pasture beyond.

The arguing grows louder. Something about one guy knowing what he saw and the others insisting that they follow orders.

I catch a glimpse of the edge of the familiar deep blue uniform and a hint of sandy hair as the Instructor turns his back to me and waves his arms. Whoever he's talking to is out of my sightline. I hold my breath and strain to hear the words while trying to remember the exact path I took around the backhoe to get to my hiding spot. If they move just a little to their right. . .

"They've found her earpiece," someone yells loud enough for me to hear over the pounding of my heart. "Let's go!"

The Instructor with the sandy hair turns in the direction of the backhoe. He cocks his head to the side and steps just out of my view.

Is he still there?

I count the seconds—waiting to be found.

Ten.

Twenty.

Forty.

Sweat drips between my breasts.

Sixty.

Still, I don't move. The muscles in my legs begin to cramp, but I stay huddled in the digger listening to my heartbeat and the sounds around me. Time seems to stand still as I wait. After ten minutes—maybe twenty—I slowly raise my head to peer over the edge of the teeth.

The field is empty, which is good because it takes several tries for me to uncurl myself from the pretzel position I am in before I can climb out of the digger. My foot catches on one of the teeth. I pitch forward and tumble out of the backhoe with a splat into the mud.

Well, if they come back, I'll at least be camouflaged. I giggle, feeling a touch insane as I push to my knees, and look for the bag I had been holding. There. Sitting in the muck next to a rock a few feet away.

Only, I—I don't think it's a rock. I tell myself to go to the barn. To leave the bag and move before the Instructors come back. Instead, I reach forward and dig into the soft, wet earth, then jerk back when I uncover enough to understand what I'm seeing.

It's a foot.

There's a body buried in this field.

SEVENTEEN

I stagger backward. My foot slips and I catch my balance before I land next to the body.

There's a dead body beneath the mud. And if there is one . . .

I turn and look at the backhoe's clawlike digger. The machine has clearly been used. Despite being out here exposed to the elements it appears in good condition. No rust. No missing pieces or flat tires. And I ask the question that I didn't ask when I was running for my life. What purpose could a backhoe have where there is nothing but a field of mud and a barn that doesn't look as well-maintained as the others I've seen?

Bile bubbles in my throat. My stomach churns as I look back at the heel poking up from the wet earth.

Last night, the man in the scrubs told someone that he wasn't needed because I was going to survive. That person was called to the infirmary because they thought they were going to have to dispose of my body. They were going to bring me here. This . . . this must be the place where they buried the bodies of those who don't survive. The place one Instructor referred to as "the pit." A graveyard of the missing and forgotten.

My skin crawls with every step. The mud sucks at my shoes until finally, I reach the fence. There is an open gate a few yards away, but I grab the top black steel bar and pull myself over to the other side. I make it to the tall grass a few feet beyond before the metallic taste filling my mouth overwhelms me. My stomach cramps and I hunch over a patch of large white lace wildflowers as hot, yellow bile burns my throat and trickles out of my mouth.

I have eaten nothing in the last twenty-four hours, but my body doesn't seem to know that. It continues to heave after the last acidic drops have been squeezed from my stomach.

Shaking, I wipe the cold sweat from my forehead. Then, after making sure no one is around, I tug off my mud-caked shoe and reach for the GPS camera.

I take pictures of the field. Of the heel peeking from the slick earth. Then, legs shaking, I trudge to the gravel road that runs near the building. The road branches in two directions—one leads through the tall grass to somewhere over the hill—away from this place. The other Isaac told me to follow. It ends on the opposite side of the barn from the body in the field I just left.

As promised, the dingy white side door is unlatched. The rusted hinges give a token protest when I ease it open and peer inside. Empty.

The barn isn't all that big, by barn standards. Maybe half the size of our small gym at school. Or maybe I just think it isn't big because other than the last few days the only time I visited a farm was when I was in elementary school and we took a field trip to a local pumpkin patch. The memories of bins of apples and gourds and ripe orange pumpkins of all sizes, the perfectly maintained red-and-white barns with brightly lit spaces filled with picnic tables for eating sack lunches, and the screens playing videos touting the importance of the farmer to our democracy stand in stark contrast to the dirt-caked concrete entrance and the earthy scents of mildew and wood.

The only light sneaks between the loose wooden boards and the closed, machine-size doors that are to my right. Despite the lack of windows, I don't chance turning on the lights. Instead, I prop open the door I came through with a small clump of dirt before walking into the barn.

A haze of dust dances in the meager light. The outline of a much larger backhoe than the one huddled inside looms in the center of the concrete floor. Shovels, hoes, rakes, and other tools with long wooden handles hang from the wall to the left of me. A bunch of filled, large white plastic bags are stacked in a corner to my right.

I peer through the crack between the door and the threshold to make sure no one is approaching from that direction, and step deeper into the shadows. A discarded wrapper crunches under my mud-caked shoe. A sturdy wooden workbench lines half of the far wall. Atop the bench on one end is a computer with a hairline crack running down the length of the screen. As the computer powers up, I yank open the first drawer and rummage through more empty wrappers, pieces of twine, and loose nuts and bolts and machine parts. Then I move on to the next. I pull out a small flashlight with triumph and find a pair of batteries rolling around the back that bring it to life.

Quickly, I work my way down the bench, pulling out drawers

and closing them when I don't immediately identify anything of use. Some are filled with surgical masks. Others with gloves and an assortment of eye protectors. I find an empty plastic water bottle, a half-eaten bag of pretzels, a pair of used socks, and three sleeves of peanut butter and cracker sandwiches that I place on a metal stool. It's only when I pull out a drawer at the end of the bench and the contents rattle that my pace slows.

The deep wooden drawer is filled with barcoded ear cuffs. Dozens of them, along with a scanner and two metal ratchet-looking things that fit the back of the ear cuff perfectly.

I run my fingers through the ear cuffs. Some are stained with grass and dirt and reddish-brown streaks that can only be blood. I hope the images I take capture it all.

Leaving the drawer with the barcode cuffs open, I head for a series of large metal cabinets like the ones my father has—had—in our garage. In the first, I find yellow coveralls. In the next—blue Instructor uniforms. All of them look way too big for me to wear, but a slightly dirty one hanging from a hook on the wall next to the cabinet might fit. I shine the flashlight in that direction and stop dead in my tracks.

Beyond the used uniforms is a floor-to-ceiling whiteboard like some of my teachers who weren't good at operating the digital class screens used. Instead of being filled with chemistry formulas, there is a black box in the corner with the word "Freedom1234" written carefully inside of it. The rest of the dingy board is covered with words written with red, black, and royal-blue ink in at least a dozen different hands. The board was probably intended to provide reminders to fellow workers. At least that is what I believe when I read the sentences in the middle.

Don't forget your gloves and masks.

Use the lime!

Speed bumps occur when you don't dig deep enough.

After the muddy field, those words make me want to scream. But the rest . . .

Do they always have to smell like animals?

The three today are finally useful.

God bless America!

Check out today's images from zone 2! They are saluting now.

Shivering, I use the recorder, then read the words again. A lot are faded—like someone brushed by the board and wiped some of the color away. There is one I start to skim over, but a word catches my attention.

Pictures

I get closer to the board and squint to make out the words.

Uploaded new pictures onto the computer. Check out the face John is making on the backhoe!

Could the picture be on this computer?

I don't have time to spend hanging around here. Still, I go back to the cracked screen and click the mouse.

Password

"Who password protects a computer in the middle of nowhere?" I can't help asking. So much for . . . Wait.

I look at the word in the corner of the board again. Could they be lazy enough to write the password on the wall? After all, it's not like they expect anyone unauthorized to come waltzing through.

I type "Freedom1234" into the password box, press Enter, and a display of dozens of desktop folders appear. First thing, I turn off the internet connection—just in case—then start going through the folders. There are backhoe manuals and forms for ordering new equipment or uniforms. Several folders are marked as requests for transfers, vacation schedules, and employee evaluations. I ignore those, but take pictures of the spreadsheet filled with schedules and dates and numbers of subjects buried as well as the work schedule of officials who work here.

A name catches my eye at the bottom of the last page and I feel like throwing up again.

Isaac Webster.

According to the spreadsheet, he was assigned to work here two days ago. He knew about the mass grave. He must have wanted me to see it so if I escaped I could tell others. And I will.

I spot a folder titled "Fun," click on it, and discover hundreds of photographs. These must be the pictures reference in red marker on the whiteboard. The first images look like the ones I saw on news segments extoling the virtues of the Great American Farm, with smiling men and women in blue uniforms standing in front of this barn. Then the images change to ones the news channel would never allow anyone to see.

Instructors wearing masks and gloves dragging bodies across the dirt.

A male Instructor peeing into a hole in the ground while others laugh.

Bodies stacked like firewood under a partially tacked tarp sprinkled with snow.

By the time I reach one with dead bodies posed with their hands on their hearts as if saluting the flag, someone has added captions. This one reads, "Bet they wish they had done this before."

I blink away tears and use the GPS recorder to capture dozens of the images. Bile burns my throat. How does anyone live with knowing this is happening? Do they think they are protecting the country? Are they too scared to voice their opinions? Or are they glad to have an excuse to be cruel?

How does one person—a few, a hundred—fight this?

From the first night I sat in the Stewards' station across from Atlas and learned about the missing words and history, I believed that people just needed to learn the truth. Once they did, they'd want to fix what was broken. But this . . .

I don't know if anything can fix this.

I turn off the computer and place my GPS recorder on the workbench with the other items I will be taking with me. I've spent more time here than I should have, but Isaac told me I'd have a better chance of escape if I ditch my "subject" clothing, so that's what I'm going to do.

I strip off the shirt and pants and stash them behind one of the white bags stacked in the corner near the entrance. Then, I spit on a rag and dab the blood and dirt from my ear before tugging on the first uniform that looks close to my size.

The slick dark blue shirt sticks to my sweaty skin. I find a scrap of rope to keep the pants from riding too low on my hips and tuck the bottoms of the pants into the top of my socks to make sure I don't trip. There aren't any boots, so I keep my mud-coated shoes and rummage through the barn until I find a small black bag with a thin leather strap to replace the mud coated one I was using. I slide the scalpel into my pocket, then use the bandages I found in the infirmary desk to protect the wound on my ear. Finally, I add a handful of discarded barcodes and one of the hand scanners to the black bag before closing all the drawers and returning the bucket to where I found it. At first glance, the interior of the barn looks like it did before I got here. Hopefully, no one will look twice.

Isaac's directions about how to get to the edge of the farm were sketchy at best. Everything is still quiet when I step out of the barn. I fill up the water bottle at the pump and drink from it as I jog toward the trees in the distance, leaving the graveyard behind me.

"Follow the road until it turns to the north," Isaac told me. "There should be a dirt path through the fields nearby that you can follow east the rest of the way."

Easier said than done, since once I follow the gravel road over the hill, the trees and bushes stop, leaving the road exposed in every direction. One large golf cart like the one used to take me to the infirmary zooms along the road back in the direction I'm pretty sure I came from—one Instructor behind the wheel while another is perched in the back cab scanning the fields.

I crouch behind a tree, wait for the cart to creep down the road, and just as I am about ready to get up spot another cart kicking up dust in the distance.

Isaac's plan for escape had been good up until now. But I don't think he was counting on people patrolling the road in search of me. Following the road is definitely out. I need a plan B.

I weave through the trees that line the top of the hill and stop every time a cart comes into sight—which is way too often. Voices yell from somewhere in the distance. I can't tell what direction or how far away they are. The chances of someone seeing me in this uniform and wondering what a lone Instructor is doing up here is going to get me in trouble sooner or later.

Another golf cart—this one with just a driver—rattles down the road. I duck beneath a bushy pine and wait for it to roll out of sight. If I have to keep stopping every few minutes I will never make it out. I need to steer clear of this road. Or maybe, I think as I watch an Instructor steer a cart into an area next to a group of white and red buildings with solar-paneled roofs and a bunch of other parked cars—maybe I'm thinking about this hiding-from-the-Instructors thing all wrong.

I can almost hear Isaac yelling at me not to do anything stupid. But he's not the one who has to make it a dozen or more miles on cramping legs and blistered feet. Sweat drips down my neck and the backs of my knees as I walk at least another mile—hiding from Instructors while keeping the buildings and the line of carts parked next to a charging station in my sight.

In a nearby field, I perch on my hands and knees in corn not quite as tall as my shoulders. The driver gets out, pulls a cable from the red-and-black charging station that resembles a smaller version of the gas stations the government says will be unnecessary in another twenty-five years. He attaches it to the cart he was driving. When a red light appears above the charging slot, the man unplugs a cart with a green light, hops in, and in seconds is sending up dust as he zooms away.

The sky goes gray. My stomach grumbles so I slowly eat the packages of stale peanut butter crackers from my perch in the rustling corn as two more Instructors in golf carts repeat the same process. One goes into the small garage-size building while the other hooks up the cables and emerges not long after, wiping her hands on her navy-blue pants with the other shouting to hurry up. No one else comes out of either of the buildings.

I slip the black leather strap of my bag over my neck and crawl farther forward between rows of corn as the sky dims. Night approaches, bringing with it darkness that will both conceal me from my pursuers and make it impossible for me to see what direction I'm going. If night arrives before I have found the dirt road Isaac said would lead me east, I will probably have a better chance of getting lost than leaving.

When this next cart comes, I have to go.

Finally, another appears. I wait for the driver to cycle through the routine. When he drives his exchanged cart down the road, I push to my feet. I grit my teeth as the edge of my shoe rubs against my raw heels, and walk across the dandelion-spotted carpet of grass toward the charging station and the four remaining carts.

All the stations are marked by red lights. I head for the far side of the station and the two carts that were charging when I first arrived. I look at one charging station display, then turn to compare it to the next as the sound of tires on gravel hits me.

Crap!

I look at the nearest building. I might be able to make it to the door before the Instructor parks his vehicle. But what then? Running will be like a flashing neon sign telling him that something is wrong, if he hasn't figured that out already. If my Dewey-created government ID allowed me to walk around Chicago in plain sight, I'm going to have to trust my Instructor uniform to help me do the same.

I smooth my hair over my ear, and hope the last rays of light don't provide enough illumination for him to see the streaks of dirt against the deep blue fabric of my uniform. As the Instructor steers toward the parking area, I walk with deliberate steps to the driver's side of the cart and unhook the charging cable. The deeply tanned, curly-haired man behind the wheel of the approaching cart waves when he sees me glance his way. I raise my hand and gesture back, certain he has to see my hands tremble and how I almost drop the cable as I return it to the charging station.

The cart kicks up stones and dust as it rolls by me. I open the door to my cart and throw my bag onto the passenger seat as the curly-haired man pulls into an empty space three cart-lengths away.

"They're all still charging?" the man asks as he cuts the motor and climbs out. A black riding crop hangs from a loop on his hip. A gun rests next to a blue and silver uniform cap on the fake tan leather of his cart's passenger seat.

I swallow and shrug as if this is typical. "Avoid the cart on the end," I warn, sliding behind my cart's steering wheel. "It's going to take forever to charge."

Now, I wonder which of the two big black buttons turns the damn cart on? And do I need a key fob to make it work?

I can feel the man's eyes on me as I kill time deciding by adjusting the rearview mirror.

"Drives me nuts," the guy says as he strolls to the charging station for the charging cable. He plugs it into the cart with a weary sigh. "You'd think we'd get the fast-charge units since we are dealing with runaway traitors, although the way I see it . . ." He grabs his hat and gun off the seat of the cart, turns, taking me in. "The search is going to be finished any minute now."

When he smiles, I'm positive he knows who I am.

Slowly, I ease my hand so it hovers near the button on the dash to the right of the wheel.

"So what do you think?" he asks, taking a step closer.

"About what?" I ask stupidly.

"Well." He edges closer. "If the subject *is* going to be taken in at any moment, no one would care if we kept each other company while the carts recharge."

Wait. What?

I blink as I understand that he isn't talking about taking me into custody. He's hitting on me.

Now what?

"Sorry." I punch what I hope is the start button. To my intense relief, the engine roars to life. "You're going to have to recharge on your own," I say with my cockiest smile as I pull the gearshift into reverse. "I have orders to follow."

Now I just have to hope I don't back into a tree!

Heart racing, I press down on the gas and spin the wheel. The cart jerks at an angle backward. The tires kick up gravel and I don't wait for the cart to come to a stop before I shift again and shoot forward.

"You're a crap driver!" the guy shouts. *No kidding,* I think as I steer the cart down the center of the bumpy road, sending up bits of rock and dust in my wake. But crap driver or not, I'm making good time.

I clutch the black plastic wheel and brave a glance over my shoulder in time to watch the man disappearing inside one of the buildings against the last gasp of dusk. Then with my eyes firmly on the road in front of me, I drive.

EIGHTEEN

The farm's green electric cart reminds me a lot of the bumper cars that Rose, Isaac, and I used to ride on when we were kids. No matter how hard I pushed the pedal to the floor, my car ambled along while the others zipped by or rammed me from behind.

The sky turns more black than gray as I perch on the edge of my seat and urge the cart to go faster. I roll by long rows of corn that look like menacing lines of shadowy soldiers against the darkening of night. The glowing slice of moon and hundreds of stars shine impossibly bright against the velvet black sky, casting the only tantalizing hints of light. The dirt road Isaac said I should look for has to be close by, but I don't know if I am going to be able to find it in the dark.

Bright white headlights appear in the distance. I clutch the wheel tight as the lights grow larger. Finally, the other cart passes me. The driver yells, "Hey! Turn on your lights" as she zooms by.

Turn on my lights? Yeah, even if I could find them, I'm not sure making it obvious this cart is on the road is a great idea. However, if I don't find the dirt path I'm looking for before another cart passes, I might have to consider taking that chance.

I hit a rock and ease off the accelerator when I almost veer off the road. I am just about to search for the headlight switch when I notice a small square on the dash has started to blink a warning red.

The cart is almost out of power.

I shove the hair fluttering in my face out of my eyes and squint into the almost completely fallen darkness in front of me for an opening between the rows of corn that is wider than the others.

No.

That's not a road, either.

Maybe there?

Without knowing how much longer the cart will drive, I have to take a chance. I yank the wheel to the right and stomp down on the pedal. The cart leaps off the road through the tall grass and wildflowers and onto the dirt path between the rows of corn that is most definitely not the road I was searching for. The front of the cart smashes into the cornstalks and barrels forward.

Stalks fly, slicing against my legs. The cart bounces and jerks and plows down the plants. I grip the wheel tighter and turn it back and forth, trying to keep the cart going in the same direction as the rows of corn. I'm leaving what might as well be a huge neon sign for the Instructors to follow with the line of destroyed corn behind me. If I'm lucky they won't notice it until dawn.

The right front wheel hits something hard, sending bits of stalks and dirt into my face. I close my eyes for just a second. When I open them there is no time to swerve as a dark shape stumbles out of the shadows. I can tell it's a woman a second before the cart mows her down.

"Oh my God. Oh my God. Oh my God."

The right side of the vehicle rises up and I'm certain it's going to tip over. Thankfully, it doesn't. The wheels return with a thud to the ground. The cart comes to a stop and I grab the black bag from the passenger seat and jump out of the cart into the shoulder-high corn. Stalks rustling and cracking, I cross to the front of the cart while fumbling to find the flashlight and almost trip on a pair of shoes. I flick the flashlight beam to low and suck in air at the sight of feet sticking out from between the two sets of wheels like something out of *The Wizard of Oz*.

More cornstalks snap, only this time it's not because of me. I turn toward the sound as another shape plows into me. The flashlight flies from my hand as we tumble into the cornstalks. I shove my attacker, roll to the side, and am about to come up swinging when I hear a familiar voice say, "Holy hell, it's you. You're alive."

"Wallace?" I scramble for the small beam of light glowing like a beacon and shine it into his dirt-streaked face. "What are you doing here?"

"Put that thing away before someone notices the light. I didn't get us this far just to get caught."

I extinguish the light, and push past Wallace to the passenger side of the cart. The woman I hit with my cart lies motionless, facedown on broken stalks of corn.

I hook my hands under her shoulders and grunt as I struggle to pull her free. When Wallace realizes what I'm doing he hurries over to help.

"I didn't see her until it was too late," I explain desperately. "She ran right in front of me."

The woman makes no sound. Not when she's being dragged the three feet to get her clear of the cart or when we roll her over so her nose isn't pressed into the dirt. And when I shine the light on the woman's round, pale face, I realize three things. I know her. She's the woman from that first day in the orientation center. The woman who said she didn't belong here—who believed her husband would help her get back home. The second is that she's no longer wearing the ear cuff. Instead, there's a huge tear where the barcode used to be. But I don't think she feels the pain from its removal. Her eyes are blank. Her chest is still.

"She's dead." I clap my hands over my mouth to keep from screaming. "I didn't see her," I whisper. "I couldn't see . . ."

"It wasn't you." Wallace grabs me by the arms and turns me so I face him.

"The wheel ran her over. I felt it." It was like going over a speed bump. That's what someone called the bodies on that whiteboard.

I swivel back to the woman on the ground. I killed her and I don't even remember her name.

"She was shot." Wallace grabs my arm again and pulls me away. "We were running. They were shooting into the field and she got hit. I got their tags off us, but they'll be searching the area. If we don't want them shooting us, we have to go."

The motor of the cart still hums. The corn rustles. Wallace points at the main road where I came from and the two pinpricks of light that are moving on the horizon.

"We should put her on the back of the cart," I say.

"There isn't time." He hops into the passenger side and waves for me to get moving. "We have to go."

I hate that he's right. There's nothing we can do for her, and taking her body with us will slow us down.

I take one last look at her lifeless face before turning on my heel.

The memory of the woman insisting her imprisonment was a mistake haunts me as I put the cart in gear and drive forward.

The red light on the dashboard still blinks.

Corn stalks crack and crumble under the cart's wheels.

Wallace twists and looks behind us.

"The lights are gone," he says, swiveling forward. "We're good for now. There's a dirt road to the left somewhere. We should try to make it there so we aren't leaving a path of destruction all the way to wherever we are going."

"I don't know how much longer the cart will drive," I say, pointing to the warning light. Still, I follow his instructions. I yank the wheel to the left and wince as the cart crashes through row after row after row of corn. Finally, I steer onto an eight-foot wide path of dirt and head east—at least, I hope I'm going east.

"This is amazing!"

"Keep your voice down!" I glance over my shoulder, waiting for someone to come rushing out of the darkness.

"Sorry," Wallace says. "I just can't believe we're here."

Wallace grins as I work to keep the cart in the center of the road. He's right. The fact that we are here—together—*is* pretty unbelievable.

"If I remember the maps I studied during my training," Wallace says, just loud enough to carry over the sound of the cart and the shuffling corn, "the fence shouldn't be too much farther. There are guard buildings near the fence line every twenty miles or so, but those are mostly there to keep people out. Ever since we started using the safety ear tags, no one ever gets this far before getting caught." He shoots me a grin. "But we did."

"Yeah," I say. A knot of unease grows in my chest and not just because I know any minute the cart will lose power. "How did you get away from the Instructors?"

"What?" He pauses, then shrugs. "Oh, we were in the fields and the alarms went off. I was certain it had to be because of you. They said you were dying, but I saw what you did with the blood. That was seriously smart."

I keep my eyes on the darkness in front of me.

Out of the corner of my eye I see Wallace frown as he continues, "Half the Instructors were called away from the fields to help search and a group of subjects a few rows over decided to take a chance. When our Instructor's attention was on them, three of us in my group decided to make a break for it. By the time the Instructors realized we were gone, we were too far away to catch us on foot so they opened fire. The man running right behind me was shot in the back. The other . . . well, you know what happened to her."

The thud of her body against the front of the cart—that's a sound I won't forget. Ever.

The red light blinks faster. I press the gas pedal to the floor, but it's no use. The cart has started to slow.

Wallace doesn't appear to notice. "How about you?" he asks. "How did you get out of the infirmary?"

I picture Isaac. He must know the Instructors haven't found me, yet. I know he must be rooting for me to get out and to help him as he helped me.

"The door didn't latch when some guy came to check on me." I glance over to look at Wallace again. "I pretended to still be drugged and when he left I snuck out."

"So you didn't convince anyone to help you? I figured you must know Instructors who help sneak people out. Some do, if the price is right."

Warning bells flash in my head.

"I didn't know that."

"Really?"

"Yes, really. Why is that so hard to believe?"

"Because it means you got damn lucky," he says quietly.

"I'd say we both got lucky," I tell him. The indicator light goes black. The motor dies and the cart bumps and sputters to a stop. "I think our luck has run out," I say in the hushed night. "We're going to have to walk from here."

"Well, it can't be that much farther." Wallace hops out. "Then . . . I guess . . ." He shakes his head and shoves his baggy shirtsleeves to his elbows.

I grab my bag, slide it over my head, and climb to the ground. "What?"

"Nothing. Once we reach the fence, I'm not sure where I'm going to go."

"Away from here would be a good start."

"That's the truth." He kicks the dirt with the tip of his boot. "I'm just not sure what I'll do once we get out. I mean, it's not like I can go back to the Marshals after all of this and who knows what story everyone I know has been told about why I suddenly disappeared. For all I know, my parents and friends think I'm dead."

The moonlight catches the side of his face giving me a clearer view of the ear where the barcode used to be embedded. There was a smear of blood at the bottom of the lobe. Other than that, his ear looked fine.

"Are you okay?" Wallace asks.

I don't think I am. All of this feels very wrong. "I was thinking about the woman you were with."

"What happened to her wasn't your fault. Hey! I think I see the fence beyond those trees." He grins at me and picks up his pace. "We're going to make it and maybe if we get back to Chicago we can try to shut this down. You know other people like us, right? You're working with people who know what this place is for and are planning to tell people about it?"

He turns to me and realizes I'm several steps behind him. "Are you okay?"

No. I'm not.

"How did you get the ear tag off without hurting yourself?" I ask quietly.

He lifts a hand to his ear. "As soon as I started pulling at it, the fastener unlatched. I guess we both needed some luck to get this far."

My stomach clenches.

"Hey, do you think you can run as far as the fence?" he asks over his shoulder. "Once we get to the other side we can talk about what we're going to do next. I think I know where we can find a phone if you have someone you want to call. . . ." Wallace glances back to where I'm standing—scanning the landscape, looking for somewhere—anywhere—that I can run. He sighs, reaches under his shirt and when he turns to face me, he's holding a gun.

How could I be so stupid?

Trust—but verify. I knew better and still I trusted everything Wallace told me because he said what I wanted to hear. I wanted to believe that the people who were tagging their neighbors and putting them in cages didn't understand what they were doing. That once they saw the truth they, too, would want all this to stop.

Wallace shakes his head. "It's always the little details that screw things up. I'll remember that in case you aren't as helpful as I think you'll be and I have to do all of this over again."

"Do what?" I ask. "I don't understand. You were in the Unity Center when I woke up. You were a prisoner, like me. You were beaten by the Instructors after we got off the truck."

"Not going to lie, letting them take those couple whacks really sucked." He rolls out his left shoulder. "But after we talked in the truck, I realized you'd need an extra incentive to trust me." Wallace smiles in the moonlight. "My boss said I was grasping at straws—that I was just looking for a way out of the crap assignment of sitting in that room day after day assessing the criminals after they were brought in. He couldn't understand why I thought you were involved with the group we've been hunting. You didn't have a tattoo. You didn't try to kill yourself in some blaze of idiotic glory to protect the other terrorists you're working with."

He tightens his grip on the gun and I hold my breath.

"But the second you opened your eyes, I knew. I could tell you were different. It didn't matter that everyone else said I was wrong or that they only let me ride here on the truck because they wanted to teach me a lesson. I knew you were the person I was sitting in that stupid room going out of my mind with boredom to find. And now they'll know I was right."

Gun still pointed at me, Wallace slides his free hand into his pocket and pulls out a personal screen.

"It's Wallace," he says to someone on the other end. I take a step to the side and Wallace moves the black-barreled gun side to side like wagging a finger at a naughty toddler.

"Send a cart to my position. I'm bringing her in." He grins as he slides the screen back into his pocket. "A team will be here to collect us soon. While we wait, how about you tell me how you knew about the Marshals and labor unions, and how you really managed to escape the infirmary? It'll be easier for you if you cooperate. I can promise you won't like the other methods they use to get information." The breeze ruffles his curly hair. "It's seriously unpleasant. Trust me."

In this one thing—I do. I trust that the Instructors will hurt me. They'll find the GPS recorder. They'll realize I'm not working alone and do whatever is necessary to get me to tell them what I know. I won't tell them what they want to hear—at least not right away. But I don't know if I can hold out forever. My mistakes put Isaac here. I'd rather die than have that happen to anyone else.

"How did you find me?" I stall for time while I ease my hand into my pocket and fumble to open Isaac's thin case.

"Security spotted you on a charging station monitor. Your uniform almost fooled them. When you climbed into that vehicle we really had to scramble to catch up."

I shift my weight and prepare to make a final run when a large, distinctive shadow moves from behind one tree to another.

Wallace shrugs. "We assumed you'd see the dirt road and take it east to the boundary. You were supposed to run into me and my tragically injured friend there. Then you—being you—would sympathetically stop to help. It never occurred to us that you'd decide to drive through the corn instead of waiting to reach the road, or that she'd have the strength to get up and run when my back was turned."

A large shadow just over Wallace's right shoulder creeps beyond the trees. I recognize the way the shadow moves as it comes toward us.

It's Atlas.

He found me!

I glance over my shoulder. Several pinpricks of light shine in the distance—and they're coming this way. Atlas doesn't know they're headed for us. He doesn't know how little time we have.

All thoughts of running, of using the scalpel on myself, disappear.

"I don't understand how you can think any of this is okay!" I raise my voice, hoping my words will mask the tread of Atlas's footsteps as he advances. "How can you pull people off the street just because they know things you don't want them to know? How can you lock people in cages and lie to their families about what's happened to them? The story of the girl—"

"Wasn't real . . ."

"It is real!" I shout.

Atlas emerges from the trees over twenty feet away from where Wallace and his gun stand.

I take a step forward as Atlas starts to run. "Every time you take someone to one of your Unity Centers," I yell, "you destroy lives while pretending to keep the country safe."

"You think anyone cares about those people?" Wallace laughs. "No one cares. No one gives a . . ."

A branch cracks.

Wallace spins. Atlas grabs Wallace's arm and shoves it up to the star-studded sky.

A shot echoes in the air as Atlas hooks a foot around the Marshal's ankle and they both hit the ground in a tangle.

Another shot explodes and I pull the scalpel from my pocket and limp forward, desperate to help as Atlas and Wallace continue to fight.

Wallace rolls away from Atlas, cocks his arm, and smashes the black metal barrel of the gun across Atlas's face. Atlas flies backward. He lands flat on the ground—hard. It takes him a second to recover. Just a second to start pushing himself up, but that is enough for Wallace to roll to his knees and raise his gun. Wallace doesn't hear me move. He's smiling when I take my own aim and bury the sharp silver knife deep into his neck.

NINETEEN

When I was a little kid, I couldn't get enough of juice pouches—especially the pink lemonade ones. I liked the look of the ice-cold, shiny silver packaging. I loved how sucking on the straw made the package shrink. Mom would let me pull the straw free from the small clumps of glue on the back of the package. Then she would remove the plastic and poke the straw into the pouch because that was a big-person job.

I can still remember the excitement of finally getting to shove the straw in all on my own. How I held it tight in my hand and punched over and over again until the pointed bottom edge of the straw bit deep into the shiny silver. How the ruby red of the fruit punch streamed up and out and over my hands.

The scalpel is a lot sharper than the edge of that plastic straw. It takes only one punch into Wallace's flesh to make him bleed like that pouch of fruit punch. His eyes widen and he screams as I grab his shoulder with my left hand and shove the knife in even deeper with my right. Then I yank it out and stab again. The gun drops from Wallace's hand into the thick grass in front of him. He lets out a wet, bubbling gurgle when I pull out the knife and jab again. Liquid flows slick and warm over my hand. I pull the knife out one last time, and gasping, he clutches his neck to stop the blood as it drains from his throat onto the ground.

"Please," he says in a wet, strangled whisper.

I clutch the bloody knife and look down at him. "You're dead," I say. He just doesn't know it yet. And I'm glad I'm the one who killed him, I think as Wallace pitches forward and with a gurgle weakly claws at the ground.

Atlas appears at my side. Seeing him snaps me back. "They're coming," I say.

The lights on the horizon are bigger and are turning in this direction. The Instructors Wallace summoned are on the way.

"He called for reinforcements just before you arrived." I drop to the ground next to Wallace and feel for his pockets hoping to find the personal screen he used.

"What are you doing?" Atlas asks, grabbing my arm.

"They're tracking his phone. If we pull the battery, they'll lose the signal. That will buy us some time."

"In another minute they aren't going to need the signal." Atlas tugs me to my feet. "We've got to get out of here."

I drop the scalpel and take one last look at Wallace lying crumpled as what is left of his life seeps into the grass. Then I turn and, together, Atlas and I run.

Atlas is faster than me on my best day. This isn't my best day. I lag behind him through the grass to the darkness of the trees, glancing over my shoulder every few seconds as the lights grow closer.

My legs are heavy. It's hard to see where we are going in the dark. I stumble over a low bush obscured by shadows and double over to catch my breath.

"You can do it, Meri," Atlas whispers. "It's not much farther. I promise."

Not much farther, I repeat to myself as we weave through bushes and trees until suddenly there is a fence in front of us—a fence that despite all our training is impossible for us to climb. It's the same style and material as the fence in the dorm courtyard. The thick black slats buried into the ground stretch up at least ten feet into the air. Beyond the fence are more trees—more shadows. Who knows what else.

Angry voices chase us on the wind.

"Is there a tree close enough to the fence for us to climb?" I ask.

"Shh." Atlas puts a finger to his lips, then lets out a low whistle.

"What—"

A higher-pitched whistle—one I might have mistaken for a bird if not for Atlas's own call into the dark—answers. The two-toned melody is coming from somewhere down the fence line to the right.

"This way," Atlas whispers, and we run again.

The snap of twigs explodes like fireworks. Each branch I bump rustles louder than a siren. I put a hand on my side and lean over trying to ease the cramping as I half run, half limp behind Atlas.

The two-toned whistle calls again—this time it's much closer.

When we hear it again, it sounds as if we are right on top of the whistler.

"There!"

I skirt around an enormous pine and follow Atlas. It isn't until I'm almost standing next to it that I see the thick black rope ladder dangling over the fence from up above.

"Jim and Elise are waiting for us on the other side. You go first."

There's no time to ask who Jim and Elise are before Atlas shoves the barrel of the gun in the waistband of his jeans. He grabs the rope to steady it as I reach up, grab the sides of the ladder, and climb.

The thick, rough rope grates against my raw, bloody hands, but I will myself upward away from the predators who are crashing through the brush and trees somewhere behind us.

When I near the top, I feel Atlas climb on the ladder below. Carefully, I ease my leg between the sharpened slats at the top of the fence. Wide-beam flashlights dance through the trees to my right as I feel with my foot for the next hemp rung.

I glance down. A man dressed in all black grabs the ladder and holds it still. "Hurry!" he urges as I start my downward climb.

Foot.

Foot.

Hand.

Hand.

I ignore the lights bounding in the darkness as the Instructors search, but I can't tune out the voices.

"Have you found anything yet?"

"Search the fence line! They can't be far."

Not yet, I think, stepping off the rope ladder onto the ground on the other side of the boundary for the Great American Farm.

I jerk as a woman slips out of the shadows on this side of the fence and heads for a rope hanging from a nearby tree.

"She's with us," the man in black assures me as lights move through the darkness on the other side of the barrier.

Branches snap.

We have to hurry, I think as Atlas swings over the top of the fence and starts his climb down. When he is a few feet from the ground, he jumps to the dirt with a loud thud.

"I heard something. Over there!"

"I think I see them!"

"Go through the trees that way." The man in black points to our right. "Look for the flashing light."

Atlas steps beside me. "What about you, Jim?"

"We need to remove the ladder so they don't know where you crossed," Jim says. "Once Elise is done, we'll clear out. Now, get going."

The familiar two-note whistle rings from above as Atlas puts a hand on my shoulder and nods.

We leave Jim and the woman to erase signs of our escape and head through the trees—both of us listening to the sounds of the night—for shouts that will tell us if Jim and Elise have been captured or our rope has been discovered. But there are no gunshots. No screams or voices calling for others to give chase. Just our ragged breathing and the crunch of leaves and dirt under our feet. Then finally I see it—a flashing blue light to our right on an incline between two pines.

Atlas starts running. I can't. Despite the fear and desperation that have propelled me forward, I can't get my legs to do more than shuffle. I am too sore. Too tired. Too weak. When Atlas realizes I'm not beside him, he starts back to help, but I shake my head and wave at him to keep going. Maybe it is stupid, but I want—I need—to make this walk by myself.

I pull the black bag tight against my chest and limp toward the light. Something cold and dark settles into my chest by the time I reach the top of the incline and spot the two cars parked on the edge of a paved, narrow road.

Hands help me ease into the perfectly air-conditioned beige back seat of an old silver sedan. Atlas slides next to me. He speaks my name. He asks if I am okay, but I can't seem to answer.

The older woman behind the wheel starts the engine. She keeps the headlights turned off when she pulls onto the road. It isn't until several minutes later, when she turns her headlights on, that I am certain there is no one giving chase. Numbly, I lean my head against the cool glass and stare into the darkness, picturing Isaac and all the others held against their will who I am leaving behind, knowing no matter what I do there is no way to save them all.

Four days.

It was just over four days ago that I walked down the streets of Chicago with Atlas certain that the plan I'd helped create was the only way to help find Isaac—to bring Atlas's father back—to return truth to those who didn't understand they were being lied to. Four days since I stood in that alley and pushed aside the fear because I was convinced what I was doing was right. That Atlas would find and break me out of the Unity Center long before the battery on the GPS recorder expired.

When I handed him the device, there was less than an hour of guaranteed power left.

Now, as I step into the shower of a stranger's house and watch the dirt and horror of my time at the Great American Farm wash down the drain, I know I should feel relieved to be free. I don't. How can I, now that I have seen people trapped in a nightmare that the country believes is part of the American dream?

The soap stings each scrape and cut even as the near-scalding water soothes my weeping muscles. I'm not sure how long I stand under the hot spray. Long enough for the red-and-gray-streaked soapy water circling the drain to run clear. Long enough to prompt the woman who owns the house—a lady named Mrs. Acosta—to knock and ask if I need her to bring different clothes.

"I can get you others if those don't fit."

Since she can hear the water running, I understand she isn't asking about the clothes. While Mrs. Acosta is at least forty years older than me, we are close to the same size. This isn't about what I will wear. She is asking if I am okay.

"These should be fine," I tell her. "Thank you."

"Let me know if you need anything."

If I need anything . . .

Well, right now I need a lot of things.

I need to scream until I am hoarse and can't scream anymore.

I need the blood to come out from under my nails. I need to feel sorry that I killed Wallace, so I know I'm not like him. That I'm not like any of them.

Only I'm not sorry, I think as I step out of the shower. I will never be sorry. So, what does that say about me?

Maybe that's why I couldn't let Atlas hold me as I cried once I knew we weren't being chased or why I pretended to sleep as the car traveled two hours down the highway to the house with the cheerful white and red country kitchen that smells of freshly baked bread. Or maybe it's because when he sees me, I know he can't help but think of his father—whom I failed to find. I know so much more now than I did when I stepped out of that alley, but I still don't have the answer Atlas most needs to hear.

Atlas and Mrs. Acosta turn to stare at me as I stand barefoot in the light at the kitchen's threshold, clutching the black bag I brought out of the farm. The shock and anger on Atlas's face as he comes out of his seat makes me cringe and the pity I see in Mrs. Acosta's rich brown eyes makes me want to cry. While the washed-out blue sweatpants and a tight black T-shirt are long enough to conceal the damage from the beating I took, there is no hiding the long gash and sickly yellow and green bruising on my right cheek or the Band-Aids haphazardly covering the gaping wound in my ear.

"Where are Jim and Elise?" I ask, breaking the silence when I realize the two who helped us scale the fence to freedom have yet to arrive. "Did they—"

"They retrieved the ladder and got away just fine." Mrs. Acosta pushes back her chair and crosses to the stove. "They checked in an hour ago to make sure you arrived safely. Have a seat. I'll bring you something to eat. Atlas here said you aren't a vegetarian so I made chicken soup. It's after midnight, but I thought you could use a little home-cooked comfort after tonight."

I take the seat next to Atlas so I don't have to meet his eyes while the compact Mrs. Acosta brings two large steaming bowls to the table. It's when she returns with a basket of bread and places it in the center of the table that I notice the tattoo on the inside of her wrist. There are blue and yellow flowers, which seem to be sitting on a decorative vase. But to my eyes the vase and the flower stems form something very different.

"You're a Steward. That's why you're helping me."

Mrs. Acosta wipes her hands on her trim white shorts and shakes her head. "I'd help you whether I was or not, but the Stewards are why they knew to send you here. Now eat up before it gets cold. I'm going to check to see about your train to the next stop."

"Train?" I ask, looking at Atlas. "What happened to your car?" I assumed this was where Atlas left it.

"Since I was planning to break you out of Marshal custody, driving myself wasn't an option," Atlas says.

"He could have gotten here without any problem," Mrs. Acosta explains. "But there would be records of his road transponder's toll payments. That wouldn't be a big deal coming, but . . ."

"If I got out the Marshals would search that information for anyone who traveled to the area from Chicago and use it to find the car on the way back."

Mrs. Acosta nods. It was like the transit cards in Chicago. Any unusual travel would send up a red flag. The government is watching.

I turn back to Atlas. "Then how did you get here so quickly?"

"A friend goes to Dixon several times a year to visit family. She was able to get me that far. While we were en route, Dewey reached out to some relocated Stewards along this train line."

"We typically relocate books or people out of Chicago. One-way tickets," Mrs. Acosta explains. "This is the first time in years anyone has ever taken a return trip. That's enough to give a lot of us hope to keep up the fight. Now you dig in before it gets cold."

"Aren't you going to eat?" I ask as she heads for the door.

Mrs. Acosta turns and shakes her cap of dark brown hair. "I ate before you arrived. If I stay around I'll be tempted to eat again. I'm not young like the two of you. I won't get to sleep if I eat this late at night."

She disappears, leaving Atlas and me alone with the ticking of the kitchen clock. The time is 12:39. Neither of us speaks. I think of the things I failed to do—the man Atlas saw me kill. I did it because he was going to shoot Atlas, but I would have done it anyway given the chance. Even in the darkness he had to have seen the satisfaction on my face of watching Wallace drown in his own blood.

I pick up my spoon and swirl it in the soup that under the bits of fragrant green herbs is filled with hunks of chicken, carrots, and spiraled noodles, looking for the words that will break the taut, uncomfortable silence between us.

"Thank you," I say as he mumbles, "I'm sorry."

We glance up at each other.

"What are you sorry for?" I ask. "You found me. If you hadn't gotten over that fence . . ." I wouldn't be in this kitchen. I wouldn't have smuggled pictures out of the farm. If Atlas hadn't come when he did, the government would have those images and I would be dead right now.

Atlas runs a hand over the back of his neck and shakes his head. "I should have gotten you out of the Unity Center before the trucks ever left the city. It's my fault you got hurt."

"No!" I drop my spoon as the simmering rage that has been building since the Marshals captured me flares to life. Soup splashes over the bowl onto the polished wood table. "You don't get to do that! None of what has happened is your fault. *I* made a choice. Me! You don't get to take that on you. That place . . ."

I think of the barcodes—the cages—the woman singing the song, looking for hope in the dark—the oath—

"Everything I saw and went through was about taking away choices. I decided the truth is important enough to fight for. I chose to let myself be captured. Those choices might have sucked, but they belong to me!"

I wait for him to shout back. To glower or storm out of the room. Instead, Atlas takes my hand as I reach for my spoon. He waits until

I stop trying to tug it free, then turns my hand over. He runs a finger lightly along each scratch and scrape of my abused palm, then lifts my hand to his lips. The ice-cold rage I've used as a shield shatters at the brush of his warm mouth against my jagged skin and the words I've been needing—hating—to admit break free.

"I didn't find him," I say, looking down at the steaming bowl on the table in front of me. "Your father. I looked for him in the cages at the Unity Center, I tried, but after—" Tears thicken my throat as I ignore Atlas telling me I have nothing to be sorry for and keep going. I have to get it out or I'm not sure I can look at him again. "I barely thought about him after they loaded me into the truck. I wanted to. I promise I did. I thought when I was put into the transport that I could find him and Isaac, but after I was told Isaac was dead . . ."

"Isaac is dead?"

"No," I say. "He isn't . . . wasn't . . . Liz thought he was and . . ."

I shake my head and pick up one of the tall glasses of milk Mrs. Acosta left on the table. And even though I've never been wild about milk when it wasn't used to dip cookies, I'm grateful for the way it coats my raw throat and settles me enough to catch my breath. "It's hard to talk about."

"You don't have to right now."

"Yes, I do," I say. I don't want to talk about it. I don't want to go back there, but Isaac risked his own life to save mine. He is waiting—counting—on me to be brave. "Did you download the GPS recorder images?"

He reaches into a bag on the chair beside him, pulls out a screen, and sets it on the table. "It finished just before you came into the kitchen."

My stomach turns. "Have you looked at the pictures?"

Atlas shakes his head. "I was waiting for you."

"You need to see them. So does Mrs. Acosta. Everyone needs to know what is happening."

Atlas places the spoon in my hand and says, "You eat. I'll get Mrs. Acosta. When you're ready, we'll look at them together."

He pushes back from the table and heads out, and I look down at the bowl in front of me and swirl the soup with my spoon. It takes only one mouthful to realize how hollowed-out my stomach feels. I almost whimper as the warm broth runs down my throat. Until this very moment, it never made sense why everyone seemed to think chicken soup was the only thing a person should eat when they felt sick. The flavorful soup is familiar and comforting and warms a part of me that the heat of the summer sun in the fields could never touch. Maybe it's because I haven't eaten much in days, but I shovel bites of chicken and noodles and vegetables in with the single-mindedness of a general preparing for battle. I contemplate licking the bottom of the bowl, but instead use a hunk of crusty bread to mop up the last of the liquid. I'm finished with both the bread and soup when Atlas and Mrs. Acosta, who has changed into a mint-green terry-cloth robe and matching slippers, step back into the kitchen.

"Atlas says you have something the Stewards on this route need to hear."

Slowly, I reach for the tablet where Atlas downloaded the images I captured and click the power button. The screen flares to life and I take a deep breath. "I am not sure how good these pictures will be, but this is what I saw."

TWENTY

REVOLUTION—(n.) The action by a celestial body of going around in an orbit or elliptical course; the period made by the regular succession of a measure of time or by a succession of similar events; a motion of any figure about a center or axis

Up until a few weeks ago, I only heard the word "revolution" used when someone was talking about a bicycle wheel or the planets' movement around the sun. Then I sat in my kitchen the day after meeting Atlas with the history textbook Dewey gave me. That's when I saw the word in a context I didn't recognize. I looked up the word in the battered Merriam-Webster collegiate dictionary I am certain Dewey never thought I would use and found the definition that our country was created with. It was the meaning of "revolution" our government no longer wanted anyone to know.

REVOLUTION—(n.) An overthrow or repudiation and the replacement of an established government or political system by the people governed

Not just finding a way to get the truth out to the country, but offering a way forward and convincing everyone that it will be better.

A combination of excitement and dread swirls in me as I climb into the back of the emergency plumbing van waiting outside Mrs. Acosta's house. People need to understand what has been taken . . . the unknown sacrifices for the safety they think they have gained. I had thought like my mother and Atticus and Dewey had before me—that if we could just get the truth out to the country, it would change others the way it had me. That the truth had so much power that once it was set free, the rest of us could step back. But there is no stepping back anymore. If the truth is to spark a revolution, it cannot do it on its own. It needs people to lead.

I look down at the book Mrs. Acosta handed me when we walked out of the house. "You should take this. It was one of my husband's favorites," she said as she pressed the book into my hands.

American Revolutions.

"I think you'll find the people here had the same problems you're trying to solve now. No one is ever chosen to start a revolution," she says, gently placing a hand on my shoulder. "Revolutions begin because people step up, marshaling their resources and doing what needs to be done."

Our driver, Craig, looks at Atlas and me settled on the floor between large tool chests and lengths of long white pipes and asks, "Ready?"

I glance behind him to Mrs. Acosta, who stands framed by the light of the open kitchen doorway. Then I look down at the book in my hand. I doubt anyone is ever ready to lead a revolution.

"Let's go," I say.

Tools and pipes rattle while the van bumps and rolls along the back roads to wherever will be our next stop, and with our fingers intertwined in the dark, we start to plan.

We agree we will have to post the pictures to *Gloss* soon. Some of the images were too dark to make out. Others were poorly framed or partially obscured by my clothing or bed sheet. I hated each blur and obstructed view, but Atlas assured me there is power in the imperfections. I hope he is right.

"The excitement the paintings of the logos and the online posts our friends are creating will only last so long," I say.

"Not to mention that we aren't the only ones who know what is happening to the disappeared people now," Atlas says. "Mrs. Acosta can convince them to wait for a while, but I spent enough time with Jim and Elise to know they won't wait for very long now that you've confirmed the rumors they've heard are real. Whatever plan we come up with, we're going to have to come up with it fast."

Atlas volunteers to go through the photos on the tablet again so I don't have to relive the horror. As if I will ever be able to forget. I know when I close my eyes to finally try to sleep they will find me. But I am glad to leave winnowing down the photographs to ones with the greatest emotional impact to him while I turn on my flashlight, settle the book onto my lap, and start to plow through the decisions that were made hundreds of years ago, looking for things that will help us now.

It's not long before we climb out of the van on the side of a two-lane road lined with grass and trees and into the cab of a land-scaper's truck while the sky is still dark. The landscaper takes us to his house, where we wait for hours in the basement before his wife loads us into her car and takes us on her daily "visit her mother" trip ten minutes down the road. She explains that we have been taken south from where we started instead of directly east. A safety precaution since the Marshals are bound to be watching all the highways that lead through Iowa to Chicago—although it doesn't feel so safe when I realize we are only a thirty-minute ride from the boundary of the Missouri portion of the Great American Farm. A direct trip from her house to the north side of Chicago would take eight hours. Ours lasts twenty-nine hours.

Carpenters.

Teachers.

Grocery store clerks.

Musicians.

Computer technicians.

College students.

Priests.

Nurses.

We are with some for a few minutes. Others drive us for hours on back roads I'm not sure appear on any map—until we reach the next person on the Stewards' train line—as we are ferried on a zig-zagging path back to Chicago.

Atlas and I talk to each of them—learning who they are, why they are helping us, and how they came to be Stewards. There are stories of finding old books in attics. Of searching for a friend who had been asking strange questions and suddenly leaves town without any notice. Of seeing something on the news that they witnessed and knowing it was not being reported correctly. Of deciding to run for mayor or the school board or the city council only to be told the Bureau of Election Certification had decided they were not qualified to be on the ballot.

Some were living new lives, having been targeted by the Marshals and forced to leave cities like Chicago and St. Louis or climb out of their dorm windows in Champaign and Wichita. We listen to their stories and answer questions about our own. One brings a phone that Atlas uses to update Dewey. He chooses his words carefully to let Dewey and the others know what I found and our thoughts about the next steps. Dewey sounds like a character out of a spy movie when he says the pot we left to simmer is now boiling, but the natives are getting restless and our friends at my former employer say the window could be closing soon. He promises he'll work with them to find the best options for all of us to have dinner when we arrive.

In the time alone between phone calls and car rides we wait in basements and back bedrooms where we try to sleep. And when I jolt awake from nightmares of callused hands on my thighs or dead bodies clawing up out of the muddy ground, I take deep breaths and choke back my screams so I don't deprive Atlas of rest. Just because I can't sleep doesn't mean he should suffer. I stare at the strong lines of his face until the worst of my terror has passed. Then, knowing those same dreams wait for me when I close my eyes, I pick up Mrs. Acosta's book and continue to read.

In school, we learned about the Declaration of Independence. How it created America. I didn't know about the war. Or that while being ruled by a faraway king was unpopular, many of the colonies would have been satisfied to stay under British rule if the taxes were eased just a bit. Especially since the war that had already started wasn't going well.

My school e-texts all showed the men who wrote the Declaration of Independence as calm. Confident. Without fear. Only the truth isn't calm, and reading between the lines—knowing what I know now—I am certain there was a great deal of fear.

Maybe it was my teacher's fault that I didn't understand that the declaration was written because the Continental Congress realized the opportunity in front of them and understood that if the moment passed and things went back to what they had been before there might never be another moment like it again. Maybe it was my lack of imagination or the privilege of growing up in what I thought was safety that I didn't see how the declaration was a rally cry—not to England, but to their friends and neighbors. It was printed and sent everywhere to be handed out to everyday people and published in newspapers to unify everyone behind the cause. There were parades and thirteen-gun salutes and the tearing down of statues of the king and burning of the royal coat of arms.

All the kinds of things I am hoping will happen when we put the photos Atlas has chosen in *Gloss*. And still those leading the revolution didn't stop. They found allies. They stood on battlefields. And they also fought by writing and publishing and giving speeches. They didn't hope the truth of their declaration would live on in everyone's memories. They did whatever was necessary to ensure that no one was allowed to forget.

By the time the Steward driving us on this leg steers the car into the lot next to a suburban park to make our next exchange, I have sent ideas to Dewey and Rose of what I think needs to happen next. I have also compiled a list of the allies we will require in order to make it work.

"I was told to give you this," our driver says, reaching into a large bag she has on the front passenger seat. To my surprise, she pulls out a gray-and-black pageboy hat complete with a jaunty yellow flower.

The five-year-old in the car seat next to me makes a grab for the hat. Her mother expertly avoids the curious hands and adds, "On the other side of the park near the pavilion is a bench. The next stop on the train is there. Katy and I will be at the swings if something happens and you need us. I don't know if you can change anything, but for my daughter's sake, I really hope so."

While she bundles Katy into the stroller, I tuck my hair under the hat, grab the bag with the book buried deep at the bottom, and head toward the next stop that will officially take Atlas and me home. We walk side by side across the grass—close enough that if I moved a half step closer I could take his hand in mine. I want to, but I don't. I can't. Not quite yet, and Atlas hasn't pushed me. It's one more thing I have to be thankful for.

Childish laughter tinkles across the sunny park as we pass the slides and the yellow-blue-and-red jungle gym. The late-morning air is comfortably warm. Atlas points out a group of local government workers in bright orange vests as they power-wash a statue close to the sidewalk. Since we don't know if the Marshals have alerted others to look for me, I keep my head angled away from them as we head for the wooden pavilion just beyond a patch of white lilies.

I spot the hat first—gray and worn—and my steps slow.

His striped, short-sleeve button-down shirt and beige pants are rumpled. There are smudges of sleeplessness and worry under his eyes. He spots us, slowly gets to his feet, and removes his hat. I walk faster and when Dewey opens his arms, I step into them without hesitation. His clothes smell like they always do—like old books and paper and the touch of cinnamon he uses in his coffee and suddenly, I feel like I'm home.

Dewey pats my back, then clears his throat and steps back. He doesn't apologize for what has happened. He doesn't ask if I'm okay. Neither does he wince at the bandage on my ear or the scrapes that makeup does nothing to conceal. He simply studies me for what feels like forever before asking, "Do you remember when we first met?"

"You said I didn't look anything like my mother."

He gives me that irritating, all-knowing smile.

"It turns out, my observation was incorrect. You look more like your mother every single day." His voice cracks. Tears shimmer in his eyes. Then he places his hat back on his head, adjusts the brim, and says, "Well, I hope you weren't expecting to rest now that you have returned. As a proverb most aptly espouses, there is no rest for the weary. A great number of people are waiting on us and there is no time to waste."

"I thought you don't drive," I say as Atlas and I follow Dewey to the parking lot. After having lived most of the last thirty years with the Stewards in the underground Lyceum, I can't imagine that Dewey has had much time to practice behind a wheel.

"Of course, I don't drive," Dewey says, opening the door of a bright blue compact car with a long scrape along the side. "Lucky for us, my friend here does."

He climbs into the front seat and slams the door. Atlas and I slide in back and come face-to-face with the same smug smile I remember seeing just before she threw a punch.

"What?" Joy asks, brushing her brown-and-blond-streaked hair behind one of her dangling gold-hooped ears. "Not who you expected to see? Didn't you tell her?" she asks Atlas, who slid into the backseat next to me.

"Tell me what?"

"Joy has family in Dixon," Atlas answers. "When I needed to get to you, she drove me the first leg out of town."

"Atlas and Dewey told us you were in trouble. When Atlas said he needed a ride out of the city from someone who wouldn't draw any attention, I offered to help." Joy shrugs. "I grew up two blocks from here, which is why anyone who might be looking for you won't think twice if they spot my car or do their locator crap on the GPS in my screen." She digs under her seat and comes up holding a paper bag. "My godmother baked cookies this morning. I was nice enough to save a couple for you."

I catch the bag that she wings back at me and ignore the tantalizing aroma of chocolate and butter long enough to ask, "Why?"

"Because eating too many cookies is bad for my health, and Dewey here is on a diet."

"I never said the word 'diet,'" Dewey protests as Joy steers the car out of the parking lot. "I'm watching my cholesterol."

"Same difference."

Atlas chuckles and reaches for the bag, while I push for an answer. "Why are you going out of your way to help us? You made it pretty clear how much you hated anyone involved with the Stewards." Especially me.

"Because Stef, Ari, and the kids are busy doing some kind of online-hacking thing and I suck at computers, so I drew the short end of the stick."

Dewey makes a *tsk*ing sound.

Joy lets out a loud huff. "Fine. Look, just because I don't agree with you on everything doesn't mean we aren't on the same side. And . . ." Joy glances at me in the rearview mirror. Her eyes lose the smart-ass glint as they meet mine. "I'm really glad you made it back, Meri. Chicago hasn't been the same since you left."

It turns out she means that—literally. As the silver, black, and glass buildings fill in the cloudless blue sky, Dewey and Joy fill us in on all the things Dewey didn't want to say on the phone about what was happening back here. About how Stef and the others continued to paint logos throughout the city both at night and also during the day, when the city had no chance of removing them before people took notice—and they hit places that the news could not ignore: the sidewalk directly in front of the main gates of Wrigley Field, the famous silver jelly bean–looking Cloud Gate statue, and on the inside of several red and blue line L cars.

"We would have lost Ari and Shep to the Marshals if Dewey hadn't told them about the Stewards' hideouts in that part of the city," Joy says.

But while Ari, Stef, and half the others are currently in lockdown in one of the old Steward stations, Amber, Jake, and the other computer whizzes continue to post online comments under various social media accounts.

"They've created dozens of fake accounts and have been getting everyone online totally stoked about *Gloss*," Joy explains. "According to the twins, the program Dewey's guy created is amazing. It gives a fake location to anyone attempting to track their position," Joy explains.

"We have another day, maybe two before the government breaks through their defenses," Dewey says.

"So, if we want them to use their fake accounts to draw people to the proof Meri brought back, we need to launch the special edition of *Gloss*—like, now," Atlas explains.

"What if it doesn't work?" I ask the question that has haunted me since those final moments at the farm with Wallace. "What if we're wrong and people don't care?"

"Meri," Dewey says as we drive across the La Salle Street Bridge. "I understand you're scared. We're all scared. But rebellion is not like fruit. It will not change colors and fall from the tree to signal that it is ready to be picked. The only way to know if the time is right is to take a bite."

He's right, I think as Joy cuts into a parking space a truck just vacated and kills the engine. There are no guarantees. Waiting a few days—a few months, a few years—won't change that. We take a stand now and hope the spark we strike becomes a blazing fire.

"If you are ready, there are a number of people waiting on your return to get this revolution started," Dewey says, opening the door of the car. "You might want to bring the cookies."

"Where are we going?" I ask, climbing out after him. "I thought we were going home to plan."

"Did you think those of us here in the city have been sitting around doing nothing?" Dewey adjusts the brim of his hat and smiles. "I know how to read books on revolution, too."

TWENTY-ONE

Perhaps when I walked out of the four-story brick building wedged in between taller structures of gleaming glass, I should have known I would be back. The Stewards chose the building for one of their stations because it was in an area where people of all shapes and sizes came and went throughout the day and night. It made sense that Dewey would direct those who had barely escaped the Marshals here to lie low.

"Substantiate." Joy reads the small plaque on the keypad while Dewey punches in the emergency code the former stationmaster gave to him when she left the city. "Never heard of it."

"I'm not surprised," I say as I follow them through the same doorway I watched my father walk through after I turned down his ultimatum and he stepped out of my life.

He never looked back to the bright, open foyer where I stood waiting for him to change his mind. It hasn't changed at all since then. Only I have.

The last time I was here, energy buzzed through the halls. We believed we had shattered the mirage of government lies, only to have that hope fade as the hours passed.

The building is tomb-quiet now.

Memories tug at the edges of my heart and then scatter at the echo of hurrying footsteps in the stairwell. When the door opens, Stef walks through. She's wearing black leggings, a dark purple tank, and a black ball cap, but the smile she gives to me is anything but dark. "Oh my God, you actually made it! You're here!"

"We're glad you're back," Ari adds from behind Stef.

"If you are going to state the obvious, perhaps it can be done while we are walking. Unless you want to waste the little time we have." Dewey maneuvers around them and continues to the silver elevator at the end of the hall. "Our newest allies are not the most patient."

"We have new allies?" Atlas stops walking.

"Are Mrs. Webster and Rose here?" I ask. "I have to tell them that I found Isaac."

"They're both at *Gloss* waiting for one of our people to bring your photos. You'll talk with Rose and Charity soon to help them finish the story they're going to print. But right now, we're late." Dewey punches a code into the elevator keypad and I stare at the dented doors as they slide open. "It seems the Marshals aren't the only ones who recognized the significance of Meri's logo. Scarlett and the other engineers found a way to contact me. They have had a change of heart."

Joy, Stef, and Ari follow Dewey inside. Atlas doesn't move.

"You want us to go to the Lyceum and work with Scarlett?" Anger sparks off Atlas's words. "Have you forgotten what she did to my father? He was your friend, Dewey. He dedicated his entire life to the Stewards and Scarlett betrayed him. He could be dead right now and it would be because of her."

Dewey sighs and pushes a button on the elevator to keep the door from closing. "I will never forget, Atlas. Your father saved my life when the Marshals were after me. He made me a Steward and gave me a place to feel as if I was making a difference. Scarlett betrayed him. Nothing can change that. But as the ancient proverb says: 'The enemy of my enemy is my friend.'"

"Does anyone understand what the hell he's talking about?" Joy's quip does nothing to break the tension.

"Scarlett isn't your friend, Dewey," Atlas snaps. "And she certainly isn't mine."

"You don't have to be friends to work with someone," Dewey replies with a calm that makes Atlas's eyes flash.

"Dewey's right," I say, my heart twisting at the betrayal and resentment that storms in Atlas eyes. "I don't like it any better than you, but if we are going to have any chance at all we need allies. We have to accept the help that's offered even if we hate where it's coming from. If we don't, we're just asking to be defeated."

Atlas turns and walks away, his hands curled into fists at his side. When I start toward him, Dewey grabs my arm and shakes his head. Atlas pounds the wall several times, then takes a deep breath and says, "Fine. Let's go."

The elevator shakes as it lowers until we reach the old pedestrian walkway with its long fluorescent lights and cracked white-and-yellow ceramic tile that Atlas's grandfather and the original Stewards walled off and repurposed for their use. Atlas's resentment radiates off his long, angry strides. Finally, we reach what was once a maintenance closet. The last time we were here, the makeshift exit the Stewards crafted at the back of the wall was blocked off as part of the lockdown protocol Scarlett put into effect. Her way of keeping danger out and the Stewards—whether they agreed with her or not—in. The concrete lockdown barrier is now gone. Once again the old streetcar tunnels, which until a few weeks ago I didn't know existed beneath my city, can be entered.

While the others follow close behind Atlas and the lamp he has lit to illuminate the way, I hang back with Dewey.

"You should have told us about Scarlett in the car," I say. "You should have given him time to get used to the idea."

"It is harder for someone to ignore the path when you are already walking it." Dewey stops walking. "Change requires sacrifice. I hope you will keep that in mind."

"What sacrifices are you making?" I ask when the glow from the lights inside the Lyceum comes into view.

"I thought that was obvious," Dewey says. "Until you came along, my life was simple. Now I have a revolution to lead."

We all pause at the threshold of the arching entrance built in the middle of a towering bookshelf. Only half of the mismatched lights swaying from the soaring ceiling of the massive underground library are currently shining, but the lack of light only enhances the magic of this cavernous place filled with piles and piles of books, ladders, and people.

So many people.

Hundreds of them lean on low shelves or sit on the colorful mismatched tile floor in various groups. Some are standing on chairs and shouting instructions, while others are weaving through the maze of books. People are passing out papers or bottles of water, and here and there I see several holding guns. From this vantage point, we can only see part of the Lyceum. How many more are there?

Atlas's eyes narrow. "There weren't this many Stewards when they locked the Lyceum down."

"Atlas!" someone yells.

"I didn't think there were this many left in the entire city," he says as one by one, heads turn to look at us.

"As Scarlett has demonstrated in the past, she does not do anything halfway." Dewey removes his hat and starts forward. "Scarlett and the remaining engineers have activated various networks—much like I did to transport you and Atlas. Stewards from a number of states responded. Many have come here, or to one of the other locations from which we will be launching our mission of truth."

Stewards wave and shout words of solidarity as Dewey leads us through the maze of books and Stewards and shelves to the back room I was in only once. The Stewards call it the firebox because that's where the fuel that propels the train forward burns. The twins and several of the other teens from Stef's group sit at the long silver-and-black table littered with bottles and wrappers, which spans the middle of the high-ceilinged space. A number of older Stewards sit across from them. All are talking rapidly to each other while punching screen keypads or tapping away on portable computers.

But it's the short, sturdy woman with a cap of white-and-dark-streaked hair that pulls my attention. She is huddled with a group of Stewards, studying maps and writing on whiteboards mounted against the far wall. I search for a flash of uncertainty or regret when she takes a tablet loaded with the images that I collected from Dewey. Instead, Scarlett looks at Atlas with a clear, unapologetic gaze and says, "Welcome back. As you saw on your way here, almost everyone who will be deployed in the city has made their way to the

Lyceum. We have divided them into groups and have been giving them preliminary instructions."

"What instructions?" I ask.

Scarlett gives me a flat, unwelcoming stare as if I were a bug that she was preparing to flick off her arm.

"Want me to punch her?" Joy whispers.

Dewey answers before I have the chance to take Joy up on her offer. "We'll have four teams. They will spring into action once Rose and her mother launch the special edition of *Gloss* tomorrow morning. The largest group will lead a protest through the streets to the mayor's office, calling for the Great American Farm to be shut down and their friends and family and neighbors to be set free. Groups of Stewards in sixteen other cities will be holding similar protests."

"Eighteen," Scarlett corrects. "Boston and Seattle have confirmed since you dropped communication and another three hundred have convened in a location near the farm. The site was chosen by the Stewards who assisted Atlas. They'll lead their team on a raid from there once we give the signal to begin."

Eighteen cities—all with protests. And a raid on the farm—where the Instructors are armed.

"What about the other teams?" Atlas asks. His voice is cold and flat. "You said there were four."

Scarlett nods and walks to one of the whiteboards. "The protests should pull the focus of both the police and the Marshals. Then..."

"We're helping with that," one of the twins says, looking up from his screen. "We're creating content that will go live once the protests start telling everyone online to go join the crowd."

"Then," Scarlett repeats, "the other two teams here in the city will have whatever weapons we have been able to manage. One will take over the Unity Center. And since our Telegraphers haven't been able to hack into the television station systems, the third team will be deployed to the National Broadcasting Company. That will allow us to air the truth about what is happening to as many people as possible before they shut the signal down."

Dewey looks directly at me. "That's where you come in."

"Me?" I glance around the room.

"Someone has to report the truth of what's happening to the people watching," Dewey explains.

"And you think it should be me?" I shake my head as Atlas steps closer to my side. "It should be someone better with words—you or Atlas or—"

"You were taken off the streets. You know what the cages are like—the lack of food, what they do to those who don't survive," Dewey explains. "They need to hear the truth from the person who not only took those photos, but is pictured in them. They need to hear from you."

I swallow hard. "How long will I need to speak?"

Scarlett turns to Huck. "How long can we hold the broadcast signal before the government overrides us?"

Huck rubs at the scruff on his chin and leans back in his chair. "Factoring in the protest and the Unity Center raid both acting as a distraction, maybe three minutes."

Three minutes?

Scarlett crosses her arms and looks at me. "You have until tomorrow morning to figure out what you are going to say. For the sake of the country, I hope it's good."

How do you convince an entire country that everything that makes them feel safe is built on a lie? What words do you use to convince them that there is a need for change?

Scarlett and the Telegraphers pull the images from the farm off the tablet I recovered and arrange for them to be taken to Rose. Then they clear the room so Atlas and Dewey can help me construct a message. Each word is debated. Each syllable and sentiment carefully conceived before I step in front of a camera run by the twins and try to bring the words to life.

Sound natural.

Don't look away from the camera or people will think you're lying.

Don't glare or they won't like you.

Don't talk so fast.

"This isn't going to work," I snap. "I can't say these words the way you want me to. I can't pretend to be George Washington or Thomas Paine or whoever. I don't know what words I am supposed to say. I just know how I felt when I was tagged like an animal and loaded onto a truck. What it was like to see people forced into labor—people starved and killed in a place that my entire life I was told was an example of how great our country was and proof that we didn't need the rest of the world. I believed in it all, and seeing someone like me saying those words in front of the camera wouldn't have changed my mind."

"Then we'll come up with words that will," Dewey says, sliding into a seat at the table with his paper and pencil.

"This seems like a good time for a break," Atlas suggests. "I could use food. I'm sure there's some quote about inspiration coming after the soul is fed or something like that. Right, Meri?"

I doubt I could keep any food in my stomach, but I agree because it's better than seeing my wooden delivery replayed on the screen again.

Once Dewey and the others are gone, Atlas asks. "Are you okay?"

I shake my head. "This is too important to screw up."

"You're not going to screw it up," he says. "Just seeing you on the screen will get people's attention. You're . . ." He gives me a smile that tugs at my heart. "Unexpected."

The word—the memory of the first time he said it—melts the ball of ice in the pit of my stomach. Slowly, I reach out and weave my fingers through his. He draws me close. I let myself lean against him—to feel his belief in me, my trust in him. We are not the same people we were last week standing in that alley, but when his lips brush mine—the warmth that pushes everything else but us away is the same.

When the kiss ends, I feel more—me—than I have since waking up in the Unity Center. More—settled. Closer to normal.

Atlas runs a finger down my scraped cheek and says, "How about you hang here while I grab food for both of us?"

"That sounds great."

He brushes his lips against mine one more time and heads out, leaving me for the first time in what feels like forever, alone. I take a tablet and stylus and sit on the floor against the back wall as voices from inside the Lyceum play in the air like a strange sort of music. I press a button on the screen and Dewey's carefully crafted words vanish like smoke. Then, hoping to forget about everything I'm doing wrong, I do the one thing I can get right. I draw.

People bathed in shadows come to life on the page. The only thing clear about each of them are their eyes—dusty hazels, deep blues, rich browns—all staring across a cavernous abyss to the sunshine-kissed hill on the other side of the screen.

Something brushes against my leg.

I look up to see George, the fluffy brown-and-white Lyceum cat staring at me with unblinking amber eyes. He bumps my leg with his head, purrs when I scratch him, and settles down beside me to snooze. The ill sensation that had been creeping up from my chest settles and I keep drawing.

When I finish adding a fluttering American flag, I put down the stylus and study what I've done. The lines are imperfect. The colors not quite right. But as I look at it I realize why people say a picture is worth a thousand words. It's because it takes almost no time to look at a picture. Words, however, take time to say. They take even more time to hear. Words take more effort than pictures, but the human voice is needed to make the powerful images real.

Atlas is right—my face on screens across the city—the same face that looked into the camera in the Unity Center with the tag in her ear—will not go unnoticed. Only, it took more than seven decades to eliminate the words that changed our entire country. There's no possible way we can convince people to wake up to the world they have been living in blissfully unaware in just three minutes.

"How do we extend the broadcast?" I ask the twins, Zain and Van, from Stef's team who are the first ones to return to the firebox.

The two look at each other and blink.

"We can't." The twin I think is Zain dumps several candy bars and a bag of cheese puffs onto the table. "Not with what we have to work with."

"What if you had more to work with?" I ask. "What would you need to keep the government from cutting the signal?"

"A couple months of nonstop hacking and a lot of luck," Van answers.

My heart sinks.

"Either that or a magic lamp and a genie to give us the override code," Zain agrees.

"What override code? What would that do?"

Another look that is a cross between exasperation and pity is exchanged before Zain replies, "It's the computer password the government uses to lock out a user."

"Typically twenty characters or more—so it's basically impossible to break," the other twin adds, with equal amounts of admiration and frustration.

Zain nods. "We can broadcast at the source because an administrator will have already put in the current authorization code. But once they realize we've hijacked the signal, someone will use the override codes and change the signal's authorization key."

"The signal will stop broadcasting until the new key is entered," Van adds. "That will effectively shut us down with no way to turn it back on."

"And if you had the codes?" I place my tablet on the table—the image of the faces yearning to cross the divide stares up at me. "Then what?"

"Then I'd basically be god of the screens," Van says.

"Until the Marshals hunt you down and prove you aren't immortal." Zain scoffs. "But yeah, if we had them when we take over the broadcast station, we could change both the authorization and override codes and make it impossible for them to shut us down remotely."

"So we could broadcast longer from the station?"

"We could broadcast longer from anywhere in the city," Van corrects.

"Anywhere in the city?" I ask. "We could broadcast from the

protest or the Unity Center raid?"

"If you want the Marshals to know exactly where to find us—"

"Do whatever you need to in order to be ready to make sure we can broadcast from the streets," I say as I grab the bag with Wallace's gun and head for the door.

"Where are you going?" Van asks.

"I'm going to get us more time."

TWENTY-TWO

The sun is starting to set. Out the window, Lake Michigan shimmers in the last of the evening sunlight below. But while the view is stunning, I stand, back straight as a rod, with my eyes on the front door of the apartment that I have, until today, been inside only once.

When the knob starts to turn, I step back out of sight and hold my breath. My eyes flick to the familiar faces smiling in silver-framed photographs on the living room wall and wait for the bump of the door opening, the click of it latching after it swings shut, the footsteps, and the deep, rich voice to say, "Rose? I know you said you needed to talk, but I have work and—"

"I don't care about your work," Rose snaps.

"If you are going to talk to me, you will not use that tone."

"Rose can use whatever tone she wants," I say stepping around the corner.

Mr. Webster turns, moves toward me, and I lift the gun I took from Wallace, immediately stopping him in his tracks. The safety is on, but he doesn't know that.

We're here because Mr. Webster kept my secret in the Unity Center. He let me leave so I could try to find his son. I believe Mr. Webster will help us get the extra time we need to broadcast the truth out to the entire country, but I have learned that just because I want something to be true doesn't make it real.

Anger whips across Mr. Webster's face like fire through dry brush. "Where is Isaac?" His eyes flick to the gun. "You claimed you were going to look for him. That's why I allowed you to leave the city."

Allowed me to leave.

I wait for him to take in the scrapes and bruises coloring my face and the bandage on my ear, but he doesn't react to them. If he is moved by the injuries inflicted on the little girl he camped with and shushed in the middle of sleepovers, he keeps it well hidden.

I fight for calm and ask, "Do you know where I was taken?"

"Did you find my son?" He steps forward.

I hold my ground. "Do you know where the Marshals send people they take off the city streets?"

"Answer her, Dad," Rose snaps. "Do you even know where Isaac was taken? And don't bother trying to lie. I know he isn't being held by the mythical street gang you and the police blamed for his disappearance."

"Rose, I can see you're upset," Mr. Webster says carefully. "But you have to realize that I did what I thought was necessary to keep you safe." He reaches for her hand. "There are things you don't understand—"

Rose yanks her arm back and walks to stand beside me. "The problem is that I do understand. And I no longer believe whatever you say."

Mr. Webster straightens his shoulders. "I don't know what

Meri has told you, but you need to trust that I know what's best."

"I know Isaac was taken because the people you work with thought he was looking for information they didn't want him to have." Rose waits for her father to deny the charge. The silence is damning. Hurt shimmers in Rose's eyes. Her lip trembles before pursing into a hard line.

Rose believed everything I told her. She convinced her mother to risk everything because she had seen the evidence of the government's lies with her own eyes—the government her father worked for. Despite all that, there was a part of her that had hoped he would deny it. I get it. I knew my father was lying when he promised to stop drinking, but every day I looked for signs that would convince me I was mistaken. And every day, my heart got broken. Just like Rose's was breaking now.

"How could you be a part of this?" Rose demands. "How could you pretend that any of this is okay?"

"I wasn't pretending!" Mr. Webster shouts. "You've never had to be scared of being robbed or shot when you walked down the street or went to school. You've never had to live in fear of our country being dragged into a war. Our country faced terrible problems. Action had to be taken."

"That's your justification for the lies?" Rose's voice cracks. "For the rewriting of history and the kidnapping of people who were guilty only of thinking something different?"

"Difficult decisions had to be made," Mr. Webster says coldly. "The ones who were in charge made the right choice."

"How do you know?" Rose pushes. "You weren't there."

"No, I wasn't," he says—his face hard as stone. "But it's too late to go back and change it. What's important is how much happier and safer the country is now."

"I don't feel happy . . . or safe. Neither does Isaac."

Taking that as my cue, I hand my gun to Rose, pull a tablet out of my pocket, and turn the illuminated screen to face Mr. Webster. His eyes latch on to the image—the one I took of Isaac before he walked out of the infirmary door. The picture isn't centered, but while the composition is poor, the hollow anguish in Isaac's eyes is clear.

"I found your son, Mr. Webster."

Rose's father takes the tablet, never taking his eyes off the face on the screen.

"Isaac helped me," I say quietly. "I wanted him to come with me, but he refused."

"Why?" Mr. Webster asks.

"He said it was because he was being used as an example to everyone in government. That if we escaped together they would never stop searching for him," I explain.

"And you just accepted that?" Mr. Webster yells.

"Don't you dare blame Meri!" Rose shouts back.

"If she had only trusted me everything would be okay!"

"Us not knowing about all of this wouldn't make things okay," Rose snaps.

"Mr. Webster," I interrupt. "When Isaac made the choice not to come with me it wasn't only because he was worried about finding a way to disappear." The last words Isaac said before leaving he infirmary play again in my mind. "He knows what will happen to his mother and Rose if the Marshals came knocking on their door. Isaac told me to tell you that he's in hell. He made the choice to stay there while I escaped to buy all of us time."

"Time for what?" Mr. Webster asks.

"To do what we can to free him," I say.

"And not just him," Rose adds, locking eyes with her father. "We're going to free everyone who you've helped hold against their will. We'll do it without your help, but we'll have a better chance of saving Isaac with it."

Mr. Webster is the first to look away. His shoulders slump as he looks at the ground and rubs at the back of his neck. When he looks up, the man I once believed was hard as stone has tears in his eyes. "Nothing will ever be the same. We won't be safe."

Rose's expression is steel. "I know."

"What do you want me to do?"

Rose glances at me, then back at her father. "Just so we're clear— if you betray me and the Marshals come, I'll fight them. I'd rather die than let them take me. Isaac and I will both be gone and it will be your fault."

Mr. Webster takes an uncertain breath. "I could never live with that."

Rose studies him. She knows him best. So when she nods that she believes him I say, "Here is what we need from you."

Rose never puts down the gun as we walk Mr. Webster through the codes we need him to deliver to us. Our request clearly surprises him. "That's it?" he asks. "The codes are in my files. I'll have to go to the office to get them." He also offers to warn us as to where and when the Marshals are dispatched after we take over the broadcast signal. With his help, the truth—and his son and daughter—might stand a chance.

Whatever else he is or has done, Mr. Webster loves his children. He helped the government conceal terrible things because he thought it would keep them safe. He'll fight them now for the same reason.

"I'll go to the office with my father. When we have the codes, I'll let you know." Rose hands the gun back to me and heads to the door.

I'm surprised when instead of immediately following his daughter, Mr. Webster turns to face me. "Meri, I really am sorry about your mother. Neither of us knew the truth when we started working for the government. The mayor called me into his office ten years ago to explain why certain choices were necessary. I haven't always agreed with what we've done, but I couldn't see an alternative. The truth will break this country; I hope you're prepared for that."

"It won't," I say. "Because it's already broken."

"And you think we can fix it?" he asks, looking at his daughter.

The question pulls me off-balance. Do I really believe that everything I've discovered can be made better? That we can simply fix what has been broken for so long?

Squaring my shoulders, I lift my chin and answer, "We have to try."

Less than thirty-six hours later, Huck climbs into the driver's seat of his van. "Scarlett just sent word," he reports. Rose and her mother have been at *Gloss* working round the clock on the special edition. It will launch any minute. My team has been in position in the underground parking garage underneath Columbus Avenue—directly below the National Broadcasting Company building—since just before the sun began to rise, waiting for *Gloss* to publish. When it does, we will jump into action, broadcast codes in hand.

Huck runs down the timing again, just in case any of us have forgotten since the last reminder. Once the new issue hits, Stef, Ari, and a dozen other members of their group will use online accounts to draw attention to screenshots of the issue and call for protests.

Minutes later, the protests will start and our team will begin its work. First here in the studio. Then, once the codes are entered we will move to the street to broadcast. We will give people the words they need to hear and the real-time images that prove to them the words are true. The Marshals will come for us. And the police. And anyone who is desperate to keep the truth shut away. We have to get in, start the broadcast, wrest control of the broadcast satellite, and get out so we can continue broadcasting from the streets—all before we get killed.

"Wait, I almost forgot," Atlas says as the twins, Huck, and the other computer geeks jammed in the van go over who will be manning the signal and the cameras and the remote vehicles. He reaches into his pocket and pulls out a thick leather bracelet. No. Not a bracelet, I realize, as he takes my hand and fastens the band on my wrist. I can see the square black face and gold numbers of the watch.

A knot uncoils in my chest as I read the numbers—9:56. "Where did you get it?"

"It was my father's. I thought after everything . . ." He closes his eyes and takes a deep breath. "I wanted you to have it."

"Thank you." And despite having so many people around us, I lean forward and brush my lips against his. After being deprived of knowing the time during my captivity, nothing he could have given me could mean more.

A few of the teens groan. Then we all settle back to wait. Atlas and I watch the gold arrows move on the face of the clock until our screens buzz with the message we have been waiting for. The twins pull out their tablets and turn the screens so we can verify the message is correct.

**AMERICANS MURDERED IN SECRET BY OUR GOVERNMENT—
THE HORROR OF THE GREAT AMERICAN FARM.**

The first shot in our revolution has been fired.

There is no turning back.

Huck cranks the ignition. The van roars to life. Computer equipment rattles and we all fight to keep our balance as he pulls out of the far back corner of the parking garage. Tires squeal as he rounds the corners. Finally, he pulls into a No Parking spot by an emergency exit where two dozen Stewards have already assembled—some carrying bags filled with tablets and portable computer equipment. The others are wearing jackets to hide that they are carrying guns the Stewards hid away years ago to use if ever they needed to defend the Lyceum. Atlas's weapon, the gun we brought back from the Great American Farm, is in the side pocket of his bag, the handle exposed so he can grab it quickly. Atlas rests a reassuring hand on my back as Huck waits for the Stewards near the front entrance to signal their readiness. If we are lucky, no one will need to fire a weapon.

The emergency door crashes open and the Steward who works in the weather department hands Huck a badge and says, "Studio B on the third floor. I'll meet you there."

The twins and two Stewards in the van drive off to get into position to meet us later. Huck takes the lead as we quietly navigate the back hallways where there are no receptionists or security guards or lines of wayward fans. Atlas stays directly behind me—guarding my back since I, like most of the techs, have no weapon.

Screens filled with smiling faces of actors and talk show hosts and audiences from the productions created in this building line the walls. We hear the shouts as we round the corner at the back of the large lobby. A bunch of Stewards are shoving each other just inside the wall of gold and glass revolving doors. When a security guard goes to break up the fight, the Steward shoves her to the ground and the other guards run to help.

Huck hurries across the back of the lobby, waves the badge at the security pad, and punches the call button. When the elevator arrives, we stream inside. My heart pounds as the numbers climb. I take deep breaths and when the door opens on the third floor I follow the others to the studio. A quick wave of the badge in front of the security panel and we're in.

The room isn't as big as I would have imagined. Several large cameras in various positions are on one side of the room. A polished wood counter with a rich blue top and station logo that is used for the evening newscasts sits empty in the front of the studio.

"Meri, take your place on set," the woman who let us into the building tells me as our team moves into their positions behind the cameras or in the control room.

One of the cameramen gives Atlas a microphone for me to wear. We fumble with snaking the cord under the back of my shirt and up through my collar as Huck and the others work their computer magic. Once the microphone is clipped to the scooped neck of my shirt, I shove the battery pack into my back pocket and follow instructions as to where to stand.

Huck nods from the doorway of the control room and one of the Stewards heads out into the hall. The first code giving us access to the broadcast feed has been entered and accepted.

It's time.

Bright white lights flare in the rafters above me.

Minutes from now, members of our team will set off smoke

bombs in the bathroom and hallway to trigger the fire alarm. People will have to evacuate. If this goes as planned, we'll sneak out in the chaos and continue the broadcast remotely.

Atlas squeezes my hand and asks, "Are you ready?"

I place a hand on my stomach.

Am I ready?

Is anyone ever ready for revolution, ready to upend her entire world—no matter how necessary?

Screens around the room flicker to life. Atlas backs out of the shot and I am alone on the screens. Bruised face. Determined eyes.

"In five," the cameraman calls, and Atlas hurries to stand next to him. "Four. Three. Two."

He holds up one finger to complete the countdown and then waves at me to start talking.

My heart pounds and all the carefully thought-out words I came up with fly out of my head.

The cameraman waves and makes a hurry-up motion.

So I lift my chin, look into the camera, and say the first thing that comes to me: "My name is Merriel Beckley, and I'm here to tell you what the government won't. I'm going to tell you the truth."

TWENTY-THREE

"Not long ago, I believed everything I saw or was told by our city and our country's leaders. I never questioned them. I never knew that could be done. My mother worked for the City Pride Department before she was killed. I was told it was an accident. It wasn't. She was murdered by the government because she learned the word 'verify,' a word that appeared in the books we recycled—that the leaders needed us to recycle—and that we no longer know. A word that means to prove something is true rather than to just believe it is. So that's what she started to do."

Something pounds on the studio doors. Someone is either doing a safety sweep to make sure everyone has heard the fire alarm and evacuated, or the Marshals have arrived sooner than we'd hoped.

Atlas turns and points his gun. I swallow my fear and keep talking.

"The ones who murdered my mother—who kidnapped me—are going to try to shut down this broadcast—" My voice cracks. *Please, let anyone watching believe me.* "They don't want you to question their leadership. They don't want you to hear my words or read them in the special edition of *Gloss* that was published this morning."

Huck appears next to the cameraman and signals me that the override code Mr. Webster gave us worked. We will still have control of the signal when we leave the studio. It's time to go.

"They will tell you not to believe your eyes and to only believe what they tell you. I'm asking you to read our words and to keep watching this screen. These are photographs I took after I allowed myself to be captured. I risked my life to show you proof of what they have done—what they are still doing. This is the truth they hoped our country would never see."

My image fades from the studio screens and is replaced by one of the first pictures I took in the Unity Center cages. People lying on the dirty concrete. Eyes staring hopelessly into the shadows. Debris and waste covering the ground.

Under the picture is a blue graphic box with the caption: "Please help us identify these people. Their families deserve to know why they have gone missing." There is a phone number listed. The phone it belongs to is turned off so it can't be traced but the voice message recorder is operating.

The image changes—this time to a shot taken through the cage bars of a dirt-streaked man huddled in a thin, foil-like blanket. The hotline number stays on the bottom of the screen along with a call to protest at city halls across the country. The messages were Dewey's ideas. He hopes people will recognize the faces. That it will give them the courage to take a stand. That the protests will encourage them to step forward. To start thinking for themselves. To push back against the things they have been told are good, but they have to know deep in their hearts are wrong.

"The Marshals are on their way! We have to go!" Huck calls to the team, and heads for the door.

"Meri!"

I glance at my watch. Nineteen minutes have passed since we first walked into the building. *Gloss* has published the truth. I've spoken it. But I know that won't keep the government from doing everything in their power to silence us all for good. That's the next truth the people need to see.

Huck opens the door and our team heads into the hall filled with flashing lights and the whooping alarm. We follow him past the main elevator bank to the stairwell. A haze of smoke greets us as we thunder down the three flights of stairs.

The smoke makes my eyes water. I'm coughing by the time we reach the bottom. Security guards in the lobby wave people toward the exits. We start to follow their direction when a guard stops and stares at me. "You!" he yells. "Stop right there!"

"He recognized Meri," Huck shouts. "This way!"

Atlas grabs my hand and we take off running, several other Stewards following behind.

Huck swipes the badge on the sound studio's two security locks and jerks the door open for us to race through. He then shoves it closed and yells, "Head for the loading dock. Hurry!"

Gunfire sounds on the other side of the door as we run deeper into the enormous sound stage. We zigzag around folding chairs, equipment, and carts filled with metal boxes until we reach an unfinished-looking movie-magic building in the center of the space.

The door behind us crashes open and the Marshals rush into the space. Huck and Atlas turn and fire, sending the Marshals diving to the floor. We reach the set piece doorway as they recover and return fire. A bullet digs into the wood above us as we bolt through the set piece entrance into . . . a hospital?

Patient rooms with beds and glass doors are on my right and left. Two Stewards have already reached the double doors in the back. Huck, Atlas, and I leap over the big desk and duck as a Marshal bursts in, takes aim, and fires.

The Stewards at the hospital's exit fire around the corner of the doorway to give cover, but every time we try to move, the Marshal resumes shooting.

A bullet rips through the desk and rams into the floor tile.

A Steward with blue-streaked hair and freckles leans around the corner. She fires at the same time a bullet punches into her stomach. Her eyes go wide and she drops to the ground.

Oh God.

"We have to get out of here," Atlas insists.

Huck agrees. "Can either of you tell where he's shooting from?"

We both shake our heads. The echo of the space and the still-whooping fire alarm make it impossible to tell. He could be right behind the desk for all we know. We need a distraction. I spot the wheels on the chairs and whisper, "I have an idea."

I stretch my leg toward the chair closest to me and kick it as hard as I can. A second after it careens to our left, a Marshal's face appears over the desk. He shoots the empty space where he assumed one of us would be. Huck takes aim. The Marshal crumples to the desk, and Atlas and I scramble out from behind the desk and race toward the exit.

The whooping alarm stops as we reach the loading dock. Huck and Atlas hide their weapons under their shirts as we go through the door.

Nine of us went inside. Six of us hurry across the concrete and around to the side of the building and make a beeline for the crowd of evacuated office and studio workers. I keep my head down as we walk, although I don't think anyone even registers us as we pass. Most are watching the public screens, which are still broadcasting the horrific images from the farm along with the accompanying hotline number, or the dozens of officers and Marshals that are racing through the front doors of the network building with guns drawn.

We turn onto the next street and are approaching the agreed-upon meeting spot when the van streaks up to the curb. Before it can stop, the back door slides open. One of the twins grins at us as we climb in and go.

There's a rhythm to these things, Dewey said. A momentum to the energy of a revolution that like a fire has to be stoked and fed or it will burn out and die. The truth is the kindling. But we are the oxygen. Oxygen is necessary if we don't want the fire to fade.

"We have your microphone frequency plugged in. Dewey's video feed at the Unity Center and the one from the Stewards outside the farm are running. Everyone is ready to move," the twins report as the van comes to a stop.

Huck swivels in the front passenger seat. "The police have the roads shut down past the bridge. Your friend's father sent a message saying this is the closest we can get."

"Then this is where we go back on the air," I say. The twins grin, grab their tablets, and scamper out while the others stash their weapons. It's important the public sees that the Marshals are the ones with the guns. From now on, our only ammunition will be words.

"Good luck," Huck says as the van door slides shut.

"You, too," I call. The screens have been playing a taped set of images. Huck and his team will be controlling the broadcast while avoiding the Marshals when we once again go live.

Mr. Webster was right. There are pedestrians everywhere on the sidewalks. Cars are bumper to bumper on the streets. Half of the public screens are playing a broadcast by the other network. The anchors with too-bright smiles are currently warning of an elaborate hoax and urging residents to stay inside. The words "STAND BY" appear in stark white against a deep blue background on the other screens.

Several people shoot me startled looks as we merge with the crowd on the other side of the La Salle Street Bridge. Police officers direct cars to turn back as hundreds, maybe thousands of people who have answered our call head down the street to the protest at City Hall.

The closer we get the denser the crowd becomes. Someone on a bullhorn or a speaker is instructing people to go inside. The banner on the other news show says ,"PRANK VIDEO," which sparks outrage in me.

I nod to my camera crew, and the screen that asked people to stand by changes. Once again, I'm pictured, and this time I am not alone. Using their tablets, the twins stream video of the ever-growing crowd, then turn their cameras back to me.

"As you can see, this is not a hoax," I say. "The photos you have seen—the people out here on the city streets—the ones who have called the hotline to report the names of their friends who have disappeared—are all real." The image on the screen changes. Puffy white clouds. Bright blue skies. A lush, sweeping rendition of "America the Beautiful" plays over video of sun-kissed fields, smiling people in overalls riding big green tractors or laughing while feeding chickens—part of an advertisement for the farm the team pulled because all of us know it.

With the faces still smiling against the beautiful farming backdrop, Van nods to me that my microphone is live and I follow the script we came up with last night. "For years special newscasts told us all to be proud of the Great American Farm. You've seen the pictures I took when I was there. This is what is happening there now."

The screen changes to the feed of the Stewards who have gathered in Iowa and launched a raid on the farm. The video is jerky. The audio cuts in and out. But the gunshots and the screams are clear.

"Look, it's Meri!" someone shouts.

"There are Marshals behind us," Atlas whispers in my ear.

"Do you see her?"

"This can't be real!" someone screams.

"Look at the screen, you idiot!" I hear as we shove our way through the crowd until it seems as if word of who is coming runs ahead and a path opens in front of us.

Our broadcast on the screens switches to the raid of the Unity Center, where Dewey and the others have overcome the small contingent of Marshals. While their camera crew captures Dewey approaching a dirty cage with a half-dozen adults and two girls a few years younger than me locked inside, I describe what those people have gone through.

"They deserve better," I say as the cage door is unlocked and those trapped inside walk free.

Someone has erected a white platform in front of the main doors of City Hall. I spot Mr. Webster standing with several other officials. Marshals are everywhere. An official with a bullhorn orders people to disperse. No one complies.

Out of the corner of my eye I see myself, sweaty and out of breath, once again on our broadcast. We got this far. I wasn't sure we would or what will happen next. The Marshals in front of the platform raise their guns and start toward me, but I don't run. I plant myself in front of the imposing stone structure of Chicago's City Hall and shout over the noise of the crowd, "You've seen the pictures and the video. The government has targeted anyone who questions them. This is your wake-up call! We need to stand together and demand the lies end!"

The screens—all of them, even the ones broadcasting the other channel—go dark. There are shouts of protests. A few cheers. Over it all I hear Atlas call, "Meri! Look out!"

I feel the punch of the bullet. The burning in my stomach that turns icy cold.

Atlas catches me and I look up into his face.

The sky behind him is impossibly blue.

And then, like the screens, everything goes black.

TWENTY-FOUR

I don't know what would have happened if I hadn't been shot in front of City Hall. If those who were assembled on the street hadn't seen for themselves the Marshal firing his weapon at me—an unarmed girl. If those people didn't verify what they witnessed with others.

Maybe our elected leaders would have found a way to put a stop to the change we started. Maybe when they regained control of the news they could have convinced everyone that I was a liar or spun a new tale about how their actions were necessary in order to make the country safer for, if not all, then the many.

I'd like to believe the truth is stronger than fabrications under any circumstances. I'd like to say that the call for change would have continued to sound if I had only broadcast from a hidden location instead of making myself a target. Or that the government would have opened the gates to the Great American Farm and the Nevada Desert Energy Fields if the Stewards hadn't publicly started the process of freeing those who had been imprisoned inside. I'd like to think once Rose and Mrs. Webster published the pictures and I appeared on the public screens that change was inevitable, but I'm not that naive. Not anymore.

The Stewards did break down the gates of the Great American Farm that led to the orientation center. Dozens were shot and killed to free those who had been ripped from their lives and forced to work for the "good of the country." The fight for that freedom happened live onscreen because even though the public screens went dark, private ones in houses and restaurants and other businesses continued to broadcast. And when those feeds were finally cut, the *Gloss* website live-streamed it, allowing even the most adamantly opposed to the truth to witness it all.

Viewers witnessed Instructor Burnett shoot Mrs. Acosta as she shielded a young subject wearing oversize pinkish-gray clothes. Then they watched as Instructor Burnett shot the terrified boy before she herself was killed.

Some of the subjects ran. Some were gunned down. Others, like Isaac, joined the Stewards in the fight.

Interspersed with that battle were videos from those held at the Unity Center haltingly telling their stories. In between each, Dewey made a public plea for doctors and nurses to come help those who were held there.

The country watched as the helpers came.

Maybe if people hadn't seen all of those things—too many to be ignored—maybe the government could have spun it all back to where we started.

But they did see. The country watched someone die on the sidewalk in front of City Hall. And even if change doesn't happen immediately, nothing will be the same. I guess I know that better than anyone.

From my hospital bed, I viewed the replay of the Marshal firing his gun at me. I watched the bullet punch into my chest. Relived my strangled cry. Atlas catching me—lowering me to the ground, and through my microphone everyone around the country heard him beg me not to die. That's when the Marshal fired again.

I guess we'll never know why Mr. Webster stepped in front of that bullet. I've watched the footage a dozen times of him jumping off the platform and charging toward us, trying to understand his thoughts in those final moments. Maybe he knew it would be worse for the government's containment attempts if the Marshal succeeded. Maybe he wanted to redeem himself in the eyes of his children. Maybe he wasn't thinking at all. Whatever his reasons, I'm alive.

The bullet that struck me fractured two ribs. I lost a lot of blood and I'm told there were some complications during surgery that scared everyone. Mr. Webster was struck in the forehead. He died before the ambulance arrived.

The doctors would not clear me to go to the funeral today. So, I sit in my hospital room alone and read the *Gloss* website obituary Rose helped to write. The photograph displays Mr. Webster's warmest smile. The accompanying article highlights his love of family and the sacrifice he made to free his son and bring truth to the country. His lifetime of government work is little more than a footnote.

Funeral details were omitted from publication—Mrs. Webster's attempt to keep the service private. I hope for Isaac's and Rose's sake she was successful. After the story of helping me escape the farm was published and his father's subsequent sacrifice, Isaac has become one of the country's heroes. When he visited me last night every nurse on the floor found an excuse to stop by. The fact that he's good-looking might also have had something to do with it. Isaac and Rose both promised to stop by after the funeral to let me know how they're doing. That's why I am surprised when it's Mrs. Webster, not Rose, who walks into my hospital room still dressed in a fitted black suit and yellow-and-black heels.

"Is Rose okay?" I ask, ignoring the twinge of pain as I sit up.

"It was a hard day," Mrs. Webster admits as she crosses to the bed. "I thought it was best to leave her at home. She and Isaac are clearing out the office so it's ready for when you're released tomorrow."

"I really appreciate you letting me stay," I say. While I'm fond of Dewey, I don't think I'm ready to start every day with ancient Greek proverbs. Besides, he has his hands full with helping Scarlett, and Stewards around the country organize daily protests and "Truth Matters" marches. They don't want to let the pressure being put on the government to subside or the horror of what we revealed to fade. Not until those in charge have been held to account and things begin to change. That will take time, although here in Chicago where the protests have been strongest, the mayor has already resigned. No one has seen him since he announced the special election where anyone—not just approved candidates—will be able to participate. According to Atlas, Scarlett plans to run.

Scarlett will never be my favorite person, but even Atlas has to admit she's effective when she puts her mind to doing something. If it weren't for Scarlett and her strategic planning we would have never gotten into the network building or mobilized Stewards from around the country.

"I hope you don't mind, but I wanted to talk to you about something." Mrs. Webster takes a seat at the foot of my hospital bed.

"Rose said Scarlett and Dewey were here yesterday. That they asked you to speak at upcoming protests and you turned them down."

"They don't really need me," I say. There are dozens of Stewards who were released from Unity Centers and the farm who can talk about their experiences. Atlas is going to speak at the next one about his father. According to government logs the Stewards uncovered, a man matching Atticus's description was killed before reaching the Unity Center on the same day he went missing. As a Steward, Atlas's father vowed to use the deadman's switch if the Marshals captured him. He told the truth.

"Have you thought about what you're going to do?" Mrs. Webster asks.

"I'm going to go back to school when it starts in a month. Maybe at some point I'll talk to my dad." He contacted the hospital after watching me get shot and asked that I call him when I'm ready. I'm not sure when that will be.

When Mrs. Webster says nothing, I add, "I guess I just want to try to feel normal again."

"After everything that has happened, I believe it's important for things to not go back to normal," Mrs. Webster says gently. "Already there are people who are determined to go back to their lives as if the truth behind your broadcast or the pictures or the protests aren't real. We can't trust the government to change unless people are paying attention to what they're doing. The protests and marches Scarlett and Dewey are organizing will help. The protests are why as of this morning the *Gloss* website is working again."

Not long after the doctors arrived at the Unity Center, the government used their power over the internet to render the *Gloss* website not viewable by anyone outside *Gloss* offices. The codes

Mr. Webster gave us were changed and despite the twins' hacking prowess, the e-zine site remained blocked from public view.

"That's great," I say.

Mrs. Webster agrees. "It is, but no matter how hard Dewey and Scarlett work, eventually the protests will end. People will go back to their lives. If we're lucky we'll have new leaders in place by then. But once people have stopped paying attention, what will stop our new leaders from making those same choices, or ones that are even worse?"

A vague sense of panic builds in my chest. "I don't know."

Mrs. Webster smiles. "You enlisted my help because it's important for people to learn the truth from a trusted source."

"Which we did."

"And in spite of everything, there are people who refuse to believe the truth. Some are determined to bury their heads in the sand. Others are already working hard to justify what was done." Mrs. Webster places her hand on mine. "The only way to make sure the truth is heard is to continue to share it. I'm hoping you'll agree to help me and the *Gloss* team do just that."

I shake my head. "I've already shared my story. You said it yourself—eventually they'll stop paying attention."

"That isn't the only story that needs to be told," Mrs. Webster insists. "The people need to hear more than the news the government wants them to hear. To make sure things don't simply go back to normal, the public needs to hear every day from someone they trust to look for the facts. When *Gloss* launches its new broadcast channel in a week, I want the people who tune in to hear from you."

Mrs. Webster is right. Things can't be allowed to return to normal. But . . .

"Why me?" I ask.

"Because the viewers understand what you've been through. They watched you stand up to the government in order to tell them what they needed to know. Until people learn how to ask their leaders tough questions and push for answers they might not want to hear, they'll trust you to do it for them," Mrs. Webster explains.

"I can't," I say, glancing at the tablet and stylus on the bedside table. "Dr. Blitzer said it would take six weeks for my ribs to heal." Which would get me excused from gym class for the first few weeks of school. Going back to class and figuring out my future is what I'm supposed to be doing. I shouldn't have to be responsible for more.

"And Dr. Blitzer assured you that as long as you're careful you'll be able to do just about everything you normally do—even travel."

"Isaac should do it," I say. "Everyone trusts him, and he'd look great on the screen."

"Isaac has decided to go back to the farm. He's going to help exhume and identify those who died there. If you agree to work with *Gloss*, Isaac has asked that you come back to the farm and report on those efforts."

Go back?

"And while you're there I'd like you to visit the other part of the farm, where the actual volunteers work."

I cocked my head to the side. "The news does a special broadcast on that part of the farm every year. Everyone already knows that story."

"How do you know what the story is until you see it for yourself?"

I just assumed the volunteer section of the farm was portrayed correctly on the news because they needed that truth to hide the lie on the other side.

"Hey." Atlas hovers in the doorway and my heart flips. He looks a touch dangerous and very attractive in the smoky-gray shirt and pants he wore to Mr. Webster's funeral. "Am I interrupting?"

"I was just about to leave." Mrs. Webster squeezes my hand. She starts to leave as Atlas steps into the room, then turns back and says, "I almost forgot. I was supposed to mention something Thomas Jefferson once said. 'Where the press is free, and every man able to read, all is safe.'"

It hurts to laugh, but I can't help it. "You've been talking with Dewey?"

"He is hard to ignore." Mrs. Webster grins. "Can I ask one more thing? Do you still think there are important questions that need to be answered?"

I don't hesitate before saying, "Of course."

"Then before you decide what you plan to do, ask yourself one thing. Do you really want to trust someone else to ask them?"

Before I can answer she turns and heads out, leaving a clearly confused Atlas in her wake.

"Is everything okay?" he asks, crossing to take my hand.

I study our entwined fingers, thinking about everything we have lost in the search for the truth, what we have gained, and what could be lost again just as quickly.

"I think it will be," I answer. But there's only one way to know for sure.

A week later, I once again step in front of City Hall with the cameras rolling and say, "I'm Meri Beckley, reporting for Gloss News."

Because as much as I want this to be the end, it is simply the beginning.

ACKNOWLEDGMENTS

Some stories are harder to tell than others. This book was incredibly difficult for me to write. The words didn't always come easily. Sometimes I wasn't sure if they would come at all. If it weren't for the unfailing support of my family, my agent, Stacia Decker, and my editor, Kristen Pettit, I'm not sure this series would exist.

I owe a debt of gratitude to Edel Rodriguez for his iconic cover art and to the incredible Harper team for taking this journey with me. Also, I cannot thank the teachers, librarians, and booksellers who have embraced this story enough. And to the journalists working here in the United States and around the globe, thank you for your work. The late Judge Damon Keith is quoted as saying, "Democracy dies behind closed doors." To every journalist working tirelessly today—thank you for shining your light.

Words matter. Facts matter. Truth matters.

I've always known those things to be true. However, in recent years I have realized how much I have taken those ideas for granted.

This series was written because I wanted to learn what could happen if those tenets of our society continue to erode and how they could be restored. I wish I could say in my historical research that I found a magic wand that can be waved. Trust me, I tried.

What I have learned is that we are all, children and adults alike, stewards of our history, our government, and our world. It is up to us to stand up for the power of words, facts, and the truth they convey, especially when it is easier to remain silent or it feels as if speaking out will do no good.

Your voice matters. Your words wherever you use them are important. Your willingness to question what you wish to believe is courageous and sets an example for others.

Thank you for reading. Thank you for sharing this story with others. But most of all, I want to thank you in advance for each time you stop and fact-check something before believing it to be true. The truth can only matter if it starts with you.